CORPO

SECO

NADIA MADDY

For my son, Akir, my source of strength,
and my greatest inspiration.
With deepest gratitude,
I dedicate this book to you,
as a testament to the profound impact
you have on my life as a mother.

Acknowledgements

Make no mistake, I stand on the shoulders of others. Every small gesture makes a difference to the magic of a writer's pen. If I have forgotten anyone, thank you in spirit.

When I had the idea Usifu Jalloh was the first person I presented it to. He told me to turn it on its head and I never looked back. Thank you Usifu. Thank you to Pede Hollist who taught me about 'in media res' and saved the story. I continue to be grateful to my mentors who have unwavering faith in me, Anni Domingo, Winston Forde, Dr Kadija George, Leslie Leigh and Patrice Naimbana. My amazing friends who fight for me, read my work, pull my ears and always give me advice and support in all things creative and quirky with no judgement, My deepest gratitude to Mark Lewis for highlighting the comic book analogy and for introducing me to Ghanaian royalty, who welcomed me into their world and revealed the beauty of Ghanaian creativity – Juliette Ibrahim and Michael Djaba (I-Factory LIVE) for trusting me with their invaluable creative support. Martin and Hannatu Gentles making sure my crazy didn't damage the story and Christine Shearer for endless belief. My sister cousin Shalimar

Garba for cheering me on relentlessly through the unglamorous writing process. Beta readers, lovers of books and fellow writers, my cousin Jemila Pratt and Oliver Burrows who kept on at me with so much enthusiasm. Deepest gratitude to the Ghana massive, my dear friend, Abena Serwaa Kirsty Osei-Bempong, Editor In Chief at akadimagazine.com thank you for writing the blog post about the Tabom, fuelling my curiosity, reading my work and Dr Kwadwo Osei-Nyame, Jnr (SOAS) who both read the early drafts and put me straight with Ghana love. João Pedro Corrêa da Silva, the kindest Brazilian I have ever met, who graciously took the time to go over the manuscript and represent his country for me. Jonathan Howard, my first die-hard fan who became a beta reader and championed my work for 6 years. May you rest in glorious peace for showing me how books touch people and bring them together. My heartfelt thanks to Jessyka Winston of HausofHoodoo, whose Instagram profile led me on a remarkable Pan-African journey, revealing the profound beauty of Ghanaian spiritual practices and sharing them with the world. Thank you, Sarah Odedina for your kind words and big heart. A big shout out to Nigel Davis, Josy Hamelburg, Rochelle Williams and Fredrica Yaa Abrefi Antwi. Naija Queen of African Romance @loveafricapress, Kiru Taye who is an inspiration to all of us for her dedication to the craft – thank you for your assistance. Allen Glenn for pushing and supporting me in the final battle to get this story out and into the hands of the reader. Your unwavering love and support know no bounds.

Akir, my son, you have listened to me discuss this story endlessly for 7 years, read it and given me your honest opinion. You are phenomenal.

CHAPTER ONE

Mosquitos danced around the Bahian plantation as if they owned it. Sugar cane fell ceremoniously under the machetes in the midday sun. The razor-sharp slices played havoc with slave hands as they hacked through its thickness. Most sugar-cane plants stood taller than the men in the field. Faron moved from one worker to the next, his determined strides setting a relentless pace. While they held mixed feelings about his attempts to make them comfortable, he was their sole reminder that water, shade and rest were possible. His presence was dedicated to facilitating their miserable existence, compelling them to keep working until they dropped. Their eyes followed him hungrily, seeking any relief from their backbreaking labour. He offered no respite, only an unending stream of water fed into parched lips and cracked mouths.

Faron's main duty was to assist in the transportation of sugar cane by cart to the mill, where the juice was extracted. This happened in haste, as the juice inside the cane deteriorated almost instantaneously. The vertical three-roller mill operated exceedingly long hours. Faron had a way of appeasing the Moedeiras – the milling women. Their work was to feed the cane back and forth between the rollers to crush it and extract the juice, but fatigue had led to lost limbs from time to time. The accidents stopped under Faron's watch. Slave master Sinhô didn't trust the help as much as he trusted Faron. A few slaves had attacked his white assistants, and some had attempted to escape. Two had killed themselves. Easing the strain on slaves with water and short breaks during trying times had been Faron's idea. Although the slaves did not care for him, they listened in silence and obeyed his commands. They knew he would not hurt them. The lower-class Portuguese assistants observed from afar, too scared to challenge Faron's self-appointed authority. As the only child of the plantation owner, he held immense power over the workers, and no one dared defy him with his potential to become the overseer of one of the biggest sugar plantations in Bahia.

The parish of Santiago do Iguape was located along the drainage basin of the Rio Ribeira de Iguapê, surrounded by the main town of Salvador in northeast Brazil. Moist forests and steep slopes crawled within the eyeline of the plantation. There had been a time when gold seeped through the veins of the Riberia. Greedy men ploughed the riverbed and its resources. Some stayed to tend rice and others sugar cane.

Day after day, slaves were ferried to the Bahian coastline and sold into servitude, driving the cost of labour down. It was of no consequence how many perished while working. But Faron's view was different; he staunchly believed in protecting the lives of his people, and wanted to demonstrate to his father that fear and anxiety could never be beneficial for business. On this day, mercifully, no one had lost their life.

With precision and grace, Ambrosina arrived at the designated spot carrying the large woven basket he'd requested. Guava, carambola and papaya spilled out in a tantalizing display. Beads of sweat glistened on her forehead from her journey across the plantation. Her dress stuck to her plump body. She wore Sabbath clothes for the occasion – a white cotton petticoat, a narrow red band across her midriff, with a blue-and-white striped shawl draped over her shoulders. She exuded a warmth and cheerfulness that drew people to her. Ambrosina was known for her hard work in the Casa Grande where she cooked and cleaned for the Sinhô. Older women saved leftovers for her, and men always asked if she needed help. Her presence seemed to lift people's spirits. Faron had attempted to speak to her on numerous occasions, but she would always just playfully tease him in response. She was one of the only people who could make him laugh at himself without feeling embarrassed or annoyed.

Purple corsage orchids were carefully arranged around the fruits in the basket. As Ambrosina walked towards Faron, a smile spreading across her full lips, his heart fluttered. He was drawn to the dimpled indentations in her cheeks that appeared every time she looked at him with adoration. Today, those dimples were a sign that he had made the right choice. It was time for Ambrosina to meet his mother; their lives were soon to be intertwined, just like his mother and the Sinhô's. His mother, Mamãe, was the only woman to bear the Sinhô a son and had theoretically become the mother of the plantation. He took Ambrosina's hand as she reached him and guided her out of the overbearing heat.

Mamãe loved flowers. She spent her time planting the freesia and camelia rosa, but her favourite was the corsage orchid, with its curved purple leaves. She placed them all around her space. A few wilted as they lingered inside the house, away from their natural habitat. Today, Mamãe knelt outside the hut, digging up the earth with a flat piece of iron. Grey cornrows pushed through a dirt brown scarf wrapped around her head. The smell of pork broth hovered over the entrance of the hut.

"Mamãe, let's go inside. I've brought you a gift." Faron buzzed with excitement.

With a groan, she pushed herself up from the ground and dusted off her hands.

Faron's cheeks flushed. "Mamãe … this is Ambrosina."

Squinting in the bright sunlight, Mamãe moved closer, peering into Ambrosina's eyes.

Ambrosina giggled. "Faron talks so much about his Mamãe. I was scared about today. We brought you these and I hope you like them. I'm grateful to meet you in your home." She handed over the basket of flowers.

Mamãe sniffed the flowers before taking the basket off Ambrosina. She guided them into the hut.

Ambrosina looked up at Faron, who responded with a reassuring smile. They followed her into the largest slave hut on the plantation. The hut was covered with banana leaves and stood at the far end of an array of slave quarters overlooking part of the estate. She had always lived apart from the others, ensuring privacy for the Sinhô's visits through the years.

"I sent a message to your Papai. Did he get it?" Mamãe asked.

"I don't know, Mamãe. I've been working."

"I don't understand why you work in the mill. You should be a bush captain."

Faron winced. A bush captain was a slave hunter who spent most of his time in the forests and swamps seeking runaways.

"Why would I want to do that?" he asked. A dull ache racked his muscles from the arduous walk across the sugar plantation to the slave huts.

Mamãe ushered them to the chairs in the room set against a small table. There were three candles held upright by a round copper chamber stick in each corner of the room. Slaves rarely had access to candles. She smiled as she waved out the window for the food to be brought in.

"Did you hear what happened in the Santana plantation? Those quilombolas took the spinning wheels from the sugar mill. They stole arms, ammunition and women, then ran back to the hills. We can't have that here. This is your legacy, Faron."

A young girl entered with bowls and placed them on the table.

"Feijoada! It smells so good. I am so grateful for this meal. Thank you, Mamãe," Ambrosina gushed as the smoke rose out of the pork broth bean stew. A pig foot surfaced as she tucked in. A rare delight for a slave. Ambrosina's eyes widened as she placed the spoon in her mouth.

"I'm glad you are enjoying it," Mamãe replied. "If you behave, you will reap a lot of rewards serving my son."

Ambrosina nodded.

"Buraco du Tatu is a good example of the Caboclo dismantling the quilombolas," Mamãe continued.

"What is quilombolas?" Ambrosina asked.

"Runaway slaves," Faron answered.

"They run away? Where do they go?"

"To the mountains. Or sometimes they stay nearby and set up towns like Buraco du Tatu."

"What? They don't get caught? It sounds dangerous," Ambrosina exclaimed.

"Quilombos everywhere!" Mamãe said. "Stealing food supplies, cattle and women from the plantation. They think they can get away with it. That's why we have captains of war, those indigenous mixed with white they call the caboclo. They do the job well, helping the police raid and destroy outside Salvador. This is what you should be doing, Faron. They cannot destroy what we are owed."

"Mamãe, they don't want the plantation. They just want to survive outside of it. When Papai dies, they won't bother us because of who we are."

Mamãe slammed the table with her fists, bulging veins stretched against the thinning skin on her hands. A mess of beans slew out of the bowls.

Faron froze.

Ambrosina's chest heaved in surprise.

"Fugitives kill their masters. Those fools from the Santana plantation even demanded a voice in the appointment of overseers. Does that sound like peace to you? Raiding cattle and stealing women? What will you do if they steal Ambrosina?" Mamãe demanded.

Ambrosina gasped.

Faron took her hand and squeezed it. "That will never happen."

"You've got that right. Eat, Ambrosina. Eat up," Mamãe retorted.

"I have no intention of becoming a bush captain, but we can consult Luíza on this if you want." Faron spoke to ease his mother's anxiety. Luíza was his mother's best friend. Both were African-born slaves who'd never settled into plantation life until Luíza's prophecy stated Faron would one day take over and rule.

"Forget Luíza," Mamãe dismissed. "She's losing her mind to old age. She tells lies and keeps filling our people's heads with dreams."

"Dreams of what?" Faron's eyes widened.

"Liberation in a matter of days. She is a crazy old woman. Forget her."

"Thank you for your hospitality, Madame," Ambrosina exclaimed. "I have never had feijoada with pigs' feet before, not even in the Sinhô's house."

Mamãe smiled and waved to the window for the children to come and clear the small table.

Faron had lost his appetite. His bean stew sat neglected. Ambrosina squeezed his hand. She remained happy to be in the company of people more important than her, and content not to understand the depth of the heated discussion that had arisen.

His mother's new revelation troubled Faron. Luíza and Mamãe were inseparable. Luíza had loved both him and Mamãe for as long as Faron had known her. She was his mother's only confidante. They spoke to each other in their own language, purposely alienating the other slaves. No one could keep them apart. Luíza had sneaked fruit into his pockets when he was old enough to work on the plantation and had taken him into her hut when the Sinhô arrived in the early hours of the morning to spend time with his mother.

"I think you know it's a sign of what's to come if you are with my son, Ambrosina. Are you up to the task?" Mamãe asked, breaking the silence.

Ambrosina's dimples hollowed, crinkling in her cheeks. Her eyes sparkled against the faint sunlight shadow in the room.

"I will never let him down. I'm his rock," she answered, gazing at Faron. "I'd give my life for him. And I am a fast learner, Madame."

Ambrosina had a habit of creating momentary peace around her.

"I am the mother of this plantation. You have a lot to learn, my dear. And you *will* learn," Mamãe said.

"Oh yes, I know," Ambrosina gushed.

"Thank you for the food, Mamãe. I'm glad that you are well. I will try to come and see you again. If not, I will send Ambrosina," Faron said.

"That's lazy. *You* come," Mamãe retorted.

Faron nodded.

Ambrosina hugged an unresponsive Mamãe, and they waved goodbye.

"She's a good woman," Ambrosina reassured him.

* * *

A few months before, Faron had set about building a hut for Ambrosina. Previously, she had shared living space with the other slaves who'd been bought alongside her, and whenever new slaves arrived, they were placed together in the same hut. Ambrosina was one of the few not to have been born on the plantation. Sold twice, she had only faded memories of her parents. Faron wanted to see Ambrosina alone whenever he could, and he didn't want to share her or have anyone listen in on their conversations. So he gathered up the strongest slaves and together they built a smaller hut over a few months. Despite becoming the envy of young women on the plantation, Ambrosina had continued to invite her companions to share a space in her new home on days when Faron wasn't around.

Later, they settled back at the hut, forgetting about Mamãe's uncompromising behaviour. Ambrosina prepared water and washed Faron's feet while he lay back and thought about his mother's words. Mamãe and Luíza had been on the same slave ship and sold together. Luíza was an important asset to the plantation. When Diogo's foot had been cut off as a punishment for running away, she was the one who attended to his stump until the swelling and infection subsided. Mamãe gathered herbs for Luíza in her spare time, and Luíza even tended to the Sinhô on occasion, when he wasn't feeling well. Mamãe would sit up on those nights, fretting for Luíza's safety. Sinhô tended to switch from pleasant to repugnant for no reason. Luíza always returned intact and Mamãe would ask for details. The white Portuguese assistants insisted on keeping Luíza away from the plantation. They disliked her being around the other slaves. On those days, Luíza searched for herbs, singing songs for all to hear. Not all the slaves liked having Luíza around. The Brazilian-born slaves hardly spoke to her, but Luíza didn't seem to notice.

Ambrosina's perspiring body rubbed against Faron's as she moved to sit next to him. He put his arms around her, but she wrenched herself away and vomited onto the ground. Faron caught her arms and pulled her back to him. He found himself grappling with her convulsing body.

"Ambrosina!" Faron shouted. He tried to calm her juddering movements before pulling her to the bed.

Ambrosina's eyes rolled back until only the whites were visible, her body going completely limp. Faron rushed to lay her on the bed, his hands shaking as he tried to process what was happening. He clutched his head in disbelief. Just moments earlier she was massaging his feet. Faron's heart pounded in his chest as he frantically tried to revive her, but her body was unresponsive, her senses completely shut down. Thick drool pooled at the corner of her mouth.

He ran out of the hut, shouting for the slaves to come. An old woman emerged from the nearest hut. He fought back the tears as he struggled to tell her what had happened.

"Go! Get Luíza, quickly!" she instructed. "I will stay with Ambrosina."

He ran faster than he had ever done in his life. Those who were still up were surprised to see Sinhô's son running frantically across the slave quarters. Some shouted after him, "What's wrong?" But he carried on creating wind beneath his feet, with one woman in mind.

As a young boy, Faron had thought Luíza fearless and powerful, despite how physically small she was. He witnessed many altercations between Luíza and the Portuguese helpers, aware of how easily the Sinhô's men could have overpowered her, but they never did. On one occasion when a Portuguese assistant spat into her eyes, Luíza didn't cry in humiliation. Instead, she cursed him.

It was her laugh that caused dismay amongst the slaves – a deep, throaty masculine snort that levelled up into hysterical squawks. A few loyal women on the plantation aided her chants and dances. The assistant who'd spat on her did not return to the plantation the following day. All remembered Luíza whistling as she carried on doing her work, binding the sugar cane into sheaves after the men had cut the cane. That assistant was sick for two months before returning to the plantation. On recovery, he was given another section to oversee, far away from Luíza.

Upon hearing the news, Luíza proclaimed, "He'll be doing more gulping and swallowing than spitting on the plantation from this day forward."

Faron remembered the looks of alarm from both black and white, the mixture of fear and disgust. It was the first time he'd witnessed a sense of trepidation in whites.

Luíza never had any children. Faron had wished she had so he could pretend to have a younger sibling. He asked her once about this, but his mother interrupted and declared that he was never to ask such questions of an elder.

But Luíza hushed Mamãe and answered him. "Not all wombs will be filled with life, Faron. Some wombs serve to comfort, feed and heal on the outside and not the inside. A woman's womb carries the spirit, grace and compassion of the human soul. She shares it with others in many ways. She gives and nurtures regardless. Do you understand this?"

Faron nodded. He tried to figure out where Luíza kept her womb and decided it must be in her hair, as its curly mass stretched to the heavens whenever she removed her head wrap.

Faron found Luíza sitting next to a log fire outside her living quarters. Heat persisted in a treacherous form as she leaned in, waving her dress around the flames as though fanning them. Her short white gown glowed against the crackling, spluttering fire. Faron's damp clothes clung to his body. He wiped the sweat away from his eyes to see the woman who could save the love of his life.

"You have come to me," Luíza spoke into the fire.

"Ambrosina is sick, Luíza. Her body is limp. Please come! I don't know what to do," Faron exclaimed in panic.

"How old are you now?" Luíza asked, keeping her eyes on the fire. "It's been a long time. I've lost count of your age."

"Twenty-four," he responded, confused.

She turned to him. "Many men die here at twenty-five …"

Faron did not know whether this was a statement or a question.

She dusted the dirt from the short white gown that covered her upper body. Her legs, hands and feet were slight and dainty. "Let's go," she said.

"I will carry you. There is no time, Luíza!" Faron motioned for her to climb on his back.

When they got back to Ambrosina's hut, Luíza walked straight in and closed the door on Faron without a word, leaving him standing on the steps alone. He blinked back tears. Folk stationed themselves outside the house, asking what had happened. A young boy consoled Faron as he sat deflated on the steps. A melancholy descended upon him as he looked around at those who observed him. He had forgotten the pain. It was steady in their eyes, no matter how much they smiled, sang and gossiped. Ambrosina was a bridge. She gave him a sense of identity. They would have a family and he would belong to something much more than just being Sinhô's only son. She was a patient and loving woman. He thought of her smile and those dimples – the only things that brought light into his darkness.

He waited over three hours before the doors were opened by the old woman who had come to his aid. Most of the slaves had gone back to their quarters, as they had to get up in a few hours to continue their toil. She ushered him inside.

Luíza sat on the bed and watched Faron as he walked in. Her expression had not changed from the one she'd had when he first came to her that night.

"What did she eat?" Luíza asked.

"What do you mean?"

"It's a simple question. What did she eat today?" she repeated.

"She ate in the Casa Grande in the morning and then we went to Mamãe's house," Faron answered.

"For what?" Luíza asked.

"I wanted her to meet Mamãe."

Luíza scoffed. "Ah yes, the mother of the plantation."

"Is she going to be okay, Luíza? She fell into my arms. What happened to her? One minute we were talking, the next she was vomiting and shaking."

"Did you eat with her?" Luíza asked.

"Is she going to be okay, Luíza?" he snapped.

"I don't know. I stabilised her, that's all I can do right now, but if you tell me what she ate then I can try to help."

"We had feijoada and Mamãe managed to get some pig's feet. I didn't eat. We had an argument about you, Luíza. Mamãe said you were losing your mind, talking about a revolution."

Luíza sat in silence as Faron waited for a response. She didn't move. Instead, she just gazed into space. Faron shifted around the bed to get closer to Ambrosina, whose rapid, shallow breathing filled the emptiness of the room. Her smooth caramel skin was saturated with sweat. Faron knelt beside the bed and laid his head next to her, holding her clammy hand. He began to pray.

"All the Africans who died on the ships coming here were carried to the hills. Their bodies were thrown into the dumps with Casa Grande rubbish and dead cows," Luíza said.

"What?"

"Your mother doesn't like to hear the truth. She cursed me for being honest with her."

"Why? What did you say?" Faron asked, surprised.

"The gods don't lie to me, Faron. Ever since I told her your prophecy, your Mamãe seeks to be a free woman on this plantation. But freedom has not yet come from you. We are tied here. I am still tied to this wretched place. This is her doing. And that devil father of yours." Luíza's voice became shrill, filling the air.

She had spoiled Faron's peace at the bed of his poor, sick beloved by badmouthing his father.

"Papai is not that bad," he snapped. "I have changed him over the years. I've made it my business to make sure there are no whippings, and everyone gets food and water when they work. No other plantation owner allows this to happen. You know this. I have succeeded in keeping everyone alive."

Luíza shrugged. "If you want me to have a chance at bringing her back to you, then you must go. I will do all I can."

Faron didn't want to leave, but Luíza was a woman of her word. Ambrosina lay unresponsive. His eyes brimmed with tears at the memory of her laughter that very evening on their walk back to the hut. She had been so excited about their trip to meet Mamãe. The beautiful array of flowers and fruits arranged in the basket demonstrated her selfless behaviour, just to please him and his mother. She was so keen to belong. But she already belonged to everyone. They all loved her.

Faron and Luíza stood outside the hut. The speckle of dawn on the horizon ridiculed the amount of time he had spent away from the Casa Grande, the big house he shared with the Sinhô. Luíza's withered frame had saved many lives and healed many hearts. He would do anything for this woman if she saved Ambrosina.

"Thank you, Luíza –"

"You may inherit this land," Luíza interrupted, "but I see nothing but death, wailing souls, bare feet bleeding with each step. Rotting corpses, burning bodies … I smell the burning, Faron. It haunts me at night. Closer and closer it gets – the fire, the smoke. I smell the burning flesh. I hear the screams. I see the struggle. I wake from my sleep shrieking almost every night!"

"Luíza, come on! You know I don't have that in me! Why do you do this?" Faron sighed.

"You are but a boy, Faron. Swear to me you will not do worse than your Sinhô," she demanded.

"No! Luíza, no. I am a good man. I just want Ambrosina back. I need her. She is everything to me."

"Then you will need to choose," she said.

"Choose what?"

"Your mother is the mother of this plantation. She removes choices. That is who she is and who she has always been. Sometimes the bitterness of life can change your destiny if you allow it. You will need to make a choice very soon, Faron. Now go. I will stay and do what I was put on this earth to do by the gods."

"Please, Luíza, I love her. I cannot live without her. Please save her."

"My father fell in love with a woman who shortened his life. He left his family. She was a demon."

"Ambrosina is not like that. She is a good girl, an Angel."

"Demons and angels are not so different. They walk the same earth as us. They are amongst us. Gods are amongst us. Some of them seduce us. Are you willing to give up everything for that which you do not know?"

Faron fell to the ground, placing his hands on Luíza's bare feet. "I'm begging you. Just do something."

Luíza pushed him away.

"Go home. We will see you tomorrow."

CHAPTER TWO

Faron stared at the ceiling as he lay on the pallet bed stuffed with straw. The draught coming in through the crack of the window enhanced the scent of the fresh flowers that filled each room of the house, the heavy smell of sweaty slaves and muddy garments forgotten. Ambrosina's serene expression flew into his mind. The strings of his heart yanked at his throat. Without Luíza, it could have been so much worse. Today, he would run errands as quickly as possible for Sinhô and get back to his beloved. He climbed out of the bed onto his knees to beg God for Ambrosina's life.

Faron made his way into the bustling town to pick up an eagerly anticipated package from a close family acquaintance. Paulo Alves was Sinhô's long-time trusted tailor. A variety of folk passed through the shop daily. Soldiers in crisp uniforms, weathered carpenters with sawdust clinging to their clothes, poor whites and free mulattos chose to take solace and catch up with the town's gossip while watching Paulo create clothes for the elite. The air was thick with fabric and sweat. Paulo and the Sinhô were good friends, and both had mulatto sons. Luca was ten years old, already learning his father's trade, his head buried in cutting and measuring cloth. Whenever the adults spoke to him, he would look up, smile and blink, before going back to cutting. Paulo Alves' establishment served as a getaway from the plantation. Faron sat for hours listening to conversations on mills, rice, gold, cattle and women. There was nothing he didn't know about the profit and loss of rich men, the risks and the next big opportunity. Whenever Faron visited with Sinhô, Paulo served his father coffee and sometimes port. The men talked and Faron listened.

This morning, Faron's presence did little to speed up his father's expected garments; instead, visitors and customers forced endless distractions upon the assistant tailors with arguments about Portugal, tax and rumours of police raids. When it was time to leave, Paulo had a message for Sinhô – he wanted to be included in the current men's club for reasons he would divulge later.

As Faron made his way home, he observed the people around him. The mountains that encased the town, looming in the distance taunted him with thoughts. He couldn't help but think about those who lived beyond them and how different their lives must be. Would he and Ambrosina end up like them? His mind raced with questions as he hurried to deliver his father's package.

Faron passed the message on as he watched his father getting dressed in his crisp, white shirt and knee-length breeches. Sinhô's instruction was to oversee the whole plantation for the first time. Faron felt a sense of responsibility wash over him. This would be the first time he oversaw the entire plantation. The heavy smell of sweat and dirty garments flooded the rooms of the Casa Grande. It was impossible to escape the stifling heat, making Faron eager for his father to finish dressing so they could leave. He needed to know how Ambrosina was doing and if she was safe amidst all this chaos.

"I set fire to the witch Luíza this morning." Sinhô's words interrupted Faron's thoughts. "Your mother told me what happened. We don't burn slaves. We never burn anyone. But she wasn't a slave, she was a witch. Nobody poisons my property."

Faron's fingers trembled as they grasped the loose buttons of his tattered shirt. His gut felt like it had been ripped out and forced back in, a visceral and agonising sensation, as if his insides were rebelling against him and attempting to escape, only to be forced back into their prison with unrelenting force. A feeling of betrayal and despair consumed him.

"You should have heard her screams," Sinhô chuckled. "She's always had a good set of lungs on her." He mimicked a woman screaming as he walked back over to the mirror. "Didn't Augusto tell you?"

"No, Papai," Faron answered, coughing to disguise the tightness in his throat. His mind whirled, his breathing became laboured. He held onto the corner of the table to keep from passing out. Was Ambrosina alive? The sound of the house slaves' bare feet moving across the floorboards and the wind against the trees interrupted the silence of the Casa Grande. The taste of bile rose in Faron's mouth.

"Ah, those tailors always keep you with them to talk, talk, talk. That's why you weren't here. Luíza confessed before she died. Curses. I don't like curses. She betrayed your mother. And you. Did you know Luíza was the one responsible for helping my slaves to run away over the years? She …" Sinhô stopped to wag his finger. "It was she who encouraged Diogo to run away. He would still have his leg if it wasn't for her. Remember that."

"Mamãe told you this, Papai?"

"Both women," Sinhô replied. "I can't have anyone on this plantation helping my slaves join these quilombos. That is betrayal and Luíza betrayed me. Your mother is good for this plantation and all the slaves, all of them know this."

"I must go, Papai. To see Mamãe," Faron insisted.

Sinhô patted his cheek. "Keep your mother close."

Faron marched towards his mother's hut. He had to get to the bottom of what had happened. How could women who loved so deeply suddenly turn on each other with such hate? Why would Mamãe get Sinhô to put Luíza to death? Where was his beloved Ambrosina? His anger increased at the sight of his mother's large hut and majestic flower garden.

Faron stormed in to find his mother eating. She waved him to sit as if expecting him.

"They set Luíza on fire!" he shouted.

Mamãe cracked the cow neck bone between her teeth and sucked at the marrow.

"You made Papai kill Luíza? Why did you lie?"

She continued to suck on the bone until the marrow was out before spitting chewed fragments into the bowl. Her elbows propped up her soiled arms. She looked him over as though he was a mosquito buzzing around, waiting to get clapped by a set of hands.

"Nobody helps anyone escape without my say so. I am the mother of the plantation. She went against you!" Mamãe pointed her oil-slick finger at him, jabbing at the air. "You will inherit this place. Nobody is going to come between us or take that away. This plantation is ours. But oh no! She doesn't want to wait. Luíza thought she could ruin what we have here? No way," Mamãe said indignantly.

"She was saving Ambrosina's life, Mamãe! Saving her life. Now I must get Ambrosina and take her away from all this planning and plotting that you have going on here. What's wrong with you? God will never forgive you for what you've done," Faron shouted.

Mamãe rose in haste, toppling her chair. "You ungrateful cockroach! Bring that feeder in here. She already has you wrapped around her finger. You think you picked her? No. She picked you. You are a child. A stupid child! You don't know women. You don't even know what plantation she came from. You trust everyone because you sleep in the Casa Grande. That woman cannot be trusted. We know nothing about her."

"What do you mean? What are you saying, Mamãe?" Faron whispered.

"You don't know women!" Mamãe slapped her chest. "I know women. They suck you into their wombs and now you want to die for them. I see how well you feed her. No! She won't get to decide! I decide."

Faron recoiled.

"What did you do, Mamãe?" he breathed.

"You go and be your father's son and do as you're told. Now get out!"

"Mamãe, did you put something in the food yesterday?"

"I said get out!" she screamed.

A heat spread across Faron's cheeks as his entire body tensed. He turned away, trying to calm the storm

21

brewing inside him. Ambrosina loved him. Luíza healed his wounds and tended to him when he was sick. He walked towards the entrance. His resignation appeared to further infuriate Mamãe.

"I am the mother of this plantation. No woman will take my place unless I grant it. They will be sold or dead before they can usurp me," Mamãe snarled.

Faron's heart stopped cold. He recoiled as his mother's shrill words pierced the air, causing him to spin round and face her seething expression. Rage and disgust flooded his body as he charged towards her and shoved her with all his might. She stumbled backwards, crashing into a table and hit her head with a sickening thud. Plates clattered to the floor. Food flew everywhere. Faron stepped back, stunned. Mamãe lay motionless on the floor, a pool of blood forming around her head. A horrified Faron froze as the deafening silence surrounded him. Mamãe lay still on the ground, her lifeblood slowly seeping from her.

Faron stooped down.

"Mamãe, I'm sorry." His breath quickened as he tried desperately to revive her, shaking her body, and calling her name. Her body was limp in his hands. A slick of blood oozed out of her scalp. "Mamãe, wake up. Mamãe, please wake up. Mamãe!"

Faron frantically pried open one of his mother's eyelids with his trembling fingers. Fear gripped him tightly as memories of Ambrosina flooded his mind, creating a feeling of déjà vu that threatened to consume him.

"No, no, God no, please. Mamãe, I didn't mean it. I love you. Please, Mamãe. Please wake up. Don't die. I'm sorry. It was a mistake. I'm sorry!"

He buried his face in her body and wept.

The afternoon sun stood still for him as he sat with his mother in his arms. He could not be seen leaving the hut, but he had to take Ambrosina away from this mess. He thought about the quilombos. It no longer seemed such a bad idea to run, but how could he? He must stay calm. This was his home. Tears and snot trickled down his cheeks and nose. He had to get it together. He was in charge. He would give his mother a good funeral. But first, the goal was to find Ambrosina and make sure she was safe.

He lifted Mamãe's large body off the floor and onto her straw bed, placing a kiss on her forehead before throwing her Sunday shawl over her face. He pulled off his blood-stained top, curling it up into a small ball as he walked out of the house.

Ambrosina's hut was empty. The slaves were all out on the plantation and the children did not recall seeing anyone enter or leave the property all day. Faron visited the old woman who lived next door. She was preparing some food and looked alarmed at the sight of Faron, hushing the children away.

"Where is she? Where is Ambrosina?" Faron asked.

"I don't know," the woman replied.

"Did you see Luíza?"

"Yes, they came and took her away early in the morning. Luíza was singing and chanting. I don't know what she was saying, but she laughed in their faces and spat at the men. They beat her to the ground. An old woman like her – they stomped her head."

Faron stood speechless.

"Nobody has seen Ambrosina." The old woman whispered. "We don't know if she lives or dies. She's just gone."

Faron searched the outskirts of the plantation for tracks, pieces of clothing, or something that confirmed her escape. There was no one on the lookout and Ambrosina was nowhere to be found. He headed home as fast as he could, slipping quietly up the stairs to his room. His bones ached from climbing, crawling, running and searching for Ambrosina. Nobody had seen or heard anything. Were the slaves hiding information from him? They should know he would never hurt her.

He needed time to consider what Ambrosina's options would have been once she woke up. Perhaps the slaves had hidden her from him? A cool breeze hit him as he entered his bedroom. One of the house slaves must have opened the window. A bowl of water stood alone on the table. Faron removed his dirty clothes. The water turned red as he wiped the dried bloody smudges from his body. It felt as if the ritual of washing the blood from his hands somehow baptised and absolved him from the sin he had committed that day. He removed any trace of the twisted, malignant love that, for as long as he could remember, his mother had abused him with.

His bedroom window overlooked animals grazing in a field of green. Faron watched the shadows of tall grass lean against the wind. The events of the day left him numb, but he knew he had to find Ambrosina. He put the bowl outside the door and slipped into fresh clothes. He needed to think about his next move before Sinhô came home that evening.

CHAPTER THREE

Faron stood on the veranda. A sea of green perennial grass rolled out farther than the eye could see, magnificent against the blue sky. The landscape, in all its beauty, had never caught his attention before, for it was no friend to the enslaved. But now, the stillness of the grounds charged through his spirit, rendering him unable to remove himself from the scenery before him. He'd wanted to run away from the plantation as a boy, but his mother convinced him to stay. Sinhô provided her with food and clothes. She had everything she wanted and was not required to work the sugar cane like the others. According to Luíza's visions, it was written that her son would inherit the land, and she just needed to be patient. Now, neither of the women were here to witness this potential future. Here he was, freshly bathed, sitting in clean clothes overlooking the plantation, and the possibility of his becoming solely responsible for the mills had surfaced. But his mother was naive. He would never become the owner of a plantation. He remained a slave, and no freed slave would ever be granted inheritance, so it was impossible. At most, he could be made an overseer.

The house slaves brought him coffee as he sat silently in his thoughts. What if Ambrosina had regained consciousness and Luíza had warned her about Mamãe, and she fled?

Had Mamãe planned this all along? Ambrosina was an impressionable girl who couldn't match the cunning of older women. She wasn't built for it. He took a mouthful of coffee and allowed the sun to embrace his body.

The walls of the house trembled as a loud and frantic pounding echoed through the rooms. Amidst the cacophony of angry voices, he could discern a cry of agony, not from a slave but from one of the assistants. Faron cautiously retreated inside to find a group of aggravated male slaves waited with clubs, whips and machetes, glowering with intent. He heard bellows outside. Half the white assistants were on the other side of the plantation overseeing the sugar cane or in the mill. The slaves had carefully orchestrated their coming to the Casa Grande without being missed. Only a handful of assistants were close to the house, and they were probably outnumbered at this point helpless to protect Faron. Several of the slaves were soaked in their blood. Their eyes narrowed as they glared at him. The smell of salty bodily fluids and dirty clothes hung in the air, suffocating the fresh flowers in vases around the room. Faron's armpits dampened. One of the bigger slaves moved forward. His name was Eduardo.

"You will pay for what you did to our mother."

Those words stung Faron's ears. Our mother. Heat flushed over him as he trembled. The weight of their accusation landed heavily on his shoulders. Her lies. They all believed her lies. The revelation of her demise, though unspoken in this moment, hung palpably in the air, threading a sinister connection between Faron's actions and the untimely loss they now mourned. Her lies. They all believed her lies. He ran into the mob with a bloodcurdling scream. His fists landed on Eduardo's jaw, sending the big man to the floor. He lashed out as hands grabbed his body, throwing him to the ground. Roars filled the rooms of the Casa Grande. Some of the grounds-men entered the house, attempting to disband the crowd. Faron clawed and punched at all the faces that attacked him. Eduardo hit him on the head with Sinhô's favourite vase.

Faron's eyes shot open, his body painfully suspended from the gnarled branches of a tall tree. His arms and legs bound tightly with coarse ropes, his skin burning from repeated lashings of a whip. The once raucous sounds of nature had fallen silent, as if in shock. Even the usual chirping of the kiskadee birds and howling of the dogs had ceased, leaving only the gentle rustle of leaves in the wind. Faron succumbed to unconsciousness, his body too weak to endure any longer.

Later, through a blur, he could make out the rugged texture of brown bark surrounded by green. They had clearly dragged him away from the house. The faces looking into his were bruised and bloody. The groundsmen must have wounded some of the crowd. There were only a few men surrounding his body compared to the numbers that had entered the house. The rest had doubtlessly been captured and were being questioned in unspeakable ways. He tried to speak, but the stinging lashes suppressed his attempts. Someone had seen him leave the hut, trying to hide his bloodied shirt. They cursed him for taking the mother of the plantation from them so brutally. They cursed the land he walked on. They cursed his life.

When they pulled him down, their attempts to grasp his blood-slick skin proved futile, and his body dropped unceremoniously to the ground. His hearing and vision distorted as he lay in the mud. The faint smell of burning wood filled the air. Eduardo's face loomed over Faron, his features twisted with malice. He spat into Faron's eyes, blinding him temporarily, before forcing his mouth open and chanting an incantation. Faron thrashed and struggled as Eduardo shoved a clump of dirt into his mouth, cutting off his air supply. The other men joined in, kicking and stomping on Faron's vulnerable body until he lost consciousness again.

* * *

He gasped.

Dirt.

The soil entered his nose and mouth, and he choked. He could hear Luíza's voice in his ears: "A union of wealth, prosperity and freedom. You will be a free man and visit many cities and people. A father's love and a mother's scorn meet to unearth a demon that walks the earth in denunciation. The ancestors prepare the land across the waters for the soul to be redeemed." A vision of his mother clapping her hands as Luíza talked of freedom and a return across the waters. Faron struggled to breathe. Soil slid around him, and his insides seized up. He should be dead. They'd buried him in a shallow grave in the bushes further out from the Casa Grande.

He speared his fingers into the dirt, clawing frantically. The voices in his head got louder. They cursed him. Luíza's voice was the clearest. "A father's love and a mother's scorn meet to unearth a demon that walks the earth in denunciation." He swallowed as the dirt fell around his face and gagged. He clawed faster, his heart battering against his chest. Finally, sunlight. He pulled himself out of the earth with the last bit of strength he had left. He wasn't safe from slaves or free men now. Wobbling, he tried to stand. Pus seeped from his open wounds. White bone pushed out of his hips and knees. His skeletal feet sank into the crumbling brown earth scattered around his grave.

Faron recoiled.

What had happened to him? Surely he hadn't been buried for that long? Fear and confusion overwhelmed Faron as he felt his body, shocked to find that it had been reduced to bones and sagging skin. The flesh on his arms had degenerated and patches of sickly yellow pus seeped from strange places. Maggots crawled through the exposed muscle tissue and wiggled around within his stomach cavity. In desperation, he slapped at his body in a futile attempt to get rid of the camouflage of gangrene and rot that riddled his being. How could this have happened? Was he going to die? How was this even possible?

The sound of gunfire echoing in the distance sent panic coursing through him. Were they coming for him? Flames consumed the sky. Faron raised his arms for a closer look at their disintegration and sobbed. What was happening to him? What affliction was this? He tried to work out how long he had been buried in the ground for. What if someone stumbled upon his empty grave? They would surely hunt him down without mercy. A series of shots made him jump. The sound was closer this time. Faron scanned the surrounding green. Everyone would track him with different intentions. The helpers would probably unite in the attempt to get rid of him, serving the interests of all concerned. With him gone, the plantation was free to return to the old ways of doing things. The longest-serving assistants would receive more for their loyalty and commitment to the plantation. His life was in danger from all sides. Faron bawled in despair. He was cursed.

The sound of snapping twigs and thumping footsteps disrupted his desolation. Figures appeared in the distance. Anyone who found him would kill him without remorse. The figures ran in different directions. Others emerged, but they were white. The feet of panic-stricken men thudding the ground drummed against Faron's ears. He backed away into the bush, hoping none of the helpers or slaves would run into him. If the assistants murdered him, they would blame it on the slaves. One of the assistants aimed his gun at a running slave and fired. The body fell onto the sodden ground. Faron backed further into the bush, away from the sounds. He could not be seen. He could not be captured. He had to get away.

He dragged himself into the surrounding forest. Creatures scurried away from his odour. He struggled over broken branches and crawled under low-hanging logs. His body weighed him down as though it yearned to be buried underneath the horrors of the topsoil. It became a gruelling challenge to move this unfamiliar physique. His skin peeled away at the scrape of a thorn or uneven sprout of leaves. He realised he had to stop before what was left of him fell apart.

Faron found a collapsed hollow trunk amongst the thick bush large enough to curl up in. He hid inside it, trying to collect his thoughts. He could hardly bear to look at his skeletal feet slipping into the soft earth. His body was unrecognisable – no longer human. The skin on his face peeled off effortlessly. He felt his mouth and his lips had disappeared, revealing bone and enamel. Faron sobbed into the moss surrounding him. No tears flowed down his rotting cheeks, he could only snort and sniffle. He was alone, and the thought of it terrified him. His mind was consumed by thoughts of all that was gone. His cries echoed through the air, a symphony of agony and loss. Each breath brought with it a sharp ache in his chest, an overwhelming sense of despair that threatened to suffocate him. No tears fell from his eyes, only terrible sounds escaped his lips – a gut-wrenching culmination of pain and anger.

He remained in the rotting trunk, oblivious to time, lying still, listening to the forest sounds, and observing the small creatures and insects that buzzed around him. From time to time, he flicked away the maggots that curled out of his seeping stomach and crushed them. He thought of his mother – this was all her doing. She had been a selfish, bitter and twisted woman. If it wasn't for his existence, she wouldn't have had any of the privileges that she enjoyed. They called her *their* mother – but that was only because she had been one of the original African slaves. They did not know what it was really like to have her as a mother. They had no idea of all that he had endured. He recalled the way they kicked and stomped on his body. They hated him. They chose to hate him. He had done no wrong to them. They chose to see only his difference and to hate him for it, labelling him and blaming him for their suffering because it was easier. Faron wanted Eduardo dead. In his mind's eye, he could see Papai's devastation at the reports of his death. His feeling of hopelessness. No body to mourn or bury. Questions of how and why this had happened. Would he be disappointed? How would he manage his anger? Was Papai safe? What would he do to those slaves that were left to tell the tale? Papai was a very unpredictable man and even the assistants would feel his wrath.

As the evening turned to night Faron felt no need to make a fire as he was unaffected by the coolness of his surroundings. He wondered, if he ventured further into the forest, whether he would need to light fires to protect himself from creatures ready to attack him. Venomous insects did not attempt to bite him, instead they veered past him and scurried away. He was not sure why. It was also becoming obvious that he did not need to eat. The terror of being hunted down and the grief of his body's unspeakable changes had him so confused that hunger eluded him. He did not even feel the need to find a spring to drink from to stay hydrated. With each revelation, he slumped further into the rotting trunk, and ignored large titan beetles feeding on the decaying wood around him. As time went by, he remained there lost in grief.

The urge to see his father grew with each passing moment. If his father knew he was alive it would change everything. The issue was to remain alive and get to the Casa Grande in one piece. Lying still for such a long time had given his body time to adjust to its new form. His skin seemed to be scraping off more slowly than before. He put his hands to his face. Bone touched bone, forehead, cheeks and jaw. Shredded skin hung off his thigh area. How was he supposed to go to the Casa Grande and not be seen? How and what was this horror? If Eduardo were still alive, he would see to it that Eduardo's suffering matched his own. Could he return to his father in this state, or was the forest destined to be his home forever? Faron punched at the soft, rotting bark that surrounded him. Someone had to pay for this. Someone had to tell him what had happened to his beloved.

He delayed himself in his thoughts, imagining the slaves subdued and the assistants comfortable. Wait too long and the momentum would slip away. Then, one sunny afternoon, Faron rose from his hiding place, determined to appeal to his father. Perhaps he was knowledgeable of this affliction. Maybe the slaves would reconcile with him once they found out the truth about his mother.

Eduardo had chanted emphatically while shoving earth into his mouth. The slaves knew something, he was sure of it, and his father understood how to get information out of anyone. He did not know if the routine of the *Casa Grande* had changed as a result of the horrendous events. It was possible but there was no way of knowing if he did not try to find out. Faron struggled to get up, an awkward dangling mass of bone and rotting flesh. His legs felt less weighty as he repositioned his skeletal form, placing one leg in front of the other. It was time to put an end to this nightmare and get back to his life. Gusts of wind blew on exposed muscle. This energised his pace. Nimble on his feet, he jumped clear of hazards that he wouldn't have noticed before. As he moved along in haste, he thought about his father's routine. A man as powerful as Sinhô had no reason to fret, the plantation owners, soldiers, and police were all family friends and relatives, ready to suppress any lingering thoughts of the slave rebellion from those who dared to imagine a different reality. Although, he had lost track of time, his body determined his thinking and pulled him towards a narrow pathway, away from the more exposed trail cut by the Portuguese for direct access to Salvador.

Sinhô preferred the indigenous trail that had widened over time from carts and wheelbarrows. Faron moved towards the trail with no doubt he would see someone from the Casa Grande, perhaps even his father. For the first time, he felt the wind sweep against his bones, bringing a strange rush to his senses. The clop of horse's hooves thudded against his ears. He wrinkled his nose at a familiar scent that he could not place. He stood still for a moment to understand it, then pushed ahead in stealth and silence. He knew his father's daily routine – he would be on his way home with Augusto.

In the distance, through the bushes, Faron spotted a female slave carrying a basket. He didn't recognise her. Her bare feet pressed firmly on the ground with the dull motion of a donkey. Faron receded into the bushes, waiting for her to walk past, but she stopped and turned around. A horse and cart trundled past her with Augusto at the helm and the Sinhô sitting next to him. Faron's stomach tightened, and his head swam. He wasn't sure whether he should reveal himself to them, but this would be his only chance before they reached the plantation. It was a safer choice.

Augusto bellowed in disgust as the horse rode past the bushes where Faron hid. The female slave cried out, covering her nose and mouth with her dress. The horse and cart stopped at Augusto's command. Sinhô stayed in his seat while Augusto climbed out of the wagon, his face sullen. Faron watched Sinhô's eyes fix on Augusto's movements and wondered how he was feeling. His father's leathery skin displayed an array of deep wrinkles across his eyes and jawline. Perhaps he was nervous, and it had troubled him to drink. Augusto marched towards the female slave. His hair had turned white since the last time Faron had seen him, probably from all the problems that had befallen them. Faron moved forwards with intent. It was not clear to him whether this was a good idea, but his body dictated that he had to get closer. They needed to see him and know that he was indeed alive. He took several steps towards the open pathway.

"What is that smell?" The female slave exclaimed. Her body heaved in response to the scent around her as she staggered back in confusion. Augusto reached her and looked in Faron's direction. Faron stopped in his tracks. The female slave covered her face as she coughed involuntarily. Augusto couldn't see Faron, but he raised his arm over his nose in response.

"Find out what that smell is, Augusto," Sinhô shouted after him.

Faron moved towards the clearing without hesitation.

Augusto's face turned ashy grey.

"Corpo Seco!" the female slave screamed. She blacked out and collapsed at Augusto's feet, her basket hitting the ground, dispersing fruit in every direction.

"Augusto, tell me! What is going on?" The Sinhô commanded.

Faron did not care about the woman. What mattered was that Augusto revealed the truth to his father – that Faron was still alive. He existed and no one would ever try to harm him or take his place again. Let Augusto see him and bear witness to the reality. It was time to go home.

Augusto's mouth fell open. His eyebrows pulled up in shock as he raised his hands to stop Faron from moving forwards.

"It's me, Augusto," Faron heard himself say. He hadn't spoken for so long that his voice came out cracked in different pitches as if it were broken.

Augusto whimpered, blocking the sight of Faron from his eyes.

"I'm alive, Augusto. I think Eduardo cursed me. I don't know what's happening, but I am well, and I am here. It's me, Faron." He took another step forward.

Augusto frantically waved his hands in the air to stop Faron from moving any closer.

"No. Stay back! It is done," he shouted.

Then he turned and ran towards the cart.

"What did you see, Augusto?" Sinhô asked. "What is it?"

Augusto did not answer. He jumped on and jolted the horse into a full-speed getaway. The female slave remained on the ground; her fruit besieged by flies.

There was nothing Faron could do but watch the cart get smaller.

CHAPTER FOUR

The forest embraced him like a mother whose child had returned home from a long day weeding crops. Trees bent over him, shutting out the intoxicating heat. Birds sang to soothe his anguish. There was no going back. The look on Augusto's face had told Faron all he needed to know. He could not present himself to his father. He could never return. Now they would look to kill him and remove any evidence of him ever existing. He wondered who would be sent to hunt him down. If Augusto told Sinhô what he'd seen, Faron would be hunted by all. He was doomed. Cursed.

This is what Luíza meant all those years ago, when she spoke of her prediction of what was to come. Faron was not sure how she'd misunderstood the vision on the day she danced around him when he was still a child, but it was clear her interpretation had changed on the last night he'd seen her. She'd snapped at him for no reason, as though she finally understood what had been revealed to her all those years earlier by her ancestors or gods or whatever they were. The woman could not even understand her own visions. Hallucinations, forethoughts and prophecies, all misinterpreted through the simple mind of the interpreter. He would never listen to the dreams and ideas of fools again.

Faron drifted away from the plantation, deeper into the Bahian jungle. Sinhô would pay men to comb the area. If the slaves knew he was still alive they might send word to the quilombos to track him. He couldn't take any chances. The lives of those he knew meant nothing now. His parents did not exist. He was dead to all. He'd lived to please his mother and the Sinhô. Every move he'd made had been dictated and monitored, but now he was free, and desperately isolated. He would remain so until he found a cure or died in the jungle.

The further he ventured into the bush, the more his surroundings changed. Thicker tree trunks, gigantic leaf spans and colours sprung out at him as if in a contest to be admired. Furry caterpillars, black grasshoppers with yellow spots, butterflies with owl eyes, and tailless scorpions all rummaged and scampered around him. He no longer paid attention to what would have bothered him before. The deeper the jungle, the less the creatures scurried away from him. The smell of his rotting body mixed with his surroundings. He spent time observing the animals and the many saplings that thrived around him. The leaves of the palla trees had been used to cover huts in his childhood, and their seeds when cooked produced a milky, chocolatey drink that he'd enjoyed with his friends. Where daylight seeped through the opening cracks of large palms, he observed ants collecting epiphyte seeds and "planting" them in nests they built in tachigali trees. He picked up fruits littering the ground in the dry forest from the fifty-foot cupuaçu tree to taste the creamy pulp dug out of the husk. The sediments remained tasteless and stuck in his throat. He spat them out and grew content with not eating. Instead, he roamed, climbed, crawled and focused on the animal life around him. Anything to cast out the memories that plagued him.

When the rains started, it became difficult to move. Faron scrambled to find a space to shield himself from the mercenary downpour slamming ferociously around him. He knew he was not yet in the deep confines of Amazonia. He intended to make his home near the borders of the New Kingdom of Granada. As a child, he'd listened to stories of the indigenous in that area; it was a place with fewer Portuguese and therefore less strife.

It was not possible to know how much time had passed since his encounter with Angelo, but he found himself thinking of the Sinhô celebrating Christmas in the usual way; drinking with the neighbouring family and frolicking with new female slaves, in his own home, when the sun disappeared from the sky. The memories remained, but the longing was gone. It was as though he was recalling the details of a painting hung on the walls of someone else's parlour. Sinhô owned two paintings. One he claimed to be of his grandfather and the other a self-portrait. Paintings were created from a thought, a memory, an experience of something beautiful. Faron decided that although paintings existed to be admired and evoke emotion, there were also times they existed to be forgotten and ignored in the presence of others. Now that the Amazon was his home, it was as though the memory of his life resembled those paintings in the Casa Grande. It could be retained, and regarded or ignored, amid the day-to-day reality around him that proved much more engaging.

Faron began building temporary shelter as the rain threatened the forest with its torrents and accompanying humidity. He leaned a broken tree branch against a larger tree and added smaller branches at different angles along it. Then he placed leaves and foliage to cover and complete his shelter. The rain signified how much time Faron had been away from the plantations, wandering around without direction. It brought him a certain unease. He felt he needed to shield himself from its rage and figured the further into the Amazon he ventured, the less the rain would bother him. It was said that it could not permeate the trees and get into the jungle. A welcoming thought. He had loved to wash in the rain as a child, but there was a different feeling to this new body. The sound of thunder exploded in his eardrums and rain drops hitting his bones sent tremors through him.

Once he had covered his shelter with foliage, he climbed in and covered his ears. Rain smashed against the broken tree. Faron was unable to comprehend why his vision blurred intermittently. His senses were increasing the further he moved into the forest. He noticed colours and sounds that no human could surely recognise. The thought of going blind terrified him as his vision dimmed. His eyelids had disintegrated into dust upon his change, so it was important to block out the rain in his shelter. He tuned in to his other senses and focused on the pungent smell of decaying vegetation to block out the angst. The smell of life in this vast forest. This was his smell. This was his world. He felt his chest rise and his lungs expand. At least his organs were hidden behind a wall of torn muscle and ribcage in his torso. The deterioration in his body no longer fazed him. He felt more alive than ever before. The rain dripped off the leaves sheltering him and made its way to the ground. Colours around him changed shape and became distorted.

Alas, his shelter could not keep the rains out. His skeletal arms and legs flailed unexpectedly as the intruding water washed over him. His eyes rolled to the back of his skull. His bones seized up. The mating calls of the cigarra cricket screeched in his eardrums as though they were beside him, fighting with the vibrations of the bulldog bat using sound to navigate at night. He languished for what seemed like hours in a world of darkness as the rains pelted his skeleton. No sound, no smell, no motion. When the rains stopped, his bones eased and slackened. He had no eyelids, but it felt as though he had experienced the sensation of deep sleep. An earnest disturbance racked his being. The moist smell of sapinho sapo frogs nearby surged into his senses.

Faron sat up, his bones covered in mud, and his shelter broken into sticks surrounded by rotting leaves. Sudden hunger pains gnawed through his form. He instinctively crouched down, sniffing the air around him. The scent of what he required was nearby. He didn't recognise the smell, but his body did. The gnawing increased. Faron looked down at his exposed intestines. They seemed to quiver ever so slightly against his pelvic bones. His nose led the way. He slapped bushes out of his path until he saw a human hiding in the trees. The human had a spear. He was a PataxÓ. Faron recognised the tribesman from his traditional red paint. A ravenous convulsion shook his body, accompanied by intolerable stinging to his trembling intestines. He felt like a puma – a large, secretive cat from the mountains with the urge to feed. The need overwhelmed him.

Faron prowled around, observing the PataxÓ boy as he hunted for small animals, not sure what he would do with him. The convulsions grew whenever he got closer. Food had long been forgotten as he'd struggled to understand his changes, making his way through the forest. The PataxÓ unsettled him. He knew the people had no communication with the invading Portuguese. They, too, knew the horror of being hunted. Yet what he was feeling was not the urge to protect one who understood his pain as a slave.

Faron followed the boy as he moved unaware through the bushes. He couldn't see the animal the boy was trailing. His compulsion blinded all other senses. The boy's skin glowed. His rib cage pushed up against his flesh. The muscles in his arms stretched taut against his skin. The boy's jet-black hair curved neatly against his forehead. Faron needed to speak to him. To touch him. To carry him away. The urge to own him was overwhelming. A craving linked to the gnawing and shivering of his intestines created an overpowering yearning for the boy.

A ring-tailed coati moved past Faron, its long nose and high tail disrupting the compulsion. Faron swung around and grabbed the tail, unsure of his motives but understanding that his body was doing the talking. The coati made a surprised "woof" sound that alerted the PataxÓ boy, who did not stop to look around but ran into the thick forest, unaware that his life had just been spared. Faron squeezed the coati in a fit of rage and the animal disintegrated into a cloud of dust. A rush of indulgence flooded his being. Bittersweet, fleeting pleasure shuddered through his bones. An instant relief, devoid of melancholy. Faron sniffed the earth for more coati – there was a band of at least twenty females nearby. A warm sensation trickled over his rotting flesh as he crouched on all fours, ready to seek out this new rush. Something told him that if he did not get it from the coati, he would seek out a human.

CHAPTER FIVE

The love affair with the ring-tailed coati didn't last very long. Faron felt like a rodent chasing a rodent, and there were only so many coatis he could find and kill. The momentary euphoria that had rattled his body left an unpleasant sensation in his core. Short-term gratification. The more animals, the less fulfilling.

He wandered around, thinking and searching for an alternative. The PataxÓ boy's smell and taste lingered on the tip of his tongue, as though he'd licked the sweat from his body. The gnawing in his stomach increased, as did the soft intestinal shifting in his abdomen. He ambled deeper into the forest, driven by the image of the PataxÓ's soft brown skin. The folds in his armpits and the damp patch between his shoulder blades carved a permanent picture in Faron's brain. The lower part of Faron's body pulled him with intent towards the human flesh. Trickles of water dripped between the tree leaves above him. He shook his shoulders involuntarily at the thought of the drops hitting him. It would get in the way, slow him down, but then he remembered that wherever there was water there were humans. They needed it for survival.

His body persisted for what seemed like an eternity, smelling, tracing and tracking, to no avail. Yet his legs marched on regardless. They did not lead him to a PataxÓ settlement as quickly as he'd have imagined, and the gnawing sensation reminded him he had to keep moving, until he saw the howler monkey. His pace slowed. Would it be possible that this creature could replace the ring-tailed coati? The snout-nosed howler monkey sensed Faron's presence and shook at the branch above him to warn the others. They clearly discerned his scent and understood his intentions, which was puzzling. How could they determine his plans just by seeing him? Many indigenous kept monkeys as pets, but he did not look like them. He was unfamiliar.

Faron's feet halted at the edge of the forest, his eyes scanning the lush greenery before him. As he took a step forward, an instinct stirred within him, urging him to climb one of the trees. He felt an energy coursing through his body, reminding him of the untapped abilities hiding within. With determination, Faron approached the nearest tree and began to scale it effortlessly, using its rough bark as footholds and handholds. To his surprise his body grew lighter and lighter with each upward movement, as he revelled in his newfound agility and strength. Finally reaching the top, he perched himself atop a thick branch, hidden from view below. His body tingled with anticipation, as he scanned his surroundings with excitement, observing and waiting for whatever came next.

Monkeys were a graduation from rodents. He did not understand anything at this point, except monkeys were larger animals and could therefore keep him sated for longer. Faron watched while the howler monkeys ate canopy leaves, together with fruit, buds, flowers and nuts. He slept and waited until they raided birds' nests then ambushed them. The first one he grabbed stunned him with a slap – a sharp reminder of how strong they could be despite their small frame. Faron grabbed it by the neck in response, and it crumbled into dust in his hand. A bolt of energy rushed through his body and dizziness sent him falling from the thirty-foot tree to the ground with a thump.

Faron blinked. That should have hurt, but it didn't. He felt prickles from the undergrowth against the backs of his legs and soles of his feet. He lifted them up in amazement. Toenails appeared where once they had not existed, while the new flesh materialising around his toe remained minimal. How was it possible that the flesh of the monkey brought flesh to his skeleton? Was this the source of his hunger? He did not feed on the animals. He had no taste buds and his throat rejected everything. Instead, he snapped them into dust, and in return they gave him flesh and blood. He did not stop to think. He could make sure his problem was a distant memory by the following day.

Faron went on a spree of obliteration, surprising packs of snout-nosed howler monkeys over a large span of the forest. One then two, two then five, five then ten. Faster and faster. He continued for several days, losing track of where he was. Hunting and ambushing. His nails grew. His flesh disappeared. No muscle grew back on his legs. His skeletal form remained. A bewildered Faron scowled as the hunger within him ebbed away. What had he discovered? That these monkeys could dampen his thirst? He couldn't attack them forever. He remembered the story of the guardians of the forest. They would seek retribution.

He decided to head for the Rio Negro – the black-water river. This would lead him to the Manau, Aruák and Trumá tribes and their settlements. Faron hoped one of them could identify and understand his predicament. He would find those that lived in the forest away from the towns and villages. There had been rumours of slavers and Jesuits also settling along the river. Jesuits pretended to keep the tribes safe by making them servants in their compounds. He remembered the stories about them in town; they kept native slaves but did not rule them like plantation owners. For that reason, the plantation owners did not like them.

He had to find a Pajé, a specialist, one who believed there was a time when humans and animals were in-distinguishable. These Pajé isolated themselves and only made human contact when necessary. They remained alone to consume tobacco, visit distant realms to speak with spirits, and ignite their healing practices. Just like Luíza, they would know him and heal him. They would talk to their spirits and reverse this curse – and he would stay with them. He had travelled further from home than anyone in Bahia had ever dared to go. He was sure he would find the Pajé more easily than most. They could end this, and then he would return to Bahia.

His hunger did not die, but it was manageable. The path became lighter, leading to rocks and stones interspersed with cacti and bromeliads. It proved a little harder to navigate the slippery stones as Faron ascended past the mist rolling down the surrounding hills. When the mist dissipated, it revealed a vast area of green covering, Morro do Pai Inacio. Faron stopped to observe the flat-top mountain and valleys in the distance. He could not remember any stories of the flat-top mountain, but he recalled its existence. Somewhere in his childhood memories, the description of the region's freedom and beauty was confirmed. Hummingbirds swooped between the surrounding leaves. The tree-filled valley beckoned to him. Rumours of diamonds dredged from the riverbeds meant the towns nearby had grown in population. He would not venture out to the waterfalls or caves that covered the area to see if the stories were true. He would not investigate rumours about water falling from the sky, or try to prove that the clearest blue water known to man lay somewhere in the caves. He no longer felt the need to be around humans and did not want to witness the labour of slaves and indigenous people breaking their backs in the rivers looking for stones.

Stories had filtered into the plantations about a valuable stone that lay in the red earth on the tops of mountains and was washed down by the great rains into the valleys below. This is where humans spent their days dredging the waters. Faron turned away from the majestic beauty because he had a purpose now – to find the Pajé.

Days turned into nights and nights turned into days. For much of the time, sunlight filtered through the forest, but dark spots remained. He took turns to run, crawl and leap over, under and around the shrubbery.

Swampy depressions and their supporting vegetation nullified the sounds of the rainforest. Faron crouched and sniffed with excitement. The Rio Negro lay before him. A dense forest hung over the magnificent stream, the sun's rays flickering across the waters. He sensed no form of human energy and so moved towards the edge of the bush, perhaps to feel and taste that which he did not desire but which still held curiosity for him. Faron bent over to dip his hand into the memory of coolness. He caught sight of his reflection. Hollow sockets securing bloodshot eyeballs in a skull casing jumped out at him. A ghastly concave existed where his nose had once sat. Bone teeth dominated where once there were fleshy lips. Muscle, the colour of blood, pushed through an intact ribcage. Pink intestines wriggled in slow motion like a bootlace worm. Faron gasped at the sight and stumbled backward. This could not be so! A sickening feeling rose inside of him. What he saw was the shadow of a horrific existence. A monster. A hideous being. How could he survive in this way amongst humans or animals? In this unimaginable form – the form of a corpse? All his life he had followed the instructions of others – adults who had their own selfish agendas – and now he had been left to exist in this abhorrent form.

Faron threw himself into the grand trunks that surrounded him. He gnashed his teeth and howled as he tried to break himself into pieces. He could not live like this. He climbed to the tops of the trees and flung himself down, only to rise from the ground with bones secure and intact. He smashed himself against tree trunks, desperately moving from one to another, snorting and bellowing. It didn't matter who heard. They could be rid of him. He repeated his efforts until his energy was sapped and he could no longer fight the madness. Watching the waters ripple in response to the birds flapping over them, he leaned over the river to see himself again. Wretchedness lay evident in the bloodshot eyes that gazed back at him, and yet those eyes showed that something of him was still in there.

The slave woman on the pathway had called him "Corpo Seco." He remembered her revulsion. The heaviness of her body as she fell to the ground. Augusto's immediate rejection. They could not wait to get away, and yet once they had laid eyes on him, they would not forget him. He would stay with them forever in their confounded minds. The curse was real. His mother had murdered his lover. His father was a monster and yet would never be punished in this life, no matter how many lives he took or how many women he raped. Sinhô's life would be filled with the joys and pleasures that all Brazil had to offer, but here Faron was, an outcast with a curse. A repugnant creature whose form was unimaginable.

Faron's stomach gnawed repeatedly, interrupting his fixation with the river. A familiar hunger arose in him as the sound of voices had him scurrying behind large leaves. He sniffed and listened. The movement was not close. It was much further away. Humans. The same humans that had collaborated in violence to create him. Immediate and scathing anger swamped him. He bounded towards the voices, roaring as if his bones were on fire.

It took a while to reach the source of the human sounds. The forest distorted his senses and his ability to measure time and distance. But he did not tire. His lower body moved without effort to the compulsion of his undeniable hunger. His sight blurred as his senses soared with cravings. There were more than a few humans – perhaps a settlement. He did not care anymore. He was a monster. The Corpo Seco. He had his place and humans had theirs.

The sharp hollow sound of hooves striking the ground urged Faron towards a small mound overlooking a pathway. A musky smell of earth, sweat and leather overwhelmed him. Flat footfall on the ground indicated at least six moving humans. Horses and humans together.

Faron waited.

A Bandeirante with a long beard and black boat hat rode a horse along the beaten pathway. He held a thick long stick. The Bandeirantes were indigenous slave catchers and explorers, always allying with one indigenous against another. The only other interests they had were in the precious stones to be found in the interiors. An indigenous man with arms and hands bound walked beside the horse. A clothed mixed-race indigenous soldier walked leisurely behind the Bandeirante, leading three naked indigenous women held together by a pole. Small children walked freely by their sides. Another indigenous hunter followed behind with a gun.

Faron sniffed and shuddered. The same compulsion that had consumed him when he came across the PataxÓ now ran rife within.

The women moved slowly to allow the children to keep up. One of the smallest, a boy, stood still for a moment and stared straight in Faron's direction. Faron was sure the child could see him. The child did not show any signs of fear. Only curiosity. The Bandeirante interrupted the boy's motionless silence by hitting him between the shoulder blades with his gun. One of the women cried out, igniting uncontrollable tremors in Faron's bones. The hunters had no right to harm the boy or these people. Another Bandeirante pulled at the pole joining the women together so that they would keep moving.

Faron bounded out of the bushes and hurtled towards the first Bandeirante. He leaped, and they fell to the ground amid screams and gunshots. The Bandeirante's body transformed into ashes in Faron's clutches. Faron roared with exhilaration and turned to face the others. The women wailed in fear as Faron stood still long enough to be seen fully by all, passing his eyes over the remaining Bandeirantes, who stared at him in horror and disbelief. One raised his gun. Faron shrieked like a caw caw as the shot echoed around the forest, missing him. Faron caught the hunter's leg and slammed his body to the ground, bloodying his face and smashing the gun from his hands. Faron lifted the body into the air and brought it down to the earth repeatedly. The body perforated. Faron's bones rattled. A sense of elation surged through him. The women huddled together, shrieking and clutching at their children, who hid their faces in their mother's bosoms.

Faron wobbled. He looked down to see new skin meshing frantically around his legs, arms and torso. He gasped. The neighing of the horse interrupted his surprise, and he looked up as the last Bandeirante galloped into the distance. Faron howled after him. The man whose arms had been bound was nowhere to be seen.

The new flesh felt like a thousand red ants crawling around his body and organs, accosting him. He raised his fleshed-out arms to the sky. The women picked up their children and ran back into the forest as the ants bit at him ferociously – a stinging, excruciating pain followed by a sudden jolt in his body that knocked him to the ground and left him panting. Pain replaced his hunger. His heart pumped harder, his joints ached, and his back cracked in several places. But then a quiet contentment spread across his bones and a sudden spark of joy overwhelmed him. He lay still on the ground until nightfall replaced blue skies.

CHAPTER SIX

Several nights passed before Faron could raise himself from the comfort of the soil. He stood up to stretch his arms and legs, now covered in familiar brown flesh. His hands and fingernails appeared lean and beautiful; his organs no longer visible. He placed his hands on his muscular abdomen and paused. The Bandeirante hunters had given him flesh. The human monsters had allowed him to become whole again. He felt no remorse. It was their turn to suffer. To die. For if he was to live again as human, he would take life from them and any slave owners that crossed his path. They did not deserve to live, nor did anyone who wronged the people of this land. The Bandeirante hunters would sell their countrymen for a good price. If he came across anyone who did not deserve to be in the same space as him, or if he sensed they were up to no good, it would be the end for that human. He would not prey on the women and children, nor on the men that protected the forest, nor on the runaway slaves. He would hunt the Bandeirante hunters and the men who wronged society. They would pay the price. He would be their retribution because, in this world, it seemed God did not care. The air was thick with sweat and fear. Faron looked around him and moved away from the scene of his change, sniffing people, water and settlements nearby.

Dead male bodies lay scattered around the settlement, burnt holes in the ground where once there stood huts and families. The settlement had been attacked and the women and men he'd encountered must have been part of those who had survived. The hunters must have divided the spoils and separated them. Faron looked around. The inhabitants had refused to give in to the Bandeirantes. They put up a fight and now their women and children were being sold off to the highest bidder. Indigenous labour was not deemed to be as valuable as African labour, and so it meant nothing to murder the menfolk attempting to protect their settlements. Faron stepped over the dead bodies. The smell of gunpowder and days-old blood captivated his senses. The spirit of the village was gone. Soon the creatures of the forest would feed on the decomposing flesh, and vegetation would flourish where families once thrived. This was the future of Amazonia.

It was difficult to adjust to the weather conditions. His skin bristled against the cold breeze and reddened from the stings of insects. The humidity had him choking and sniffing as the air changed around him. Faron sat among the dead, contemplating his fate, on a grassy knoll in plain sight. What was to become of his flesh and how long would it last? His calves were no longer threads of hanging skin but were now full of bloodied muscle. He patted and squeezed the skin on his face spontaneously and blinked rapidly to make sure his eyelids were real. He pursed his lips to whistle. This miracle posed as a curse. His flesh could only be gotten from humans. He recognised that this was the hunger that had come over him when he came across the PataxÓ boy. The urge had been so great, tormenting him for days, if not weeks. The howler monkey and rodents were merely appetisers. He needed human flesh. But to what end? He had no idea how long he had spent in the jungle. No idea of time or space. One thing was definite – no matter how much time had passed, human existence remained miserable for many. The Portuguese continued to pursue, sell and punish the people of this land.

The deserted settlement reminded him of the plantation, even though it was a tiny sample of the human habitat. He thought about the plantation and how he'd become the man everyone hated by serving to please both parents. He remembered the day Sinhô tested him at just twelve years old.

Diogo had been caught stealing a chicken from the farm. Diogo was two years older than Faron and they engaged in conversation many times while stripping sugar cane and played together on occasion.

Now Faron thought about it, it could not have been Diogo's idea. Stealing a whole chicken? He must have been out of his mind. He ended up breaking the chicken's neck because of the fuss it was making, and the Portuguese assistants caught him with the dead bird.

Diogo was forced to undress, escorted from the barn in full sight of all those around, and beaten until his body streamed with blood. Faron watched in horror as his friend's screams pierced his ears. The Sinhô interrupted Faron's protest by grabbing his shoulders and demanding he take the waiting pitch of boiling oil and pour it, slowly, all over Diogo. The Sinhô's narrowed eyes and thin lips promised more terror than Diogo's screams.

The pitcher slipped in Faron's sweating hands, and his legs faltered as he approached his friend. He wept while pouring the oil over Diogo's bleeding back. High-pitched screams filled the air, overwhelming Faron's senses and causing him to cough and splutter. He begged for mercy for his friend with each attempt to pour the oil. The sides of the Sinhô's mouth turned up before he ordered Faron to stop.

When the men left the scene, Faron assisted Luíza with the washing of Diogo's back with country pepper mixed with salt and water. Diogo was tied to a plank covered with a cloth. They dug a hole in the ground and put him in an upright position, with only his head out, and left him there all night. It was because of Diogo's pain that the Sinhô started paying attention to Faron. Whenever he caught sight of him, Sinhô would grab him and look him over before pushing him away into the dirt.

Sinhô never married, and there were no women in the Casa Grande apart from slaves. Those who were dragged to the Casa Grande were released, and impaired in one way or another. Some had their faces gashed and teeth knocked out. Others limped permanently. Faron always wondered why Sinhô never harmed his mother. Once, one of the slave girls was found hanging from a tree. Most said she had hanged herself because of what had happened with the Sinhô.

Mamãe heard the news, shook her head, and said, "She'll never get into heaven now."

This puzzled Faron. "It's not her fault."

The force of Mamãe's clap slap on his ear sent him sprawling. His vision spun. A ringing in his ears created havoc with his balance as he struggled to get off the floor. Mamãe glared at him in disgust. They never spoke of it again.

Less than a month after Diogo's whipping, Faron was ordered to saddle up, groom the horses, and bring in the firewood. This was a higher position for a slave and his first time away from the plantation. At the back of the barn he found Vitor, an older slave who had personally served the Sinhô for years, surrounded by the Portuguese assistants as they accused him of assisting Diogo in a plan to escape. Both Vitor and Diogo had iron collars around their necks. On each side were hooks fastened to a branch of a tree. Faron froze, aghast, as the assistants accosted him. They ordered him to leave the horses and wait. Sinhô was on his way to settle the situation. One of Sinhô's assistants started whipping Vitor.

A mixture of anger and despair racked Faron's body. What was Diogo thinking? And to drag Vitor into this unfortunate situation was criminal. How could they do this to their wives and mothers? How could they do this to the Sinhô? Diogo had barely recovered from his wounds from the previous incident. Why had he decided that now would be the right time?

Sinhô arrived and immediately placed a whip in Faron's hand, commanding him to begin. Faron could feel Sinhô's eyes boring into his back as he tried to compose himself in what felt like a gruesome dream. He steadied his trembling limbs and closed his eyes. Lifting the whip, he lashed Diogo on the back with everything he had. Sweat, dust and blood swirled around the men. Faron numbed out the pain as he thrashed to please Sinhô.

Diogo immediately keeled over when the ropes were untied. The Portuguese assistants stretched out his limbs. They were not done with him. The tallest assistant wielding an axe nodded at Sinhô and brought it down on

Diogo's ankle. Diogo snorted and gagged, writhing under the grip of the assistants. Sinhô turned to Faron.

Faron remembered that moment. His arms covered his belly as nausea rose to his throat. He remembered that moment because Sinhô had a twinkle in his eye when he asked Faron to decide who should be hanged. The assistants turned to stare; their faces full of disapproval. He'd seen those expressions before. It was a look that told you that at some point on the plantation, when you least expected it, trouble was coming for you because you needed to be reminded of your station. Some laid down their tools and waited. Faron lowered his gaze to the earth. He dug his feet into the soil to steady himself. His hands shook as he tried to control his breathing. Somehow, he hoped the attention was a fluke and that Sinhô would interrupt this conversation and laugh it off with the assistants. Faron looked up to see Sinhô's eyes brighten, even though he did not smile. This was the moment Luíza had predicted. The moment his mother had spoken of long before. The moment to please his father. This moment would seal their fates and freedom forever. He felt the sting of his mother's slap and her disgruntled murmurs. This was a test.

Faron chose Vitor, the older man.

Sinhô brought out the empty barrel himself. He showed Faron how to tie one end of the rope to the tree, the other end around the neck, and how to remove the iron collar. Vitor was made to stand on the barrel. Sinhô gave the signal, raising his hand, and Faron kicked the barrel away with the help of the assistants. He immediately fell to his knees, no longer able to hold down the nausea that swirled through his being. He vomited. The

Portuguese assistants laughed at him. The Sinhô patted his back and grabbed his elbows, guiding him to stand up. Sinhô had never touched him with gentle persuasion before. Faron looked up, afraid of what the response might be to his showing signs of weakness, but Sinhô merely instructed Faron to collect his belongings from his mother's house that night.

Faron wilted under the sun as he staggered back to the hut he had shared with his mother his whole life. He did not know how she would take the news. Most of the slaves were still out working. He manoeuvred around the playing children, whose giggles and shouts drowned out the cries and groans of the plantation workers in the distance. Mamãe was tending to her garden. She stopped as he approached. She already knew what was happening because she dropped her makeshift spade and put her hands together in prayer, lifting them up to the sky.

"The gods have answered my prayer. The words of Luíza have come true."

Faron stood at the entrance feeling dejected. He wanted her to weep over him, hold him, give him instructions and wipe the sweat from his brow. He wanted her to plead with him to be a good boy and cling to him in sadness. Instead, she told him to get his stuff and get going – the sooner the better for both of them. Her face lit up in farewell. "Make me proud," were the only words spoken before turning back to rooting out the weeds in the Roca Garden.

He should have known what his mother was all about at that moment. She was not sad to see him go. He had liked to think she wept after him in private, that she sang songs to console herself in his absence. Now, he figured she must have been relieved. Luíza's prophecy was all that she had held on to, and so she was not sorry to see her son leave. No, she was not.

Faron remembered that day because he was given one of the smaller rooms in the back. The view overlooked a section of the plantation. The night sky covered the estate with calm and grace. He remembered the wooden shutters and the stained sheets that covered his worn body. His heaven had just begun, but when he closed his eyes the last expression on Vitor's face, bloated and shifted before he died, revisited him through the night.

Slaves did not exist to make choices, but for Faron, this was not the case. His life was never meant to be simple. The time came when he had to choose a side, and they made him choose, both his mother and his father. He was the only mestiço, the only "person of mixture," on the plantation. The others were sold off as soon as they were born. From an early age, Faron questioned why he had not been sold off with the others, until he realised, he was the only male. Faron remembered what it was like to return to his mother's shack after a long day of driving away birds and cleaning the sugar plantation. Sinhô made sure Faron stayed out of his own home for long hours, sometimes with a kick in the stomach before shutting him out. Faron joined the worn-out slaves sitting outside in the mud. Other times he visited Luíza, his mother's closest friend. She fed and comforted him until he was called home. His mother brought him to bed in the middle of the night when Sinhô was gone.

He did not look much like his mother. She was dark with small features, upturned lips and beady eyes. His complexion almost matched the Sinhô's, were it not so sunburnt. Freckles covered his upper torso and face. No one else on the plantation had these freckles. It had never been hard to spot him amongst the other children. Even now, with his new skin, his freckles came back to him.

The children of mixed stock were sold off for being the offspring of the Portuguese assistants who worked for the Sinhô on the plantation. Many of these men did not favour his presence and were not afraid to show it either. It was all coming back to him as he sat around the dead. He recalled, when he was around seven years old, an assistant pulling him away from his mother by the scruff of his neck. Her body quivered, but she made no sound. The assistant pointed to two pardo children being hauled onto a waiting cart and made him watch as the cart rolled away.

"There's no special treatment around here," the assistant snarled. "The only reason you haven't been sold is you're not worth as much as them. You are too small, too skinny."

He was never singled out for special treatment. The first time he was flogged, they stripped him naked and told him to crouch down with knees to chest. Sinhô himself tied Faron's arms around his bent knees before whipping him until he fainted.

His mother waited to untie him and had the slaves carry him to Luíza. Tribal scars on each cheek moved as she spoke. Both women communicated in the language of their birthplace. Faron was the only one allowed to witness this. He understood the language and kept this secret. Luíza told him it was too sacred for others to learn.

On the day of the whipping, Luíza's followers invoked the ancestors with their drums, singing and dancing in ceremonies. They laid Faron out on a table in Luíza's home and left him alone with her. She wore a feathered headdress and walked around him, mumbling to herself. After cutting down the stalk of the pau-cigarra, known for healing scarred tissues, and crushing the seeds of the *Copaifera reticulata* that reduced infection, she rubbed the solution into his wounds. Luíza never started her work without the árvore da cigarra. She left him to perform dancing rituals, leaping around, crying out and falling to the floor as though in grief. Faron lay motionless, his body immobilised. He could hear the chanting. A cool sensation snaked around him, reducing the pain. He drifted off and saw himself sitting on a throne dripping in blood. He sat up instantly, realising he must have been dreaming. His mother and Luíza stood shouting over the slaves lying still on the floor. A wave of drowsiness fell over him. He felt his body raised to a sitting position by his mother. It confused him. He thought he was being lifted off the table into the air. Luíza slapped his face across each cheek before revealing the ancestors' vision.

"A union of wealth, prosperity and freedom. You will be a free man and visit many cities and people. A father's love and a mother's scorn meet to unearth a demon that walks the earth in denunciation. The ancestors prepare the land across the waters for the soul to be redeemed."

"We all know that the Sinhô is a demon, but what does it mean?" Faron heard his mother ask.

"He will never be sold or taken away from you. The gods favour him," Luíza answered.

Mamãe raised her hands to the heavens.

"He will never leave you or stop loving you. His father will treat him better, and he will inherit the land. I see wealth," Luíza continued.

"How can this be possible?"

"It is what the ancestors show me. They show me the ocean … the waters … relief."

"The ocean? We will no longer be a slave, Luíza? Is Faron to be given his freedom? Are we to go home? Away from here? Will Jesus shower us with freedom and favour like the whites?" Mamãe cried out.

"The ancestors show me this! Nobody else! They will not leave his side. They will show themselves to him. He will be healed across the waters," Luíza said.

"Our freedom is near, Luíza. We must be patient. Can you see? Freedom. Freedom to leave this plantation, freedom to talk. Will we no longer speak the language that changes the very nature of our essence? You say we will go back and be as we once were. Is this even possible? How can this be?" Mamãe exclaimed.

"I cannot question what is given to me. The ancestors never lie. They send me messages," Luíza said.

"But how can this be, Luíza?" Mamãe insisted.

"Do not question it!" Luíza countered. "It is done. Your work is to prepare him."

Mamãe's arms encased his body as she wept.

CHAPTER SEVEN

Faron slept amongst the dead bodies that night. The heaviness in the space pulled him to the ground – a secret and caressing hum to death that most could not fathom. Stillness has its own melody. The harmony played out among the active biospheres. His eyelids grew heavy, his hearing distant and distorted, and fatigue forced him to his knees. Sleep carried him into the arms of the river where he floated among river snakes, bôto, the river dolphins, and otters. The cool water immersed him as his body made its way downstream into the darkness of sleep. He was not afraid to exist in this space. There was no fear or repulsion, just the flow of the tide reassuring him that he could be carried to a still and serene abyss forever. The spirits of those he lay with did not come to him.

A faint force of the breeze against his new skin woke him up. He opened his eyes and blinked at the sea of green surrounding the trees above him. A large form flapped its gigantic wings overhead. Was this a flying human? A monkey jumping at him? He turned to where the moving image had settled, a few feet away on top of one of the slain bodies. A heavy cream-white bulk with shaggy feathers and a hunched-over stance stared back at him. It had a thick, strong beak, ready to shred flesh. Red-orange skin flopped over the beak; thick claws gripped the corpse underneath it. Faron raised himself up. The bird continued to stare. He recognised the colourful feathers around its neck – blue, red, orange and yellow.

An urubu - a king vulture. The whites of its eyes glistened as it watched his movements. Faron checked his skin and patted his face, finding his form still human from the previous night's incident. Flies and insects engulfed the area. He inhaled, wondering if the king vulture was there to give him a message. Everyone knew the dead came to the living through animals. The tales of the indigenous filtered onto the plantations and into the open mouths of wide-eyed children sitting around on cool nights. The king vulture watched Faron rise in haste and step over fallen men as he moved across the settlement, away from its distorted landscape. They were gone, and he was alive. This incomprehensible stretch of experience. He considered his new skin, his fatigue, and the fact that he had lain among the corpses as if they were his sleeping relatives without a care in the world. The floating river dream, with all its creatures, had pacified his spirit. Did the dream mean he was among the dead, even though he lived? All the answers would come from a Pajé. Faron looked back to the settlement. There would be more killings, kidnappings and murder. There would be more indigenous slain for land, slavery and rivalry. The king vulture opened the splendour of its wingspan for him to see, before the settlement was out of sight, and flapped repeatedly without making a sound.

The river lay adjacent to the settlement and its murmurs and rumbles. Faron wanted to see the extent of the changes to his form. He had to see himself again. The sounds of the river got louder on his approach.

Faron stared at the reflection of the man looking back at him. His luminous skin, freckles covering his torso, large black curls, and full lips. He was Faron again, wearing his skin, but his eyes denoted something else. A never-ending wilderness. A desolate feral endlessness in his gaze. His eyes conveyed his predicament, but only he could know this. Humans would not be able to interpret it. The storm presiding in his pupils could suck out the souls of men. A single flame appeared in the reflection of his eyes. He peered in further to see. He blinked, and it disappeared. He would never fully be himself again. That Faron had disappeared forever. His eyes displayed an animalistic entity that he could not disguise. Faron lifted his face up to the beating sun and raised his arms to the sky. He was free and alive – never to be taken in again. His skin absorbed the smouldering heat. This was his life. It was time to live in a world that he owned.

The humidity of the riverbed lay in the moisture drenching the shrubs and bushes on the pathway as he walked away. His thoughts cleared as he remembered the last movements of his time on the plantation. Mamãe poisoned Ambrosina in fear that she would be replaced and someone else would have control over him. She'd lied to Sinhô about her friend, Luíza, who did not share her dream of freedom and ownership on the plantation. Instead, Luíza wanted true freedom away from the plantation, making it her mission to encourage slaves to run away, and Mamãe found out. His mother's lust for power and the impossible had made her a monster and turned him into one. She'd cursed him. He was his mother's curse. His punishment was to sit in his own curse, isolated, reliving the experience of ending his mother's life.

The Amazonia was his home now. He would protect it and its people from those whose lust for power and money caused suffering. He would wear their skin and take their lives, living his own to the fullest.

Within a few moons, Faron encountered a Jesuit priest and a slave on a hidden trail. The strong smell of men from afar had him tracking them instantly. The difference in human odour was usually determined by how much material wrapped itself around the body in the unforgiving heat. Feverish greed seized Faron's being. He followed the stench of the men until a clearing gave way. A black cloak and apparel covered the pale skin of the Jesuit priest – the slave was bare-chested. The two men walked in solemn contemplation. A large cross adorned the chest of the balding Jesuit. They walked slowly but with intent, as if going home. This meant there was a building nearby, probably full of indigenous and black slaves. Faron knew of the Jesuit colleges and seminaries in Salvador – places he would never be allowed to set foot in.

As Faron emerged from the dense foliage, his bare form caught the attention of the men along the trail. At first, they observed him from a distance, their curiosity piqued by the sight of a naked man approaching. But as he drew nearer, their initial intrigue gave way to a mixture of surprise and discomfort. Each man's expression shifted as Faron stood before them, his nakedness unmistakable and confronting. The black slave slowed significantly, instinctively knowing something bad was going to happen, but unsure whether he would be included. The

Jesuit hesitated. Was this man standing in front of them a vengeful quilombo? The Jesuit remembered his own authority and power. He called out to Faron, holding up the large silver crucifix hanging from his neck. The key to submission from all natives, slaves and Portuguese alike.

Faron positioned himself squarely in their path, his gaze fixed upon them with an intensity that left no room for doubt as they stopped short to take stock of his arrogance. Blocking the pathway in this unspeakable manner meant severe punishment. He sneered in response to their confusion, to the dismay of the slave and disbelief of the Jesuit. The Jesuit gestured for the slave to move upfront and speak to Faron, assuming there was a language barrier. This confirmed the slave was African-born, like Faron's mother.

Faron smirked, then strode towards the men. The Jesuit priest commanded him to stop, but Faron just quickened his pace. He chuckled before leaping and bellowing as he landed on the priest, knocking him to the ground. The priest gasped and grappled, with one hand going for the crucifix on his necklace, but Faron plunged his fingers into the man's torso, ripping open his flesh through the cassock. The priest screamed in agony. A feeling of release soared through Faron's body as his fingers spread further into the struggling priest. He laughed with elation, his face contorting from skeleton to skin as the source of his fix dissipated into dust.

The male slave stood transfixed in terror.

Skin stretched around Faron's body – the source initiated further renewal of his organs, sucking out all the agony. The sensation pushed and shoved like a shoal of fish swimming through his carcass, and a sudden surge of strength rose in his core. Faron laughed repeatedly, full of flesh and even stronger. He turned to the male slave, whose terror had him frozen to the spot.

"Tell them about me," he growled, his voice now an intense resonant bass that filled his prey with absolute dread. "I will come for anyone who crosses my path and lives for greed. I will eat their souls and I will hunt them. I am Corpo Seco. I am the Amazonia. This is my home, and my home will not be destroyed. Nor will it have the blood of the indigenous and slaves run through its rivers unless those I speak of seek to enslave their own."

A trickle of urine spread around the slave's legs. He backed away and ran for his life.

Corpo Seco – the legend had been born.

The forests belonged to him. He pulverised humans who did not stick to the pathways in the forests. Mothers told their children tales of the shadow lurking in the jungle and of the men that perished by his hands. A reputation of death and terror accumulated over many moons. He took just enough to survive as half-human in the jungle but not enough to go back to being human. He could hardly remember his former self and had no need to. It was no longer a desire. His body, unsheathed and unwholesome in its form, basked in its own glory. The very sanctuary of skin and flesh that he'd sought after was no longer a burning necessity. His duty was to protect the forest from the Portuguese soldiers hunting slaves and gold. He avoided the PataxÓ and any other indigenous. They sensed him sometimes in the bush when they moved around. He would see the men look up and around the trees curiously, their eyes trailing the formations of birds, monkeys and other animals that dwelled within. They stopped and stared for a while, before waving their women and children away from the area he sought refuge in for that time. His makeshift existence eased his torment. He roamed, slept and fed when the need arose for some skin to add to his torso. The memory of the life he had once lived evaporated. He could no longer remember Ambrosina's dimples. Mamãe's words disappeared into the void, and Sinhô's actions slipped from his recollection as he submitted to his surroundings.

His was a simple existence through extensive rainy seasons. He crawled and sniffed, ignoring the animals who ignored him and growling at those who dared to let curiosity get the better of them. He forgot about the world and the world stayed away from him.

This existence remained uninterrupted for many moons, until he saw billowing smoke rising from a nearby settlement, an unusual thing in those parts. What went on in the cities and towns near the river was none of his concern, but there was a disquiet to this black smoke funnelling into the sky. Faron placed his ears to the ground and heard a thunderous stomping, rapid heartbeats and panic. A heightened sense of agitation filled the air around him. He moved towards the chaos. The threat of the malign engulfed his being, but he was Corpo Seco after all.

Smouldering fumes engulfed the surrounding green as Faron pushed through it, resorting to all fours in order not to be seen. He stopped in the clearing at the sight of frantic villagers running back and forth as fire raged through their huts. He sniffed again, realising the fumes were not limited to this one settlement. If he moved on, he would find another burning. He looked for an enemy, but what he saw was war. Mestiço, indigenous, caboclo and some poor whites in possession of knives and sticks with hooks, fighting against soldiers. Faron stiffened. His muscles tightened. How could this be? The people attacked more than they defended. Soldiers fell against the swords of the caboclo.

He moved in to get a closer look but stopped short to see an unarmed elderly indigenous man turn in his direction. The villagers ran around him as though they did not heed his presence. Empty, hollow eye sockets had replaced his eyeballs. The noise of war faded into a soundless massacre and the air grew thin. The sudden weight on Faron's chest alarmed him.

"Leave here." The man's mouth moved soundlessly, but his voice rang in Faron's ears. "This is not your freedom. War is coming. The place you seek is where you came from. Go home."

An immobilised Faron watched as the elderly man turned and walked through the raging fights around him. A spear suddenly punctured his neck and his body fell to the ground. Faron dropped back, gasping for air. It was not fear but shock that disarmed him. He instinctively picked himself up and ran towards the fight, but the closer he got, the emptier the settlement became, until he stood in the middle of what was once full of human life. He looked around for bodies but there were no signs of life or death, only burnt-out huts. Intense, light-headed anger prevailed.

Enraged, he ran around the empty huts bellowing for frightened humans or soldiers to show themselves, but the stillness filled him with an unnerving emptiness – an abandoned, deserted feeling of isolation. In a moment of overwhelming solitude, he raised his hands to his head as if trying to contain a scream within himself. But the weight of it all was too much, and with a loud crash, he collapsed to the ground. His mind went blank, the noise of the world fading away until there was nothing left but the raw emotion pulsing through his veins. He waited for the shallow breathing to fall away, and the sinking feeling of forsakenness to leave. He did not want to stay here or feel this way ever again. If he could have, he would have put an end to his life right there and then. His spirit hurt for the first time in the most hostile way. One thing stuck in his mind as the pain reverberated around his brain and body – no one had touched him for as long as he could remember. How could anyone exist without touch? He wanted it to end.

CHAPTER EIGHT

Faron's mind raced as he circled through the dense jungle. This place had its own ecosystem, weather, animals and people. He moved back into the rainforest as the image of the old man haunted him. The sight of the spear unexpectedly piercing the old man's neck, sending him crashing to the ground, unsettled Faron, but he discounted what he'd seen and lingered in the familiar. Power and mystery lay with Corpo Seco, after all. He sought to regain his composure in intimate settings, but his concentration faltered, and it became increasingly difficult to focus. Low energy usurped his being. He spent time resting in the hollows of dead trees, away from the sunlight, through sunsets and rising tides. His skin peeled off and rot encased his torso. Weakness wormed its way around his bones. Irritability set in at the slightest sound and movement. When he managed to sit up, a feeling of hopelessness encapsulated him. The beauty of the jungle no longer soothed him. He slept without care until he awakened to a black-and-white world where colour ceased to exist. Something was fighting him. The smog from his brain lifted after several rain showers. Images of the old man became faint. The weight remained in Faron's chest.

Had the old man been a Pajé? The words stayed with him, forcing him to consider the smells and tastes of Bahia. He recalled the contorted expressions of the slaves and the smell of the purple corsage orchid that Mamãe cherished so much. He could no longer see in colour, but he could imagine it. He tried to evoke the memory of Ambrosina's laughter. In fragmented recollections, the world that had felt so far away spun back, ridding him of his numbness and lethargy. He possessed the ability to turn himself back to flesh and reach his father, but he was not so sure he wanted to. To be alive as a black man was to live in a nightmare, a waking hell, already cursed in life and in death. How could being human comfort the spirit or the soul? He did not understand why the visions of this old man haunted him. His mission had been to seek out a Pajé, but he had not found one. Perhaps they had found him, for he had made himself known to the people in myth and reality. But if it was them reaching him, he did not understand the command to, "Go home."

Home was his nightmare.

He had not expected the old man to be killed so instantly. The image of the spear ruined his sleep. Whether or not he believed what he had seen, he knew what he felt and he wanted it to stop. If he went back to Bahia, he could enter the state as a human. He did not know how many years had passed, or if he would be safe, but he was no longer human, and this had its advantages. He could kill everyone on the plantation if he needed to. No one could defeat him. He decided to move in the direction of home, to see if it would make a difference to his lethargy, though he went with hesitancy for his love of the forest knew no end. Every bit of this paradise gave him the sensations of safety and responsibility. Although the world remained black and white for a while, the feeling of desertion and isolation ebbed away as he ventured towards Bahia. The aches in his mind and body dwindled. His lacklustre steps grew more enthused as he slapped branches and palms out of his way. Obeying the stranger's words brought his strength back, so he did not stop. He was faster and stronger than he had ever been before he discovered his abilities. A jaguar could not have caught up with him. The world blurred around him as he pressed on. His body grew lighter. He did not know what he was going back to, but colour resurged around him. What power was this? What was waiting for him as he ambled his way through the jungle? Surely, his existence could not sustain itself in the towns and villages surrounding Bahia? There were too many people. They would find him out in the end. How could he exist and survive there? He would have to be very careful. Memories of whippings returned. Was he to finish off his family by killing his father? How could he exist in the same space as Eduardo? He did not know how long he had been away, or whether his father would even recognise him. Surely by now he would have been replaced with another child from another slave.

Bahia smelt different. He remembered the remarks of the Portuguese helpers about the smell of the slaves – the belief that their odour was distinguishable from that of the Portuguese, and that soap and water would not banish the smell of the blacks. It was said that runaway slaves were tracked in the wilderness through the pungent odour that came off their African bodies. And yet, as the world grew colourful around him, Faron noticed no pungent smell that could determine black bodies, just an increasing smell of fear coming from the human towns.

Whispers amongst the slaves rolled through the streets of Bahia to the Palace Square. The towns and villages seemed to be filled with additional people and houses. Huts were scattered across the plains where trees once stood. The area had changed tremendously, but mutterings mushroomed from the scene of change. Whispers and murmurs flowed from the homes of former slaves to the homes of those who could not afford to own them. Words thrust themselves into an atmosphere of deliverance, creating an energy that drew conflict, curiosity and fear into its town's bosom. Something was going to happen, but no one knew what.

Faron did not like to leave the jungle, but this contagion of terror swelled through the towns and their people and entered his space. It grew hour by hour, and he needed to find out why, because this time the fear was not centred on him.

Faron lurked in the shadows, listening to the quivering whispers that slipped through the morning mist. He sniffed the emerging scent of panic, just as the African slaves crested the hill. They marched into the jailhouse, weapons glinting in the sunlight, demanding their leader, Pacifico Licutan, be freed. The prison guards beat them back. It surprised Faron to see the slaves revolt like this, but these were men who hadn't been born into slavery, and their assimilation into Bahian life had been unsuccessful. Faron watched the slaves pull back, following them from the rooftops and trees. He almost didn't recognise the larger and more glamorous Church of the Third Order of Saint Francis, which had previously been closed for repair, "1835" proudly marking the building entrance.

A stunned Faron lost his balance in the branches and had to grip the trunks to prevent himself from falling into the chaos unfolding beneath him. 1835? This was not possible. He had left the plantation around the year 1703. A young man! He was able to read numbers, but these must be wrong, or he must have forgotten how. There was no way more than one hundred years had passed. The town had changed and so had the landscape – it was busier and overpopulated – but that did not mean the impossible. He read the dates aloud, repeatedly, unable to comprehend the situation. He read sparingly like a child, but Sinhô had made sure he knew his numbers. Was he truly dead, and was this his version of hell?

The circumstances did not give him time to ponder. The slaves below banged on the doors of other collaborators, shouting their names. Another group joined the commotion. It was all happening too quickly. The panic and anxiety of the town expanded around him, drowning out his own sense of shock and confusion. The gathering marched on, shouting vengeance. Faron tailed them, observing from the safety of rooftops and trees as the slaves regrouped in Água de Meninos. Everything was changing. In Amazonia, he had seen the caboclos and indigenous fighting soldiers, and now this. But there were few slaves left; they were ambushed at every turn and lacked any real firepower. Faron counted less than a hundred men. He shook his head as a contingent of mounted soldiers from the Municipal Cavalry tore into the remaining slaves. Something was very different about the soldiers – they were not Portuguese. These were Brazilian-born men. Again, something that he was not used to. A bloody battle ensued and played out quickly.

Some of the African slaves surrendered, others were killed. Many attempted to escape by swimming into the sea, others made for the woods. The sounds of war and death drew the animals further back into the forests.

War.

The smell of blood lingered in the streets for days after the executions. Not all the men were executed – some were savagely whipped in front of crowds in the Palace Square. The nightmare of violence was being played out in the streets of his hometown yet again. Why had he been brought back to Bahia? This dreadful reminder of human life sickened him, the memory becoming a painful reality once again. Had he been hallucinating in the jungle? How could he have been away for so long? He did not recognise any of the slaves or Portuguese men. The town was larger, busier and filled with discontent. This no longer felt like home. New buildings and faces. People wearing clothes he was unfamiliar with. He hadn't wanted to visit the plantation for fear of being recognised, but the more he observed from afar, the more he noticed the changes he was witnessing were far-reaching. Free men and women existed and moved differently. He could differentiate between Portuguese and Brazilian-born. Every transformation he noticed only increased his fears about the date on the building. Faron didn't want to witness the unpleasantness of further executions, so he attempted to leave the outskirts of the town. The swarms of soldiers combing the forest for runaway slaves made his escape tricky, too many people everywhere. He skirted the forested coastline, biding his time. The soldiers were extremely unsettled and intent on destroying any chance of another slave revolt.

Faron moved along the coast, trying to find a place to settle and reflect. In doing so, he witnessed slaves boarding a ship at the port of Bahia. Some were African Muslims who had been involved in the revolt, others were parents cradling children. In Faron's day, slaves had been bought and sold as readily as milk and bread. Sometimes, it had been better to be on the plantation, believing your life had some worth, than on the docks being reminded of how expendable you were. But this time, freed slaves were boarding a ship with their possessions. This was something no one had ever witnessed before. Faron lingered with an urge to find out what was going on.

His odour repelled the dockside workers. They looked up and around in disgust, shouting obscenities, unable to figure out where the smell was coming from. This was bad. He could not be seen here and recognised as Corpo Seco. This place had too many folks with too many guns and too much time on their hands. He needed to become Faron to find out what was taking place before him. He wanted to know how slaves could move freely without fear of ships that would take them away. This should be impossible. Everything he was witnessing was unfeasible.

One of the dockside workers most affected by the smell walked straight into the bush, determined to find the culprit spoiling the blast of fresh sea air. Faron moved back into the forest, luring him further from his kinfolk. The man rippled with muscles from heavy lifting and showed no fear, only irritation. Faron allowed the worker to scour his surroundings before he sauntered into the clearing in full view of his opponent. The man turned white. His mouth hung open. He coughed, gagged and turned to leave, but Faron reached out, grabbed him and pulled him close, so the worker could see the full effect of the maggots and bones of his assailant. Fear shut down his victim's vocal cords. Faron had his arms around the man's back and squeezed him almost to death before spearing his hands into his torso. Skin constructed itself around Faron's body. Still only half-formed, he followed the path of his victim back to where his friends sat facing the ships. Faron grabbed the first one from his stool and lifted him until his feet waved above the ground.

"What year is it?" he growled.

The other men sat dumbfounded.

"What year is it?" He turned to the frightened faces.

One drew a knife from his pocket and moved towards him.

"1886! 1886!" the man he'd lifted from the floor answered.

The answer caused Faron's blood to boil. He rammed his fingers into the man's soft belly.

A knife slashed him across the back, on his new skin. Faron threw the corpse into the water and turned to pulverise those who had witnessed his movements. In the jungle, his form was inconsequential, but around humans there were drawbacks.

Under the moon, by the coast, Faron delighted in his skin. He felt lighter and knew that he had the strength of many men, to the point of being essentially indestructible. But all this was strange to him, and he needed time to come to terms with the years he had been away. One hundred and eighty-three years gone and lost. While he built his reputation of terror in Amazonia, his father, the slaves and the home he'd once known had all gone. No one would know or remember him. He had no documents to prove he was a free man. He had no witnesses to explain his identity. His level of insignificance was overwhelming.

What was he here for? How could he survive as a human in this situation? How had he lived this long? Everyone wanted to live longer, but what was the point when your world no longer existed and the people you once knew were no longer with you? What was to be gained from a long life surrounded by strangers, with strange words and strange ways? And he was in the skin of a young man. How did this curse work? Was it eternal life? Would he never age if he kept killing to remain in human skin? His head hurt with questions and a feeling of gloom.

He should have stayed in Amazonia.

At sunrise, he headed back to the port to find out more about the ship his people had climbed into without fear. This was the only interesting and enlightening thing to experience here. After that, he would leave this place and never return. Faron wore the clothes of the men he killed and drew closer to hear the whispers of the foreign white men who surrounded the slaves boarding the ship. Their language was unfamiliar to him. They were paler, with different coloured hair that made them appear to have no eyebrows. The Portuguese were darker, with more robust features. He did not know white men could look so different. He moved around unnoticed, listening to their discussions with Portuguese dock workers.

It appeared they oversaw the *SS Salisbury* – the ship his people voluntarily climbed onto with their belongings. More rebels followed the freed slaves with no display of panic. He heard the white Brazilian-born soldiers sitting on the docks deriding those who chose to board. The ship was owned by the English, and this pleased the Portuguese and white Brazilians. The rebels were being sent away so they could cause no more trouble.

> *"A union of wealth, prosperity and freedom. You will be a free man and visit many cities and people. A father's love and a mother's scorn meet to unearth a demon that walks the earth in denunciation. The ancestors prepare the land across the waters for the soul to be redeemed."*

It was all so clear now. Luíza's words and his mother's tears. Faron had to know if it was true. Were they going back to Africa? He had to be on that ship. His existence had been without hope. His name was spoken with fear and trepidation, he served justice where it could not otherwise be administered, and he made grown men quiver and beg. He spilled blood with threats, capturing spirits from unsuspecting innocents, harbouring flesh from others, tasting fear accompanied by an unnerving, selfish satisfaction. But his freedom in the Bahian Forest was not the freedom Luíza had spoken of. Here was the promise of landing on African soil to relieve the ongoing torment of his existence. These had been the words uttered by Luíza. Her warped truth had been riddled with misinterpretation, but now there was no ambiguity. This was the only chance he would have to begin all over again, away from this land stained with the blood of his people. The place that had involuntarily created him. His cure was in a place where people were more powerful than Luíza. The place where she'd learned everything. A place where there would be no misinterpretation, and no mistakes. A place where spirituality could find a real solution to this sickness that afflicted his body and spirit. A place he could call home. No one would know his history and he could start afresh. This was a chance to find his truth.

The men talked of the trip taking six weeks. He moved among the dockworkers and soldiers at night while they slept or huddled in a drunken stupor, and stole as much human energy as he could, to conceal that which humankind could not stand to see. No one could know of his true form. He must discover his freedom and live once again as a fragile human. Faron shuddered within the confines of his new flesh. This was the first time he'd trounced so many men in such a short space of time. In the Amazonia, he could go for many moons and sunrises without the need to take spirits, but now he could not risk any chances. He would not allow himself to run out of skin, of flesh. His strength soared. If it were true that a hundred and eighty-three years had passed in his absence, then his life had been over for a long time. The skin he lived in captured him at the age he'd been when he had left the Bahia. He had the wisdom of an old man while still being a new man. He would leave these shores, never to be seen again, and remain a mythological legend in the forests of the Amazon and the Bahia.

The ship sailed two days later.

CHAPTER NINE

Everyone complained of the rancid drinking water, which was stored in casks that had previously carried oil, vinegar and wine. Faron listened to their discomfort. The African-born slaves were a little suspicious of him because he was Brazilian-born. Many of the Crioulo were spies and reported plans of revolt to the soldiers. He didn't mind their guarded behaviour – it was better for them to ignore him and let him be. The men and women were given salt meat and forced to pick out the weevils from the flour, rice and hard bread. The women huddled together. They spoke to no one except their menfolk. They sat around looking dejected, not sure if their decision to travel back to Africa had been the right one. The ship was infested with rats, and it wasn't long before some died from the dreaded typhoid fever.

Every morning began with the Africans scrubbing and swashing the decks before breakfast. The sailors had their own duties and ignored the Africans most of the time. The captain of the ship never appeared. For most of the day the sailors busied themselves with rigging, greasing, tarring and painting, except on Sundays. There were other men on the ship who watched their work closely. Faron had assumed a sailor's life to be pleasant but, on this ship, it seemed it was not. He was grateful to leave the decks after the cleaning.

He sat alone when the Africans ate. The first time he had tried to eat, he choked and gagged on the salt meat. His eyes watered as the meat stuck to his throat. The taste disgusted him. That experience took the wind out of his sails. When he was offered water, his gagging worsened. Although he looked human, he could never eat and drink as one. His throat and tongue constricted as soon as anything foreign was introduced. A new discovery he had to deal with. For the rest of the time, he accepted the food, sat alone and pretended to eat. When no one was looking he passed it over to the children, who could never have enough. Other times he would start conversations to deflect the attention from his habits. One of the men pulled a stem cutting from a mature cassava plant.

"You brought cassava with you?" Faron asked surprised.

"Money will run out, and when it does how will we eat?"

Another man unwrapped a cluster of cashew seeds from a small cloth. Faron nodded, a little ashamed that he did not have to worry about such things. The men were prepared for everything.

The ship rode the waves and wind like a bucking horse. A storm tore many of the ship's sails. Men vomited. Cargo flew from one side of the ship to the other. There was no point in salvaging anything until the storms subsided. Faron strapped himself to his bunk and hung on to the nearest post. The whites and Africans prayed loudly for their gods to ease the storms. Children screamed and women wailed.

When the storm subsided, they were allowed to roam around the ship in a small, contained area. In the cloudless sky, the sun burnt the white men until their skin reddened, dried and produced folds. The Africans missed the sun, having been shut inside the confines of the deck below, and so it was a chance to talk, pray and observe the sea with trepidation. The ship's sailmaker sat on the deck to mend the sails with his needle and thread, using his palm like a thimble to help push the needle through the many layers of canvas. Faron watched him, fascinated at the ebb and flow of the needle and the patience of the sailmaker, who hummed while he worked. It was a reminder of days out to the tailor with his father – all those people now returned to dust. The sailmaker nodded but never spoke. As soon as the sails were mended, the sailors climbed up the tall rigging and set them in place once again.

Several Africans fell sick with typhoid and were left to fend for themselves below deck. Their women were taken up to the deck to remain there until the men got better. They were told they would help in the galley and serve the men on deck. Faron noticed one of the sailors had his eye on one of the women. Her grief and concern for her husband stopped her from seeing why she had been chosen to stay on deck with the sailors. Faron watched the women leave. It appeared that everywhere he went, evil prevailed. As much as this experience was not the dreadful story his mother had told him of her journey to Brazil, remnants remained. Once they got off the ship, he would never have to deal with these people again.

One thing was for certain – he learned new things about himself. He could not eat or drink anymore, and the urge to feed on humans had not surfaced. He wondered if this was because of the many men he'd killed before he boarded the ship. There had been no cravings in his short time in Bahia. He attacked the men because he thought it necessary. The Africans did not notice anything strange about him, and nor did the sailors. This was a good sign. Just the way he had envisaged it. Perhaps crossing the ocean would be his cure. He wondered what would happen once they landed. The sailors did not talk much, except to say that arrangements had been made for their wellbeing for a few months once they disembarked. Faron wondered what Africa must be like. Was it like Brazil? Did they have an endless array of mountains and forests? Mamãe had told him that Africa was full of colour, and that the earth was red.

Life grew tedious as they waited for their miracle. The miracle of existing freely in the motherland with no more fear. Faron surveyed the younger sailors practicing knots while others played games of dice and cards. Sometimes he joined the Africans in complaining about the putrid smell below deck and the stale food and caskets holding water and vinegar. The Africans blamed the water for the sickness. Faron found reassurance in cleaning the decks with them. He blended in just enough to alleviate any form of complete distrust. Once off the ship, they would need to stick together in this strange new world. They didn't have to like him, but they could tolerate him.

Relief swamped the ship's men at the first sign of land. The ship stopped at several ports, and the Africans chose where to get off. Many left at the first port in Lagos, where they knew the land and people. Lagos mirrored the name of the town in Portugal where some had been bought and sold. A bittersweet name that brought ironic relief. Faron decided to stay on until the ship reached the lands of the Ashanti, Fante and Ga people – the sailors called it the "Gold Coast," and declared that would be its name in the future. This was according to the captain and his steward, who had dealings with the British crown. Faron thought about his mother's impossible wish for him to be the owner of a plantation in Bahia, but looking out into the bay, he had no doubt that his destiny would soon be digging gold from the red earth in these forests laid out before him, rich with vegetation.

The *Salisbury* docked in the port at Cape Coast. The freed slaves disembarked with their belongings. Faron observed the low hills and rolling plains spread out before him. The humid overtones were no different from those in the Bahia. But he saw Africans who had never been slaves. They walked around, oblivious to what was unfolding, moving with intention, heads straight, shoulders back. They spoke aloud to each other without cowering. Most did not look in the direction of the Europeans. Indeed, there was no fear in their faces. Some stared and giggled at the sight of the white men's reddening skin under the harsh rays of the sun. No chains or ropes to be seen around anyone, except for securing the boats. The pain he felt at that moment was that his eyes were the only ones to witness this absolute freedom from his plantation.

Upon disembarking the ship and walking onto the land, some of the women began to cry. Men pushed their chests out. Others fell to their knees in Muslim prayer, giving thanks with their heads bowed to the ground. Faron spotted an albino child clinging to his mother's wrapper as she stood with her wares balanced on her head. The little boy scrutinised Faron as he stood among the crowd, awaiting instruction from the ship's captain. The sights and sounds were overwhelming. Faron's head felt as though two invisible palms were squeezing it together. He squinted in pain, wondering if it was already time to get his skin. He raised his forearms – everything was fine.

The ship's steward appeared. A small man with a pinched nose and nasal voice. He spoke, but they could not understand his language. In the confusion, a Portuguese seaman from the ship was asked to translate.

The crowd of men listened to the translation, but Faron remained distracted. The little boy gaped at him, ignoring his mother's attempts to move away from the curious crowds forming. Faron thought it somewhat strange that he had arrived in the land of his people, and the first thing he saw was an albino – a child of the moon.

The first albino was believed to have been sent to the Guna people of Gran Columbia by their god, Baba, the father of the sun. Faron had spotted the Guna people, with albinos in the shadows, in the days of his transformation. According to the Guna, the children of the moon were blessings from the father of the sun, and now here, on the western coast of Africa, one of them had noticed him. The mother of the moon child navigated her little boy away towards the main road. Faron watched them manoeuvre through the crowds, wondering if his own mother was trying to reach him.

CHAPTER TEN

The Ga Mantse, Nii Ankrah of Otublohum, welcomed the Brazilians as guests into Ga territory. A wrapper encircled the King's bulky body before draping over one shoulder, and around his neck was a solid-gold necklace that dazzled the eyes of the Brazilians. A few men stood over the King with umbrellas and fans, surrounding him with fanfare. The King nodded as the translator spoke and smiled when he told the Brazilians they would be given a place to stay until a later date, free of charge.

The Brazilians were supplied with food and water. Everyone made enthusiastic hand gestures to communicate. The headmen arrived to have a discussion on the unfolding events. It was strange to Faron that the African slaves who had fought the Portuguese were considered Brazilian rather than African once they landed. But the men did not protest. They accepted their new identity with poise and appreciated the brief encounter with the King. They were taken to stay within a collection of wattle-and-daub households with pitched thatched roofs in Otublohum near Swalaba. As the first night drew in, Faron sat with several Brazilian men who could not sleep. They enthused about the feel of the soil under their feet and the glorious and magnificent composure of the King. Truly, nobody had imagined this experience while undergoing the hardships of sailing to the unknown. Some of the Brazilians disclosed that they had purchased their freedom. Faron had never heard of this possibility. He remembered the vision of war in the Amazonia where the poor fought the soldiers. A certain comradery. Freed men? His time in the Amazon had left him isolated with a limited understanding of the Bahia he found himself in, but here in the Gold Coast it would be different. They were all on the same playing field in this new world. The Ga people received them with such grace and joy – language did not seem to be a barrier here. Some of the men tried to speak words they could remember from their mother tongue and a few members of the crowd recognised it. Tears and laughter erupted amongst the people. It had been an exhilarating day full of unimaginable emotion. They talked amongst themselves long into the night. There was speculation of who would continue to travel further and who would stay in the Gold Coast. Fatigue hit the group at the same time, and it wasn't long before sleeping ensued.

Ga Mantse Tackie Komeh I offered land to the Brazilians for farming around Fonafor Valley and Akwandor. Faron decided to take land far from the various larger households. There was plenty of virgin land in and around the coastal areas. Faron was stunned with the offer of land as it represented the ultimate power tool for the Brazilians. Their entire existence revolved around the land as a means of survival. But here, land was more than just a means of survival; it was their way of life, ingrained in every aspect of their being. Land represented power and prosperity. The scent of freshly turned earth clung to their clothes, a testament to their unyielding dedication to the land. and this was the definitive economic dream come true for all of them. The Brazilians who brought cashews and casava with hopes to farm and feed themselves as best they could, would now develop crops on farmland like the masters they served – an unimaginable experience.

As the Brazilians separated between households and towns, a few left for further inland, creating coastal and inland settler groups. Faron went with them. Although the coastal areas were good for fishing and trading prospects, Faron knew he would venture as far out as possible, not just because he was familiar with farming but because the white men unsettled him. Anything could happen next to the open waters, and their presence meant that a permanent plan to control was certain. Faron had no wish to risk being part of the changes that would inevitably lead to power over him. A familiar agrarian lifestyle would be his to live without any manipulation or consequence.

The men set about marking out their plots to harvest mangos and cassava. Together they cleared the land of all grass, brush and trees. Toiling tirelessly under the sweltering heat was a sweet reminder of freedom and ownership. Every evening, they retired to one of the rectangular rooms, constructed from wattle and daub with fanciful animal designs on the walls, in the courtyard of the local chief. They were soon referred to as the "Tabom people" by the Ga after hearing the Brazilians in many conversations answer, "Tudo bom" when asked, "Are you okay?" The villagers invited them to stay in their homes and assisted with preparing the cassava plantations. Soon, the Brazilians began building their own homes. Faron set about gathering palm leaves cut to tiered shapes to finish the roof of his new home. Smiling children and women greeted him in the morning with food. The Ga wanted nothing more than to share their wealth and knowledge of the land, and the Brazilians realised the Africans would benefit from their skills developed on the plantations. Some of the men gave up on farming just as soon as they started and returned to the coast, others decided to travel further afield after hearing about the "Aguda," the ex-slaves who settled in Nigeria, Benin and Togo after realising that they could indeed return from whence they came originally and engage in palm oil and tobacco farming and trade. The possibilities were endless across the West African coast.

The albino child of the moon appeared to Faron several times while he cleared the land of bushes. He watched the young boy running past with his friends. Translucent skin displayed blotches of malice inflicted by the sun. The bottom half of his body draped with a cloth obstructing nothing during play. Faron waved when the boy stopped to stare. The boy's response was to laugh and run off with his friends. Weeks later, when the land was cleared, the ploughing started. The child of the moon came back to point at Faron while he worked. Faron gestured him to come closer. The boy moved in, unsure of himself.

"Where is your mother?" Faron asked.

The boy pointed into the distance to the next village.

"What is your name?"

"My name is Jojo, Owura," the boy answered before running back to his friends. Faron watched the boy walk off into the distance, realising it had been a long time since his last interaction with a child.

The physical demands of endless enthusiastic labour took their toll on Faron's body and drained his strength. The muscles in his legs and arms cramped, interrupting the process of building his home. He ignored the symptoms at first, wanting to believe that in this paradise he was finally mortal like everyone else. But the cramping got worse. His arms seized up as he cut down bushes. He took short breaks, snapping at offers by others to take over. He fought the urge as hard as he could. His new life was whole and pure, as were the people who surrounded him. Yet again, he was reminded that his existence did not depend on the luxury of choice. At night, he lay in bed sweating with chills. He shook with force on his mat. He grew thinner into skin on bone. Skin shed from his body. The villagers believed he was afflicted with malaria. One of his compatriots from the *Salisbury* visited and told him the herbalist would come the next day. This news dismayed Faron. The Brazilian covered him with a large cloth and brought him water. Herbalists were also spiritualists, which could develop into an immediate problem. His jaw clenched shut when he tried to protest. His compatriot patted him gently to comfort him.

Faron had no choice but to force himself out of his bed and home. He was here to find answers. He had believed his affliction would be lifted the day his feet touched African soil, but it was clear there was no miracle to be had. Life was as real here as it had been in Brazil, except now he was desperate. Desperate to live beyond the curse, to find a solution. For without one he seemed doomed to destroy the very people he had hoped would save him. They treated him without malice or suspicion, and now he was to be their demon.

Silence slipped into the homes of families as dusk fell on the small towns and villages. The puffing of sleeping men and the soft sighs of womenfolk drifted into muted stillness of the night. Those who chose to defy the night sky met their peril as ghosts sought out wandering men in the forest.

Faron slipped unseen into the bush to pursue men who should have been at home with their wives and left a trail of dust that flooded the night skyline. With each euphoric moment, his body grew lighter and stronger. Afterwards, he retired to his room to sleep and forget his living nightmare.

He was the only person who had been sick among the Brazilians, but later that month it became a concern when the elders fell sick, one by one, suffering from abdominal pain and nausea. As the villagers buried their dead, children started experiencing fever and diarrhoea. The Brazilians discovered the source of the problem – stagnant water from the nearby village. The locals had been gathering water from this spot for weeks. Faron and his compatriots held council with the villagers to discuss plans for water drilling. They were asked to visit the neighbouring villages to determine whether the illness had spread and examine where they would begin water drilling. It was on this occasion that Faron met the moon child once again.

The sickness was far worse in the neighbouring village. Each household had at least one sick member, and it was clear that the problem needed to be tackled straight away. The moon child lived in the second compound in a small hut with his mother. She lay weak in bed with fever. When Faron walked in, the mother recognised him and beckoned him closer. The translator stood between them as she spoke. Her son lay next to her, stroking her face.

"She says her son thinks you are an albino, but you are not," the translator said.

Faron nodded.

The woman's wrapper was damp with sweat. Faron picked up the enamel cup from the floor and peered in to see turbid sludge. He looked at the translator.

"Why is she drinking this?" he asked.

The translator shook his head. "We have a severe drought on our hands. Water has been a problem for months."

"She doesn't stand a chance drinking this," Faron said.

"What can we do, Owura? She is a severe case."

"We will dig holes in nearby swamps to gain access to pockets of water."

The moon child's mother spoke to the translator. The boy gently wiped the sweat from her face with the cloth and murmured softly to her. Faron observed the bare room.

"She wants you to take the child," the translator said.

Faron flinched.

"She says she knows the child will have a better life with you."

"There is no room in my life for this responsibility. I cannot," Faron retorted.

The translator shook his head.

The mother spoke faster with urgency to the translator.

"We have to go, Tabom." The man he'd travelled with to the village voice drifted through the door. He pushed his head into the room to make his point.

"Owura, she says she will be with her husband soon, and her son has no brothers or sisters. Her husband passed away a few years ago from the same problem. Her relatives can look after the boy, but you, Owura, can change his life," the translator explained.

The woman struggled to sit up and address him directly.

The moon child climbed on the bed and pushed his mother's shoulders so that she would lie down again.

"She says you should take him now," the translator continued.

"I can't do that. It's not my problem," Faron replied, aghast at the proposal.

"Owura, we raise children together, not alone. He has guinea-worm infection, and we are helping him to get rid of it. You will not be alone with the boy. You will be with us."

"Why give away your children? Where I come from, we spend all our time trying to keep children close to us, so they won't get taken away."

The translator patted him on the shoulder, sensing his frustration.

It was true this woman was dying, but he should not have to bear the burden. She lived in a large compound amongst dozens of people.

"The boy is only five years old. He does not remember his father. When he saw you on the boat, he thought you were his father. He thought you were an albino like him," the translator explained.

The translator moved over to the bed. The woman slipped under the covers, panting and sweating. Her son lay down next to her, covering her face with his palms. It didn't look as though she was going to get any better.

Faron turned and walked out of the room to join the waiting group of Brazilians at the compound entrance.

CHAPTER ELEVEN

The interpreter stood outside Faron's door. His fingers grasped the moon child's shoulder as if to steady him. The boy's mother had died overnight and had repeated her request that Faron raise her son. This was not something he had anticipated. Those that lived in the compound gathered around, ogling the boy, clapping in amusement as Faron appeared to greet his uninvited guests. They heaved into his room to determine what was needed for the boy to make it work. A mixture of anger and helplessness swirled around him as he argued with the interpreter, trying to be heard amongst the excited chattering around them. The desperation in the sick woman's eyes had alarmed him. A mother who thought her son would be safe with him? Of course, he would not harm the boy – how could he? He had been harmed as a young boy by parents who, he believed, had secretly detested what he represented. The interpreter and others chuckled at his excuses – they saw his fear as weakness. This "Tabom" from across the waters was afraid to raise a young boy. They saw it as a duty he was worthy of.

The moon child had no one, and yet everyone was available to help. The women took turns to make sure he was washed and dressed. He ate food from next door while Faron was out ploughing the land. Occasionally, the boy would visit him as he worked and ask endless questions: "Why are you digging? Why are you planting cassava? What is cassava? Why don't you speak like we do? Why aren't you an albino?"

Faron tried answering the questions. He had to – no one had ever answered his. He tried to remember the age he'd stopped asking questions. At night, he watched the boy sleeping on the mat beside him. The boy slept soundly, without a care in the world. Freedom was truly a remarkable thing. A child born free to go where he pleased, eat what he wanted, be who he wanted to be. His plump body shone. Faron recalled so many evenings spent sitting in the mud outside his mother's hut, waiting for Sinhô to leave so that he could eat the leftover scraps.

No, he would not let this boy down.

Faron told Jojo the story about the children of the moon in Gran Colombia who were considered a blessing, and of the indigenous people who believed that "if they looked after albinos with care, they would arrive at that special place in the heavens."

And then, a few weeks later, he arrived home from the farm late one evening to find Jojo sitting up on the mat, wide awake in the dark, holding a wooden cooking spoon as though it were a weapon.

"What are you doing? You should be asleep!"

"You said the creature with wings will swallow the moon if I don't watch for it. This is the job of the children of the moon. They protect their people from harm."

Faron threw his head back and laughed.

Confusion ran through Jojo's face.

"Why are you laughing?" Jojo asked.

"We are in the safest place, Jojo. Nobody can touch us here," Faron responded.

"But I must protect our house because you are not albino. When they come, they will come for you – only I can stop them," Jojo said.

Faron did not answer. He did not know what to say.

"You are my Papa. And I can stop all the bad things because I am albino. I can stop them coming for you," Jojo continued.

"Nobody is coming today, Jojo," Faron whispered.

Jojo placed the wooden spoon carefully on the ground beside him and lay down. Faron stroked the boy's yellow hair until he fell asleep.

Life was a little better once there was control over the situation. Jojo didn't know that owning the land and choosing to live in this village meant Faron could finally face the consequences of his own choices. He purposely moved away from the town area where the English and Dutch merchants resided, not trusting them not to capture him or any other African and take them back into slavery. He was safer elsewhere. Tales of slavers raiding villages buzzed around in the markets. Faron removed himself from any danger that would result in him unleashing his anger. His urges were confined to a controlled forest area. This made it harder to detect him. He was safe, Jojo was safe, and that was all that mattered.

Now a free man, it was time to make decisions on how to earn his keep and get better at it. Gold-dust currency was used by the Asante and Akan tribes, and cowries were mainly used in the savannah. Crops like kola nut were sold to Hausa caravan traders, who took them back to the north. Gold and palm oil were sold to the Europeans by the coast. Growing demand for cocoa and timber from the south led to the construction of railways.

Faron sometimes worked as a labourer on the railroads to discover insider tips on the future plans for the region. Some of the Brazilians set their sights on growing rubber trees – a promising, easy project as deliberate cultivation was unnecessary. Faron chose to harvest cocoa beans, which had to be planted deliberately and could only grow in the forests. He teamed up with other Brazilians to buy barrels that could be rolled along forest tracks in the hopes of transporting cocoa beans while the railway construction was taking place. An abundance of land in the region created multiple opportunities. Akyem and Ashanti chiefs leased and sold land to the Gas, Shais, Akwapims and strangers alike. Faron set his sights on buying more land, but in the meantime determined the cocoa beans a long-term project. The amelonado cocoa trees took between four and seven years to produce beans and thirty years to reach their full potential. He planted and produced crops that would grow tall and provide shade for the cocoa trees, so that he could trade while waiting on his investment. The Brazilians mirrored other Africans and acted in groups, organising financing and negotiating prices on long-term credit.

Life settled into a groove under the ebb and flow of the sun against the blue sky. Jojo's hair and eyebrows faded to match the colour of sand as he grew older. The sun was cruel to his skin, leaving a testimonial of red blotches and burns all over his body. Sometimes the villagers would rub red clay on Jojo's torso in the morning for protection. Faron came across a Wolof merchant carrying long narrow strips of woven cotton in the market. One on his head and the others on his shoulders, each a different colour, style and price. He bought all three for Jojo to wear, and a skimmer straw hat to shield his eyes. Jojo helped with the harvesting. He was slow to clear the bushes. He sweated. His translucent skin reddened. Several times he tripped over objects in plain sight. Sometimes groups of children running past stopped to mock him.

There was an incident where one threw a stone at his head. Faron witnessed it, though he was further away. He threw down his machete and stormed over to the commotion. Jojo continued working without looking up. Faron snorted and flashed black eyes at the children. They howled in fear, running away as fast as their short legs could carry them. He knew that, because they were children, no one would believe what they said about him.

"What just happened to your eyes?" Jojo asked.

"It's a trick," Faron snapped.

It bothered Faron that Jojo hadn't responded to the children's jeering. He knew who they were, and this was not the first time they had mocked him. Faron understood that being different brought out the worst in other people. In their effort to understand the difference, people sometimes treated the person with indifference. It would be easy to hurt them, make them squeal and beg for mercy, but for now he liked his peace. Jojo would have to take a stand.

Jojo interrupted Faron's thoughts. "Papa, they are just children. They don't understand what they are doing."

"You are almost a man. You show them it is not acceptable, or I will … and you won't like the way I do it!" Faron barked.

He would not allow Jojo to become complacent. He wouldn't survive – not in the cruelty Faron had seen in this world. It was frustrating to experience this lethargy while his people were dying like flies in another land. Complacency was for fools.

Jojo bowed his head and nodded.

It became apparent that Jojo's inheritance was to be denied the pleasure of the sun. In time, he ventured out only in the early mornings and evenings. Faron took his concerns to the local chief to discuss Jojo's predicament, which included increased uncontrollable eye movements. Jojo's eyes moved from side to side and sometimes in a circular motion when he was stressed. Faron lost sleep, believing Jojo was losing his sight. The chief reassured him that with albinos such eye movements were common. There were a few albinos within the chiefdom and much of Jojo's difference was not uncommon.

The chief spoke reassuringly. "It's not him doing it, Tabom. That's just how it is."

* * *

Many of the Brazilians found wives and settled down. Those who already had wives put down roots in the Accra region away from Cape Coast. It had not occurred to Faron that he might be expected to do the same. Some of the women showed an interest, but he wanted to be left alone. It was custom to reach a certain age and choose a wife, but he knew he could not take that risk. He thought back to Jojo's mother and her insistence that he take him in. Upon reflection, this arrangement had worked out for him on all sides. He was no longer alone and did not need to take a wife if he had a child.

Jojo had the habit of pointing out oddities that Faron took for granted. This was useful because it kept them safe. The more time passed, the more Faron realised how important it was that no one be included in their lives. But for Jojo, it brought frustration.

"Why do you not eat with us, Papa?" he asked, tired of eating food with the other people in the compound.

"I have a small stomach," Faron replied, tapping at his belly.

Jojo squinted. "But you never eat with me or anyone!"

"I was poisoned by my slave master and my stomach shrank. I eat and drink very little, Jojo. It is not something I can control."

"Were you eating too much food?"

"I didn't behave, and it was a punishment. So now I cannot eat so well. You know I don't like people watching me eat, Jojo."

"What about me? Why can't I watch you eat?" Jojo asked with frustration.

"You have always eaten with your friends and neighbours. You think you are too old to eat with them?"

"I want to eat with you! Some of my friends eat with their fathers and the men. They don't eat with the small boys anymore."

It had not occurred to Faron that the mere act of eating was a ritual to manhood and that Jojo would miss out on it. He would have to get him to eat with the Brazilians who never asked questions. They worked together to build wealth and did not bother themselves with Faron's peculiarities. They all had families now.

"You don't have to eat with the small boys, Jojo. You will represent our house and eat with the men of the village, but I cannot join you."

Faron took his share of fried fish in a separate bowl and beckoned to Jojo to join him at the back of the house. He placed a portion of fish in his mouth. His throat shut immediately, and the spices burst into his sinuses. Faron coughed and spluttered. Jojo sprang up to get some water. Faron spat out the rest of the fish and shook his head at Jojo's offering, but then decided to show Jojo what would transpire. He took the cup and allowed a slither of coolness to slide down his throat. His diaphragm contracted and nausea overtook him. He pushed back, not wanting to alarm an already regretful and wide-eyed Jojo, but the muscles of his abdominal walls contracted vigorously, and he retched until his eyes watered.

Jojo did not ask Faron to join him again. Instead, he grew larger by eating meals offered by the local wives, who rotated their cooking weekly. Their routine worked well with entertaining late evenings, sitting amongst the neighbours, talking while the women roasted peanuts, listening to stories and disputes until it was time for bed. Jojo was a deep sleeper, so it was never an issue for Faron to leave him to go hunting for "his skin" – as he liked to think of it. He did not need to hunt as much at first. His strength was stable, which surprised and helped him. The guilt he had felt the first time robbed him of the pleasure of flesh and strength. He had come "home" and was now responsible for the killing of people who had given him land and family. It crossed his mind that he could have hunted the whites, but their village was far from the main cities and ports. He could only hold on to guilt for so long. He had to survive until he found a cure.

He remained out of sight whenever the herbalists were called to heal the sick or give advice. Their chants and lectures echoed in his ears as they danced the spirits away. He would have to reach out to one at some point, but they would be far away from this village. If they believed their people to be in danger, they would turn on him and possibly the other Tabom who worked so hard to learn the language and build a home there.

There was a time when one of them entered the compound and stood outside his home in silence. Faron remained inside cleaning. He sensed a presence but did not go outside. Jojo sat eating at the entrance. The herbalist stopped and stared right through him. Jojo ignored him until the other villagers called the man away.

"Papa, did you see that man – the herbalist? He was staring at me," Jojo called out to Faron.

"Really?" Faron replied. He did not engage because questions begat questions.

A curious Jojo decided to follow the herbalist to the end of the compound.

Jojo asked, "Did you see something?"

The herbalist replied, "Did you?"

CHAPTER TWELVE

It was as if the herbalist knew.

Jojo was supposed to be asleep at home, tired after working on the farm like everyone else. The soundless dark night allowed Faron a short stroll to his next prospect. The victim was taking a piss on the outskirts of the village and was not someone Faron recognised. He snuck up behind the man, grabbed his neck, and slammed him to the ground. He thought he heard something in the bushes but carried on pulverising his victim as quickly as he could.

Faron smelt fear and familiarity. He leaped into the bushes to seize the human hiding within them. Jojo's translucent skin shone in the moonlight.

"What the hell are you doing here?" Faron roared.

"I'm sorry, Owura! Don't kill me," Jojo whimpered, shaking with terror. His eyes blinked rapidly over rolling pupils.

Faron let go of Jojo's shirt.

The boy fell to the ground wailing, "Please don't kill me, Owura!"

Faron's lungs burnt in response to Jojo's terror. A short sharp breathlessness followed. This was not how it was supposed to turn out. A puncture sensation pricked its way through his chest as he watched the human he cherished most writhe on the ground.

His dark lashes brimmed with tears as the sobs drove him to his knees.

It was Jojo who brought him home. Faron couldn't look him in the eye. Shame choked him and stole his appetite. Humiliation danced upon his dignity and kicked it into the dust. That night, Jojo sat staring at Faron, gripping his wooden spoon with white knuckles. It was time. The villagers would try to kill him tomorrow. They would strip him naked and teach him a lesson. They had invited him into their homes, given him land, a livelihood and freedom. And he had brought death to their doorstep.

As daylight gleamed through the door, Jojo quietly left the house. Faron didn't move from under his covers. He couldn't. He waited and worried. Jojo was not used to being out in the sun for so long. His skin would burn, and they were running out of the red clay that protected his torso. Faron thought about where he would go. He didn't want to leave – this was his home. He was happy there. Jojo reappeared with Waakye rice and beans stew. He ate in silence until the bowl was empty. He placed it on the floor then threw questions at Faron.

"I want to know, Owura. Why did you kill that man? What did he do to you? Why do you go out at night? Is that what you have been doing, Owura? Is this the kind of man you are? Are you killing women, too? Do you care? Why are you looking after me? Are you going to kill me, too?"

"No! Jojo, I would never do anything to hurt you."

"What are you doing? Are you going to kill people in the village?"

"No."

"Why did you kill that man?"

How could Faron answer the question? Nothing had prepared him for this onslaught, but he knew that now he would have to face his demons.

Jojo yanked the covers away from Faron's face. "I want to know why you did it. What did he do to you? Why didn't you consult the elders before attacking him?"

Faron did not answer.

"If you can kill a man, then you can take the life of anybody. Why did you take me in? Do you have plans for me, Owura?"

"I told you, Jojo. It is my duty to look after you and make sure your life is full of abundance."

"I don't believe you!" Jojo yelled.

"Jojo, you are my son."

Jojo paced around the room. His agitation grew. He slapped his palms against the walls of the hut and his head nodded randomly.

"Is that why you don't eat? And why you always vomit the drink you are given behind the house? Why did you do it, Owura? Why?"

"Because … I have to," Faron answered.

"You are a killer, Owura? Is that what you are? Is that who raised me?" Jojo scoffed. Faron could hear the loathing in his voice.

"No, Jojo. It is not my wish to do what I do. There is no pleasure to be derived from it."

"Then why?" Jojo asked again.

Faron reached out. Jojo shifted in response, creating a physical distance.

"Jojo," Faron pleaded, his voice quivering. He swallowed to repeat his son's name. "Jojo, please listen to me. This is not what I asked for. What you must know is that I am cursed. I am begging you to believe me. My mother murdered the woman I loved, and my father was an evil man, a slave owner. He bought your people as slaves, and he murdered them for pleasure. I am a creation of their madness. It is because of them that I am left with this curse. I came here to begin a new life, never thinking the curse would follow me. I tried so hard not to be this beast. So hard …"

Faron choked on his words. This was the first time he had spoken about his parents since arriving on African soil. It felt wrong and painful, as if mentioning their existence tainted everything that was beautiful about this place.

Jojo's eyes flickered as they scanned from left to right.

"Let me die, Jojo. Let me die in my home on this floor. I won't go out. I will stay here and wither away. You can watch me. If I can repent and give away this miserable existence, I will do it for you."

Jojo stood up and walked out of the house.

* * *

Faron lay still for a week alone in the house. Jojo did not return. Some of the Brazilians visited him to inform him that Jojo had gone back to his village to visit his relatives. Faron's heart thumped against his chest. Sweat trickled down the back of his neck. His legs twitched. Perhaps he had gone to seek advice, and the villagers were discussing what to do with him. The Brazilians did not give anything away. They brought him food and drink and discussed the success of irrigation on the land. He dreamed of his mother's angry words and his father's laughter amidst whippings and torture. He had never felt so alone.

It was a month before Faron felt the first symptom. By this time, the villagers had come to see him one by one, believing he had sent Jojo away while he recovered from malaria. Their remedies, nibima, the root of cryptolepis, lay untouched on the floor next to his mat. His excessive sweating, runny nose and abdominal cramping worried the villagers. They sat at his bedside, taking turns looking after him during the night. He ignored them. It was time. He knew the only way he could die with dignity was to give up on taking lives. This would prove to Jojo that he was a man of his word. Jojo would know that he had done it for him. Perhaps he could be forgiven for taking his mother's life. The anger still boiled within him, but maybe this was the only way to reach redemption. His muscles stiffened and his joints ached as he turned in his bed. He sipped a drop of water offered from time to time, but this brought on violent contractions, and he spewed forth bile and water from his coughing. His sight became distorted, he struggled to sit up, and his body could no longer retain heat. Visitors became more frequent, but he could not recognise faces or hear what they were saying. Blisters appeared on his skin and lingered for days before rupturing. He was unable to regulate the fluids that left his mouth and leaked through his nose. Thoughts on the past and present dissipated. A distinctive odour oozed from under his sheets and leaked into the atmosphere. His transition didn't bother him. The horror that awaited the village upon his transformation was no longer his concern. The faces of those who had met their deaths through him circulated in his space. He was not afraid. Their emotionless faces hovered as he embraced the inevitable. A peaceful stillness and his mother's singing lulled him to sleep.

It was time.

Faron drifted off into the peace he had yearned for nearly two hundred years. A crowd of hands carried him through the clouds, voices whispered around him. His weightless body soared through the atmosphere. The whispers grew louder as the hands groped him.

"Owura … Owura! Papa!"

Faron felt someone trying to lift him, but his eyes were plastered shut.

"Owura! His flesh is rotting, get water. Water, now!"

Wet hands rubbed water into his face. A wet cloth shoved in his mouth.

"Suck! Suck!"

Water trickled down the sides of his mouth.

"Suck, Papa. Suck."

He tried to open his eyes to see if the Sinhô was calling him to work on the horses.

"Suck! Clear the room. Leave us alone. Go!"

Faron tried to suck the cloth. He didn't know why, but he tried.

* * *

He didn't remember much. After a while, he recognised his son's voice. He didn't know when Jojo had returned. It was hard to know what was going through his mind. The boy had spent two months away; they had never spent that much time apart. There was no purpose without the boy – but Jojo was no longer a boy.

He was eighteen years old.

Jojo woke Faron abruptly in the middle of the night and pulled m out of bed half-naked. He dragged and carried him to a place under a cottonwood tree. Faron steadied himself against the tree as Jojo struggled to get his breath back.

"Are you leaving me here to die?" Faron asked, perplexed. He leaned into the trunk of the tree, hard and uneven against his back.

Jojo stood upright after catching his breath. Faron could see his son's strength had been sapped, even though he was lighter than usual.

"I leave you here to take care of the bad men. They will come here and find you. God does not like these men. They are for you. I will be at home waiting for you when you are done," Jojo replied.

Faron watched his son walk off into the distance, aware his life had changed forever. Jojo now carried with him a burden that could end up crushing his spirit. He did not deserve this. A sudden rustling, followed by advancing footsteps, interrupted Faron's thoughts. He put his ear to the ground. His food fix was coming.

Jojo sat in silence when Faron entered the house later.

"Owura, I want to know the truth. I want to know who you are and why you came here."

"It is not a good story, Jojo. I am thankful that you came back, and I don't want to lose you again, but I cannot help who I am. That is why it would have been better for me to die than to continue. I don't want you to be ashamed."

"I am not ashamed of you. I want to know the truth. What happened in the slave land?"

It felt like a violation, telling Jojo about his childhood: Luíza's predictions, his mother's plotting, Ambrosina's poisoning and the murder of Luíza. He watched the changing emotions on Jojo's face as he described the whippings, the torture, the countless deaths. His father's invitation to join him in the plantation house, his mother's ambitions and his father's lust for torture. Leaving out the description of his mother's death, he focused instead on his father's actions and the slaves' anger.

Jojo learned about Luíza's curse and how the slaves took Faron's life, only for him to find that he could not die.

"I did not choose my life, Jojo. I wish I could stop, but I can't. I'm sorry I have let you and your people down."

Jojo's eyes brimmed with tears. "Owura, I did not know this happened in the land of slaves. I did not know this is what they were doing over the water. I did not know."

"It doesn't matter," Faron replied. The weakness and nausea slid back into his body.

"I forgive you, Owura. You are a good person, who has been good to the village. You have saved lives, fed us and given me a home. The ancestors favour you. They will repay you. You took care of me."

"Things haven't changed, Jojo. I cannot deny what I have become."

"We will find a solution, Owura. It will come, I know it will. I won't stop trying to find one."

Weariness filtered into Faron's body, and he was unable to respond.

CHAPTER THIRTEEN

It took three years for rumours to surface about a demon attacking innocent people in the bush. Problems arose when visitors from another village arrived to discuss a potential marriage. Faron was away on the plantation the whole day and into the evening, unaware that these visitors would stay long into the night and leave when it suited them. Their eyes were accustomed to the night sky and familiar with the surroundings and pathways, so they were in no hurry to leave. He needed to feed that night and was surprised to encounter four men wandering through the forest. His attack was fast, so as not to be seen by his victims. This meant coming at them from behind and knocking them out, but Faron did not have the heart to destroy all four. Two of the men made it home to tell the tale. After that, men with weapons from both villages hunted the culprit under the midnight sky. Women were terrified to go to the outhouse to relieve themselves. Accounts of the attack changed from woman to man, from child to merchant. Children reported sightings of a multicoloured dwarf demon with red eyes and huge claws. Neighbours eyed each other with suspicion. Who was responsible for this affliction? Who was the jealous one? Who wanted power? Which of the wives was struggling to bear children or sought favour from the man of the house? The eyes of the village altered, observing what they had not before. Faron's agelessness hadn't gone unnoticed. Suspicions heightened. Questions sprouted as to how Faron remained young, and why Jojo had failed to pick out a wife.

It was time to move.

Jojo chose the village where his mother had grown up before she married. It was further inland, nearer to the Akan people. She had left it as a young girl to live with her future husband's family, as was the custom. Jojo shared his own desire to take a wife. He figured it would be better to find a woman in his mother's village. Although they ventured further into the country, changes from the outside world continued to seep into their existence. The British proclaimed the former coastal protectorate a crown colony. They called it the Gold Coast Colony. Soon, bronze and silver coins brought in by the British, French and Germans pushed their way into the countryside, overlapping with the cowrie-based monetary system.

Faron and Jojo built a house far from the villagers' compound as their interests lay in farming and the plantation. They made sure not to engage with the villagers in their daily lives, understanding that the spotlight was not designed for them. Jojo's lucent skin tone gave the impression he was older than he was, so he introduced Faron as a distant relative without family brought in from the coast. In his spare time, Faron set about cutting bushes and trees once more, to show the villagers how to set up a cassava plantation. All appreciated the new guests and their contribution to feeding their children. The demand for cocoa beans grew and for the next five years Faron ventured into palm-oil farming with others, as it was being used as fuel for lamps. The railway had turned out to be a disappointment, serving the British only, and not the cash-crop farmers. The outside world was infringing on the way of life everywhere, bringing in change with a focus on profit and labour.

Jojo's fruitless search for a wife turned to discontent. The family of a woman Jojo had chosen declared she would marry another. A man with no immediate family was looked upon with suspicion. His own mother was a distant memory for the village as she had left when very young. Her sisters had married to men in other villagers and her parents were dead. When her husband died, she'd chosen not to go back home. Jojo had only one relative who remembered her – a blind, elderly aunt who spoke incoherently and liked to shout at the goats. He grew weary of the land and disliked the slow pace, the women and the lifestyle. Five years of palm-nut planting and another five spent realising village life was not what he lived for. Jojo was strong but did not enjoy the farming. His interests lay in the picture books left by missionaries with their stories of life in Cape Coast. Encounters with traders were filled with eager questions from Jojo. One trader invited him to visit the north and stay for a while. Jojo politely declined, telling the trader he could not leave his father and needed to find a wife.

Faron recognised that his influence had caused Jojo to speculate about the unknown. He was, after all, brought up on stories of Brazil – a whole world opposite to this one in many ways. These stories had filtered into

Jojo's adulthood, creating a restless and bored individual. Jojo declared he had nothing in common with the villagers and that his farming contribution didn't make him feel much like a man. He certainly did not have the strength or stamina of his father.

"What would you have me do, Jojo? Where will we go? I can't keep starting plantations. I am not a workhorse," Faron insisted.

"We should go to Accra, Owura," Jojo answered.

Faron raised his eyebrows in surprise. The city could spell disaster for him.

"I have heard from several sources that Cape Coast is no longer the administrative capital. Accra is now the capital. It also has a port and is full of people," Jojo continued.

"The British are turning the area into claimed organised territory. They are bringing in laws to limit the way of life. I don't like the idea of watching our people trying to get control of their land back from them."

"Papa, you heard that more Brazilians have come to our coastline?"

"I heard this – several boats with freed people."

"Imagine! And now they even have their own chief, Papa, Nii Azuma I. How can you think your people won't be safe? Your chief will represent anything you want to say. If you are not happy you will tell him, and it will be resolved."

"Yes, I heard about that."

Jojo looked thoughtful. "Think about it, Papa. No one knows who we are. We can start all over again, begin our lives afresh. I can find a woman, and you can build a house like that of your Papa."

"Is that what this is about? There are many women here. Pick one," Faron scoffed.

"Don't you see, Owura? If we go to the city, we don't have to work on a farm or cut trees or … or stay out in the sun all day," Jojo persisted.

"But Jojo, you didn't go to school. I don't know what kind of jobs are available for you there as an adult. Neither of us are educated like those city people."

"I am a big man, and I will find work." Jojo hit back.

Faron did not answer.

* * *

The elders of the village had several suggestions for marriage, but Jojo promptly declined them. Instead, he focused on business ideas and how to sell the cocoa beans and palm oil to other traders and businesses, before pointing out that it wouldn't be long before the Brazilians noticed that while they were embracing the signs of middle age, Faron still looked as though he had arrived yesterday. This startled Faron, as he had not anticipated difficulties with the Brazilians, but Jojo was right. Jojo's initial idea of introducing Faron as a distant cousin would not work forever.

Faron spent sleepless nights wondering how he would end all this and leave Jojo behind. Things were getting complicated, and this was not fair for Jojo. How could he find a cure in a place where he was increasingly vulnerable? He was not a native and did not know the land as well as he should, so he could not simply search for an answer or listen to others for guidance. It was not possible to ask for a herbalist or spiritualist as if he were asking for directions to market.

He resigned himself to his predicament. He had promised Jojo to hunt only wicked and corrupt men, not innocents out for a midnight trip to relieve themselves, and he tried his best to keep it that way. But he was not always successful. They could only stay so long before he made a mistake that would jeopardise their security.

* * *

A few years passed before Jojo brought the subject up again. Rumours spread like wildfire through the villages, carrying tales of chiefs secretly and deceptively recruiting strong young men at the behest of the British. Under false pretences of taking on prestigious messenger roles, the men were being sent off to fight in a distant war, far from their homes and loved ones. Jojo was unsettled by the constant chatter of the villagers. He knew they would be better off getting away from the watchful gaze of others, especially since they had no family to protect them. The villagers would surely suggest them as scapegoats to the chief. Being two able-bodied men without any family put them at a disadvantage. He'd also learned that a Tabom quarter had been created specifically for the Brazilian communities in Accra called Jamestown, and that they had appointed delegates to the Otublohum chief's court. Many had made a home in Jamestown and their children were attending schools and acquiring jobs.

"You could be the grandson of the Tabom. Nobody would know, Owura."

This was true. The villagers still believed that Jojo was the elder between them when questioned.

"I am the elder, I am in my thirties," Jojo declared. "Once we have settled, I will get married. I need a wife, Owura. This is not how I planned my life to be. We should sell some of our land and seek our fortune in Accra, the most important city of the Gold Coast. Everything is happening there without us."

"I cannot stop you from claiming your destiny, Jojo."

Faron listened with sadness to Jojo's demands. Perhaps he shouldn't have told him about Salvador, or the Amazonia, or the different settlements along the Black River. Or the story of the children of the moon who served a purpose to the people. These tales had given Jojo a thirst for life – an idea that he could mean something more to others.

Faron didn't relish company or attention, but perhaps having access to more people who were strangers in a large city would help him feed his fix without being discovered or even creating a sense of fear in the area. He could live in the city and satisfy himself far out of the way. Jojo needed to have a life before he ran out of steam.

"So, there is no more to discuss. We will sell most of the land. You will be the child of the Tabom, and I will find a wife. We go to Accra!" Jojo exclaimed.

CHAPTER FOURTEEN

Accra boasted tribal gowns, kente wrappers and lappas. Large men threw wide pieces of cloth over their shoulders as they talked. Elaborate hairstyles adorned the heads of women and girls. Gowns swayed against the slow pace of their owners through the streets. Africans and Europeans rode bicycles. There were many whites in Accra – a reminder that no matter where you went, an omnipotent threat of brutality followed you. The difference here was nobody walked around in chains or fear. But an aura remained that left a bittersweet taste in Faron's mouth. Whites lived on different streets to the locals and gathered in places that were mostly off-limits. No different to Bahia.

Unpatched streets created broad lanes, lined on either side with two-storey stone buildings that faced each other in competition. Accra Central Station stood proud, boasting a magnificent set of rail tracks that connected the coast to mining areas and the city of Kumasi. Horses pulled small carts. The sea breeze from the coast calmed the stagnating heat. Accra's plains were dotted with lagoons and rivers, rich with fish and salt, but Faron's feet led him to Jamestown – the residence and declared hometown of the Tabom. He needed the familiar.

There had been a major fire in Jamestown long before they arrived, which some had seen as a tactic by the British to force evictions for the reordering and development of the area. Houses were no longer huddled together, and they had improved ventilation and drainage. African properties were blue and European establishments red. Indeed, Jamestown held its own privileges. The Mantse Kojo Ababio, Paramount Chief of Jamestown, was given a five hundred pound, newly built house in the Alata Quarter, with streetlamps that allowed pedestrians to walk around it. However, this did not extend to the rest of the area, where people still carried lamps to see the way through Jamestown at night.

Faron and Jojo had no suitable clothes for this fast-paced, contemporary city, and so they embarked upon a search to find a pant and shirt maker. Jojo did not necessarily need a tailor. He preferred to wrap his patterned cloth around his long lean body, but this sudden thrust into the throes of European influence had Faron remembering the cuffs and seams of his father's shirts and trousers, having never believed that there would be a time when he would feel the seamless designs against his own skin. This was his time, and he would have it no other way.

They were directed to a small hut in Osu. An old woman sat in front of the house. She stopped spinning cotton and placed the stick wrapped in white plant fibre over a half-filled calabash to bellow her son's name at their request.

"Danso!"

The ear-splitting shriek took both men by surprise.

A younger man, short in stature, appeared. His eyes lit up at the sight of the men. He nodded and ushered them in. They followed him to the back of the house where his black sewing machine sat amongst plants yielding cucumbers. Jojo had found the tailor through word of mouth. His name was Danso, and they would have to wait two months for their pants and shirts. Faron attempted to negotiate the price, but Jojo insisted on interrupting with questions about the black whirring machine that stopped and started as they spoke. An excited Jojo explored the untidy desktop full of measuring tapes, scissors, needles and unfinished customer garments. Danso alternated his conversation effortlessly between both men, clearly amused. It was as though both were visiting him with separate intentions and sought to sabotage each other. Jojo stood over Danso while he sewed, talking until he was invited to place himself behind the sewing machine and let his foot engage the pedal. He fit himself at the back of the machine and pressed his foot down in excitement. Danso's attention stayed on Jojo, instructing him to push the fabric under the needle with his hands. The whirring machine drowned out Faron's interrogation, forcing him to pause and observe the end of the material flowing through the thrusting needle. Danso's patience with Jojo and his eagerness to please had Jojo looking up at the end of the hum with fire in his eyes.

"Many orders, Owura. I have many customers' orders to fill, but it's just me," Danso explained. He gave Jojo a pat on the back for his effort. "A good stitch, Sir, it's a good stitch."

Jojo nodded in response.

"Would you like a bigger space, with help?" Faron asked.

Danso's head tilted as if his eyes were ears, straining to hear what Faron asked. "You want to give me space to sew?"

"Would you like a larger space to work?"

Danso broke out into confused laughter.

Faron and Jojo locked eyes, until Jojo nodded in agreement.

* * *

Danso's mother made them eat at the same time every day, deliberately interrupting the sewing ritual taking place at the back of her house. Faron politely refused, explaining he had a sister who would take offence as she cooked his meals. He listened to the hypnotising chomp of the sewing needle during the first few visits and thought about Paulo Alves' room in Bahia, full of enthused Portuguese men blowing at needles, pedalling to the rhythm of their bodies, and folding cloth meticulously. His father had sent him many times to pick up his shirts and pants from the tailors in the town. The memories lit up an energy inside him that he had never felt before. Here, on the other side of the world, he could wear the clothes his father wore and live the way his father lived, without remorse or trepidation.

He set about searching for a larger room that they could work in without interruptions from an impatient mother needing attention and acclamation for her cooking skills. A room to inspire a sense of pride and accomplishment.

Faron found himself back with the Tabom. The elders who knew him had either passed away or were at home telling stories to the young of a place far away that treated them as less than human. They did not walk in the midday sun or find themselves in the local bars hidden away at the back of the compounds. They were too old. He would not bump into them. The name Tabom insinuated a new culture without boundaries. The young were surprised to find out that some Brazilians had moved further inland away from the comfort of familiarity. They listened to his life and his wishes, and after a long search, they introduced him to a building in Swalaba on the border of Jamestown. A single-story rusty stone block house, bound by local clay mortar. A family of seven had recently departed. It was a good deal.

The young Tabom in Accra moved around with vigour, unaware of the disparities between their lives versus those of their parents. They did not know of the miserable existence and constant dread experienced by their ancestors waking under the warmth of the morning sun. And yet, here was a miracle that only Faron got to experience in his own exile. A certain loneliness embraced him whenever he witnessed these miracles. It did not feel good. It felt empty. To think that the people he once knew and loved would never experience this. Most would have had short lives. They would never have known what it meant to open your eyes as a free man, with relief, gratitude and vigour, harbouring a zest for life and love without despair. Only he experienced it, and his very existence depended on spilling blood. And yet a trickle of hope seeped from his pores every time he opened his eyes to the crow of the rooster.

The newly acquired building stood before the men in all its splendour, built by those who survived slavery and the *SS Salisbury*. They woke up every day with an understanding that their life belonged to them, and this building was their gift and their legacy.

Jojo and Danso stood in awe in the middle of the floor looking around.

"Owura, is this the Tabom building?" asked Danso.

"It is," Faron replied. "And we have work to do."

"What shall we call it?" Jojo asked.

"Scissor House." Faron replied.

Danso clapped his hands and laughed.

"We will sleep here until it is done," Jojo replied, stomping on the uneven floor to find a good place for them to rest.

Scissor House was unveiled to the public one year later. This was the first establishment dedicated solely to designing and sewing clothes. Seamstresses and tailors always worked from home, so this was an entirely new experience. It allowed the new establishment to charge higher prices. The Scissor House created a modern understanding around the making and purchasing of handmade clothes. Prospective customers could walk in, converse with the two tailors, bump into acquaintances, and meet other customers. Jojo's distinctive appearance became synonymous with the head of Scissor House. Danso's reputation spiralled and another Tabom, Nelson, a man whose sewing skills had been handed down by his fathers, joined them not long after. The growing native elite liked the idea of walking through the doors and telling their friends they knew Jojo, Danso and Nelson. Faron remained discreet – visiting to check the books with the occasional greetings to patrons.

The success of Scissor House caught the attention of the British civil servants. Clerks within government were the ones with the most contact. It was always useful to be acquainted with those working in the post office, railway and so forth. Faron was not surprised to hear of their inquisitiveness. He knew it was only a matter of time before a clerk appeared to scan the property and get acquainted.

He was careful not to meet the Tabom elders and mindful that no one paid him more attention than needed. His fleeting visits to Scissor House lessened as he looked for land elsewhere. The quest for a better life continued with his determination to find a home that mirrored what he felt he and Jojo deserved – a life that emulated their differences and desires. They had slept on the floor without covers, sharing space with ants, cockroaches and other formidable creatures that surfaced in the night. Woken by crickets, they toiled in the day to preserve their legacy. Danso arrived early every morning with aasana and lamugin ginger, lemon and cloves. Danso's mother passed through on the long afternoons with kenkey-fermented maize dumplings, fried fish and hot pepper sauce. Jojo and Nelson ate to their heart's content. Faron insisted on eating his later. Jojo put on weight.

He kept the house he was building in Jamestown a secret from Jojo. The scramble for land to grow cocoa and palm oil had created an opportunity for Faron. Rumblings of World War I reverberated across continents, even the shores of Ghana felt the tremors of global conflict. The demand for resources and manpower for the war effort led to a surge in cocoa production to meet the escalating demands of the British. This was good for landowners. He sold his assets to the highest bidder. There was enough money left over from the Scissor House to build a home only Luíza could have predicted. A two-storey, three-bedroom house with a sustainable outside latrine and a storage tank on the roof to collect rainwater. It took close to a year to complete. Faron managed the construction, digging holes, preparing and unloading materials, breaking down temporary structures, and talking to workers. This meant he arrived back at Scissor House late and fell asleep without conversation. Jojo didn't seem to notice as he was making new friends and receiving invitations to visit other families in different compounds. Jojo was his own man now, and the new bungalow would solidify his presence in the community.

When the house was complete, Faron brought an unsuspecting Jojo for a viewing on a muggy Saturday afternoon. Jojo walked around the compound, examining the exterior.

"What do you think?" Faron asked.

"Owura, you did not tell me," Jojo declared.

"You don't need to know everything."

"How is your demon, Owura? Has it been visiting you?"

The question took Faron by surprise, which swiftly turned into dread. He had not needed his fix for a while. Wasn't that a good thing?

"It has subsided, but I don't know for how long."

"You must go to the places bad men visit," Jojo reminded him.

"Of course. You find out where they go and I'll take myself there," Faron said.

They walked into the house and surveyed the rooms.

"What I need is a cure, Jojo," Faron announced.

"You must speak to and forgive the people in Brazil for what they did to you," Jojo responded.

"How can I? They are long dead."

"No. They are here, minding their own business until you speak to them."

Faron's chest tightened at the words. Was he to go to church and meet the Catholic Portuguese and Spanish priests settled here? Confess to them? They should be confessing to him – begging his forgiveness. These Gold Coast people did not understand the brutality that his kind had endured, which was why he did not enter churches or mosques, why he did not acknowledge the British, and why he could not speak so easily to…

"You must forgive us, too. Slaves captured from war were sold. We did not know what it would lead to. Greed creates monsters." Jojo interrupted his thoughts.

Their eyes locked in a split second.

"And yourself. A lot of forgiving." Jojo smiled before adding quickly, "I have found a wife, Papa."

"A wife?" Faron exclaimed. "Did you marry her already?"

"No, Papa, she must know who you are first."

"And what is the price?"

Jojo smiled. "First, we must speak to her family, and then we will marry as soon as we can."

"You are bringing her here to live with us?"

"No, Papa. I will live in another compound with her family."

Jojo was no longer waiting for the sun to set. Faron had taken time for granted. His son would be in his mid-thirties very soon. He said the word "Papa," gently as if trying not to hurt him.

"You must find yourself a wife, Papa. Women ease our suffering. They wash it away or carry it in secret for us. Most of the time we don't know they are carrying it. We think our load is lighter because of what we are doing, but it is the women who remove it and place it on their heads permanently. You need one, Papa, to live long."

"You want me to find one, Jojo? Will it make you happy?" Faron laughed.

"It will allow me to stop worrying and enjoy my own comforts," Jojo replied.

"Then I will find one."

CHAPTER FIFTEEN

Empire Day.

A procession crowded the street, made up of horses and carriages, starched and crisp white-collar school uniforms in single file, Wolseley khaki pith helmets complimenting decorated military uniforms, civil servants and locals. Young students marched gallantly, saluting the British Union Flag, following a chorus of familiar patriotic songs like "Jerusalem" and "God Save the King." The Governor gave inspirational speeches, with stories from across the empire. The day was filled with the excitement of new encounters, including an invitation to the Governor's garden party. The request was of no consequence to Jojo, but Faron insisted that the Scissor House partnership needed to extend outside of its premises and others had to understand this. The invitation came as no surprise – the reputation and success of Scissor House was increasingly apparent, but it was also accompanied by an uneasy atmosphere of anticipation. The festivities offered a temporary escape from the growing unease that had taken hold of the nation. As the largest employer of wage labour in the Gold Coast, the government found itself at the centre of mounting frustration. The Public Works Department workers sparked a wave of rebellion by protesting ongoing wage payment delays. It was always in the interest of government officials to have a good working relationship with the elite and the chiefs, and now Faron was one of them.

The garden party boasted servants sporting white gloves, along with an array of summer dresses with accompanying parasols. Jojo spotted a few chiefs sheltering from the sun as they made their way through the crowds. He regretted the ivory linen jazz-suit trousers that rose high on his waist with a flat, slim fit over the hips and down his leg. His body had no room to breathe, and witnessing the ceremonial cloth of the royal guests increased his agitation. Faron himself did not care for the surrounding company and knew the invite was just an avenue for scrutiny. It was never in his best interests to be well known. Unfortunately, he had no choice but to attend. Jojo needed to get used to the process of becoming a successful businessman. He would remain the face of Scissor House for as long as it took. Faron contemplated the future. Perhaps in ten years he would leave and sail to another west-coast colony. Sierra Leone sounded interesting. It was, after all, the residence of the British colonial governor responsible for the administration of Sierra Leone, the Gold Coast and the Gambia settlements.

A pleasant greeting and polite conversation were had with a Ga member of the Legislative Council. Nearby, the Governor and his wife were being introduced to guests by a senior civil servant. The legislative council member stood to attention when the senior civil servant recognised them both and thanked them for attending the celebrations on Empire Day. The Governor, a handsome man with thick blond moustache and teal blue eyes, nodded as Faron and Jojo were introduced.

"Governor Piggersill and Mrs Piggersill the owners of Scissor House"

His wife wore a tight-fitting cloche hat, held low over the forehead and nape. The Governor complemented Scissor House, and his wife appeared both enthralled and excited to hear about the establishment.

"Scissor House … and you are Brazilian, a Tabom, I hear?" Her eyes lit up with curiosity.

"That I am, Madame," Faron answered.

"How are you finding the changes to Jamestown?" she asked. "It was the least sanitary district of all. The government's resolve to clear away the rubble and construct new wide streets was a much-needed decision that will help with new initiatives such as yours."

"Yes, I am aware of the proposed regulations for public health," Faron answered.

"Well, the fire definitely sped things up," Mrs Piggersill replied.

The men fell silent. The civil servant pushed his tortoise-shell glasses up his face with his index finger. "That was an unpleasant experience for the unfortunate inhabitants of the town." He placed a light tap on Faron's shoulder "We have Mr Vivo here to thank for revitalising the area in the business of suits."

"And what a delightful enterprise!"

"Indeed," the Governor concluded. "Well done."

The Governor's wife's eyes were on him. He smelt her curiosity as he engaged with the Governor, the civil servant and the councillor. Her silk, hydrangea-print dress rustled against the breeze; endless stockings matched her skin tone. He sensed adrenaline rushing through her as she moved her parasol from left to right, impatient with her immediate company. The sounds drowned out his surroundings. She turned her focus on Jojo, who said something discreetly so the others could not hear. She threw her head back in hysterical laughter. The men turned their attention to Jojo, who stood in bemusement. She repeated Jojo's words to the others, who also laughed. Faron looked at his watch as Jojo further explained himself. He observed the insides of the civil servant's mouth in laughter and the Governor's stoic demeanour. His arms behind his back. His eyes filled with curiosity. It looked like they would be here longer than expected. As much as he tried, this world did not interest him, and he wanted to get back to his own. The Governor and his wife moved on to the next guests.

Jojo chuckled. "Look how far we have come, Owura."

"I know."

"And yet you are discontented? Today, I will go home and tell everyone I made the Governor's wife laugh till she cried."

"She didn't quite cry, Jojo." Faron narrowed his eyes.

"Yes, but my story must continue after I am long gone."

* * *

A repertoire of bird songs and calls filled the morning sky every day in the new house, allowing Faron to remove himself from the covers of sleep. He spent his first few days in his large home walking around and admiring the joinery and craftsmanship that adorned the four corners of the building. The street was quiet most days and the whitewashed wall that surrounded the house did not allow for peeping Toms or nosy neighbours. Faron enjoyed the calm and serenity. He did not miss company. For the first time in a long while, he could move around without planning his life around others. There were no visitors and no surprises. Faron marvelled at the privacy he had been unable to experience for most of his life. Wealth and privacy were a team. He had never realised this until now, and he basked in his isolation until Jojo turned up a few mornings later with a skinny, bald man called Kwabla.

"He will be your night watchman, to make sure you are safe," Jojo stated.

Faron glared at Jojo.

"I have paid him a month's wages. He is here to get anything you need. He starts work today," Jojo continued. "Kwabla is a special man who understands the ancestors' doings, so he will not question you or anything he sees."

Kwabla nodded and pointed to the outhouse. "Good evening, Sah. Mr Jojo has shown me around your yard, and it is looking dirty, so I will go and clean it." He smiled and went off to search for a broom.

"Why are you bringing strangers into my home?" Faron snapped. "I don't need anyone here. I am perfectly capable. We discussed this. No strangers!"

"Owura, Kwabla is a good, spiritual man. You will never have to worry about him."

"For god's sake, Jojo, what have you told him?"

"I am going to be very busy for the next month, Papa. Very busy. I will soon have a wife. So, I cannot look after you like before."

"What do you mean, 'look after me'? Am I a child? Jojo, you don't bring strangers into our lives like this. What are you thinking?"

"Papa, I have people from my mother's family coming to Accra in a few weeks. My mother's sisters who left home. I sent word to them."

"You mean the women who didn't come forward to raise you when your mother died? Now they want to come to your wedding?"

"Owura, they knew you were the better option … were you not the better option? Anyway … they must bring gifts and dowry to my lady's parents to agree on the marriage."

"Why? Does the woman not want to marry you? Are you forcing her?"

Jojo laughed. "Papa, this is custom. We must ask permission in this way and give a bride price. They need to see if they want our families to come together."

"How many are coming?"

"I don't know. A few. Maybe five."

Faron sighed.

Jojo laughed.

"They will stay in the compound with me, Papa. Don't worry. You will deal with Kwabla and nobody else."

"You know me so well, Jojo."

"Yes, exactly. So, don't question. That is all." Jojo waved goodbye before Faron could answer.

Faron hadn't realised how much Jojo enjoyed the company of others. It was true, Jojo loved to talk with the customers all day long. He shared jokes with the other tailors, and the fruit-and-vegetable traders passing by the shop all knew his name. Faron had not expected Jojo to blossom in this environment so fast. This was indeed the best experience yet for his son. Jojo had found a companion – a woman. They barely discussed women in any detail. Faron totally neglected that part of himself, and now his son was taking the lead with a female and was soon to be married. Faron had never experienced a wedding before, either as a friend or a relative. For this marriage, he was to pretend to be a cousin or nephew of sorts and leave the woman's family to focus on the travelling relatives, who were much more fluent in Ga.

A few days later, an unsuspecting barefoot young man in short tan pants turned up at his gates. The boy stretched his hand out, holding a white envelope.

"Madame sent me. This is for you."

Faron opened the envelope, knowing the course of his life was set to change.

> Dear Faron,
>
> It was a pleasure to meet your acquaintance and I wish to learn much more about the Tabom. Afternoon tea on Tuesday will be at your discretion. Yours respectfully,
>
> A

Faron folded the scented letter and pushed it into his pocket. What would possess a woman to be so bold? Indeed, he was not used to this and had never imagined such liaisons took place in the Gold Coast. He was not one of her kinfolk, even if he was from another country. This was a busy time for him as he sought to furnish his new home and attend Jojo's forthcoming wedding, with all its traditions and complications. It was almost amusing that interaction with women was suddenly possible, but Annie Piggersill was a dangerous distraction. Jojo's circumstances demanded focus and time. His son was getting married. Faron decided not to ponder on the issue of Annie Piggersill until it was time to visit her.

Three relatives arrived on the day in question and visited his home. Jojo had warned Faron that he would recognise one of the guests, but not to worry. This was not the time to further question his stressed son, so Faron nodded and let it be. Jojo arrived with the guests, professing that it was a short visit. Faron welcomed them in for a quick drink and some snacks. A middle-aged man and his wife introduced themselves. Faron immediately recognised the third man as the translator who had stood by the foot of Jojo's mother's bed and informed him of his destiny. He steadied his hands as he spoke. It was important not to show his unease. They were his guests. The translator was now an old man with a stoop, who smiled warmly and called him "Tabom."

Faron couldn't remember his name.

"Kumi," the translator said.

Why had he not realised at the time that this man, this translator, was related to Jojo? Why had he not intervened on the day Jojo's mother died?

"It is wonderful to see Jojo is a tailor in this big, big city. I never would have imagined it," Kumi exclaimed.

"Ah, people underestimated me," Jojo laughed.

"It was his choice. I merely facilitated," Faron answered.

Kumi nodded. "A blessing … lots of blessings to you, Sir."

"I did not know that you were Jojo's uncle," Faron said.

"I am the translator. I will be the one talking on behalf of the family tomorrow. Jojo, you will stand outside until asked to enter the house."

Jojo nodded in acknowledgment.

"Will you need me there?" Faron asked. "I am not familiar with the customs of the betrothed."

"You will come. You are his nephew. Let me do the talking and just follow whatever I say," Kumi replied.

Whatever Kumi was feeling, Faron could not pick up on it – no sweat or odour to detect. It confused him, and Jojo refused to disclose what he had shared with Kumi, just as with Kwabla. Now the wedding preparations were starting, that conversation would have to wait.

On the day in question, they arrived at the compound, observed by all as they walked towards the home of the bride. Jojo and a young boy brought an endless supply of akpetishie – the local alcohol. Kumi carried a bag full of money. Faron packed sandals, a gift for the chief, two full pieces of white cloth, a cutlass, an umbrella and beads.

"Who are you? What is the purpose of this visit?" a man called out, standing before the entrance of the home of the bride.

"We are here to ask for the rose. Our son wants your daughter!" Kumi responded.

The door to the hut opened. Faron and the relatives took the remaining bags of akpetishie from Jojo and walked into the bride's home. Faron winked at Jojo to calm his nerves. He had forgotten the impact Jojo's albinism could have, and now the compound's people were staring at him, their eyes speaking their thoughts. They both had battles to get through, and acceptance was not the only challenge.

Inside the room, four male elders sat amongst two middle-aged women. A young man in his thirties stood at the back. The potential bride was nowhere to be seen. Kumi prostrated before being offered a place to sit, and the others followed his actions. The gifts were heavy and Faron was glad to sit with the trunk and bags on the floor.

"My name is Kumi. I will talk on behalf of the family," Kumi said, before introducing Faron and the other relatives.

The father was long and lean, rather like Jojo. He wiped his face with a handkerchief, closed his eyes, and listened as Kumi informed them of Jojo's intention to marry their daughter. The mother, plump with a warm-hearted smile, sat on the floor. Kumi said something to make the observers in the room laugh. The father opened his eyes and asked a question.

Kumi turned to Faron. "He asks how a Tabom is related to Jojo?"

"I was orphaned. Jojo's family took me in and gave me a home," Faron answered.

Kumi presented the drinks and gifts to the bride's family. They accepted them with smiles. The father spoke to the young male observer, and he disappeared.

"Afua … Afua!" The mother called out.

"They are calling the bride to ask her if she knows the man who wants to marry her."

They waited.

Afua entered the room. Fresh braided lines across her scalp, glowing skin and a wrap lined firmly across her person. She moved to the side of the audience. Her father uttered a few words, which she answered. Kumi leaned into Faron and whispered, "He is asking her if she wants to be married and if she is going to accept."

The replies of "Yes" were crisp and clear.

The entrance door opened, and Jojo was brought into the house. The bride's mother snapped her fingers. Refreshments were ushered in and shared.

* * *

The next day was Tuesday. The same young man in short pants and barefoot knocked on the front door for Faron, who was not dressed. He had not forgotten, but he had received no actual instructions as to where this meeting with Annie Piggersill would take place.

"Madam sent me to take you to her house," the boy said.

"Do you know the address?" Faron asked.

He nodded in response.

"Tell me the address and I will go there myself." Faron placed a shilling into the boy's hand for his wasted trip.

He met her in a private European-styled bungalow surrounded by green forest on the outskirts of Accra. A perfect hideaway. Tea was waiting for him on the porch in the shade. She stood with a smile as he approached. Her blonde hair was a little dishevelled, as if she'd been running her hand through it.

He had underestimated her loneliness; it seeped through her pores and strangled his senses as he approached her. Her eyes lit up with anticipation and excitement at the sight of him. She stood upright, petite, but robust in stature. She kept her distance and spoke to him about England – she called it the mother country and painted that world with colourful images. A world everyone would want to create a copy of and repeat in their own environment. A world full of invention, with a clear understanding of men and God. It was important that he showed an interest in what she had to say about England. She needed him to believe this story. He spoke light-heartedly of a Portuguese-styled Brazil that his Tabom parents shared.

She lit a cigarette while he pretended to sip the tea and declined the scones. The jam jelly smelt sweet enough to eat, but he had no intention of gagging in front of her. She wiped the jam and cream off her fingers with the serviette provided.

"You must be wondering what you are doing here?"

Faron remained silent.

She crossed her legs and laughed. "Oh, come now, don't be such a stick-in-the-mud!

"My apologies, I shall endeavour to be more jovial." Faron replied.

"Have you heard of Henry Poole?" she asked.

"I can't say that I have."

"Henry Poole is the largest establishment on Savile Row, in England. Savile Row is the most dedicated and well-known home for working tailors – only the best, of course." She blew smoke from her mouth and continued. "Henry Poole employs three hundred tailors and fourteen cutters and makes twelve thousand bespoke garments annually. Are you impressed?"

"You have my attention," Faron answered.

"My husband and I may leave for England in approximately twelve months. His Governance is coming to an end. As much as we love the Gold Coast, in all honesty, we won't be back." She paused. "May I call you Faron?"

"Of course," he answered and moved back in his seat, waiting to hear what they wanted from him.

"Perhaps you would think of joining us in England to open an establishment? First in Liverpool, where we reside, and then later in London. Of course, we would see that all the legalities are taken care of – like a partnership of sorts. We feel there may be room for exponential growth in England. Liverpool is a rich city and London is the centre of the British Empire and English style. British cloth and tailoring are internationally considered to be the best. So, why not join us on a venture?"

> *"A union of wealth, prosperity, and freedom. You will be a free man and visit many cities and people…"*

The words of that dreaded prophecy. It sounded so good at the time. An unimaginable possibility. And now he had an offer to visit the home of the British Empire with an upper-class duo – the Governor no less. And yet, his heart did not sing with joy.

He sighed.

Annie crossed her legs as she puffed on her cigarette.

He wouldn't let her down today.

"What am I thinking?" Annie asked again.

Faron's lips lifted into a hard smile.

"The possibilities are endless," Faron answered.

146

"I will think about the offer. Thank you for the invitation. I bid you good day."

Faron moved alone through the yard towards the exit. He sensed the short breaths of the watchman in his quarters. Probably a loyal servant who relayed secrets to the nearby village with an understanding that the separation of locals and whites meant it would take a long time for the rumours to crawl up the ladder. Where was the Governor and why had she invited him to the house with no one there. It did not sit well with him. Whatever plotting and planning was going on – there could be no witnesses to spread rumours.

Faron entered the watchman's quarters, disrupting the afternoon nap of the young man. The man's shock turned to horror as Faron faced him with black pupils and gnarly teeth. There was no need to search the darkness for his fix tonight. It was right here waiting for him, young and strong.

CHAPTER SIXTEEN

Faron was not obliged to speak or participate in the wedding arrangements, just to provide resources and cover costs. He was a Tabom, and this made things less complex. Language barriers and lack of understanding of the culture made the family ignore him for the most part. Jojo's version of their lives together got more interesting by the minute. As the story went, both were orphans. Jojo's aunt took in the Tabom child, and Jojo helped her raise Faron. The tale fit into the ideals of hope and satisfied the palette of non-conformists. It made life simple for those who desired simplicity at its best. They were stubborn, those kinds of people. They didn't want anything to rock their simplistic existence. So, those with power created an existence for them in which they did not have to feel threatened. The wheel would turn exactly as it was meant to.

Faron entertained the idea of marriage many times, but it became a fallacy. A simple part of human existence that he could not participate in, having lived for over two hundred years with no real idea of how his future would turn out, apart from his eternal youthfulness and hunger for human tissue. Women were attracted to his strangeness. His detachment intrigued some, and there were those who thought he would choose them.

Annie sent another note, via the same young boy. Faron placed a shilling into the boy's hand with a message that he had a wedding to attend and would be recovering for a few days.

That was not a lie.

The scale of how things were managed and organised, and the hierarchy of responsibility, were not things Faron had prepared for. Although he remained in the background, the orders, requests and interruptions to daily life left him weary. Even though Danso and Nelson carried on with customer orders, it was clear they needed a helping hand. Faron permitted them to hire an apprentice in his absence. The orders could not suffer. Faron counted the days until the wedding. He wanted it over and done with – even if it meant he and Jojo would never share a place to sleep again.

On the day of the wedding, the okyeame from the bride's side made his announcements. A stout grandfather, holding a calabash filled with schnapps, lowered the cloth from his left shoulder and recited incantations, invoking and speaking to the gods while pouring the drink on the ground, to commit the couple into God's hands. He pleaded for the ancestors to protect their union. All around him responded in cohesive murmurs. He implored the ancestors to keep curses away. The muttered responses grew louder until he put the calabash to his mouth and sipped the alcohol dry.

Jojo's bride appeared, adorned with white beads around her neck and wrists, her body decorated with paintings and wrapped exclusively in white cloth, leaving her shoulders bare. The two families, traditional leaders and guests all wore beads, including the children. The chief wore a single gold bead around his neck. Faron watched the young dance and sing against the cool sea breeze that wound its way through the party with deliberation, easing the discomfort of the crowd on this special day. Smiles and laughter evoked a quietness within him. He forgot who he was as an individual, as the graceful communal offering of shared joy permitted him, just for a moment, to believe all was forgiven. This was the place Luíza had foreseen. His peace. His redemption. His death and rebirth, amongst those who lived in a communality without fear, holding a deep respect for those gone before. He remembered his mother's loathing. If she could have seen him now, would she be proud or envious? Was this her doing? If only for an instant, he was at peace. He owed it to the people of this land – the Gold Coast – to rid himself of the curse. He would have to find out how. It was time.

Jojo was no longer his. Their brief greetings, before and during the ceremony, were usurped by the guests, who all wished to be associated with the important people of the day. Faron watched his friend bask in the love of those he had just met. All his life he had been scooped up and loved by those around him without question. He had also been treated with indifference and Faron had to put a stop to children jeering several times over the years. Jojo had been the recipient of emotional contradiction, but the outcome always remained the same. Faron pondered on what it must be like to continuously be supported by those who believe this was the only way to live. The new bride smiled and laughed

– her eyes shone whenever she looked at her new husband. Faron had never witnessed this look in any of the females around him growing up. It startled him. She glowed, as if Jojo were the only man in the compound. Jojo, his son, was no longer a young man and their relationship had changed. Faron's mind ran to Annie. Perhaps he should accept the offer. He could leave Jojo to manage Scissor House and take one tailor with him. On the other hand, the idea of being completely isolated in a white man's country left him feeling unsettled. He would be at their mercy, and they could turn on him at any moment. Here he had the protection of his people. Would they protect him with the same loyalty and ferocity? Why couldn't they just find a tailor out there and set up with one of their own? There was also unfinished business he had to attend to in the Gold Coast – his cure.

* * *

Annie saved round flat Welsh tea cakes for him. She informed him there would be a party that evening – but he was to keep this a secret from the Governor. She dragged on her cigarette and watched him bite into the tea cake. The sharp tinge of the raisins hit the roof of his mouth as he bit into its chewy texture. It surprised him to taste something. She poured him tea from an impressive China teapot. He swallowed very little – allowing his Adam's apple to dip as proof that it was possible for him to eat.

"It's been rather busy since I last saw you. My watchman disappeared on the day you visited, and his family declared he never went home. It's been such a bother trying to convince them that they can't be paid for services owed. I'm having a dinner party this evening, by the way."

The meshed residue of flour and raisin plastered itself to the top of his mouth. He had mastered the art of pretending to swallow.

"You are always so serious, Faron. Your sombreness is intriguing. I wonder what's going on behind those eyes."

"Life and death," he replied.

"Why would you trouble yourself with that in such peaceful conditions? Surely you know that the experiences of your parents are not yours."

"The troubles do not remove themselves by magic," he replied.

"But you did not experience them," she countered.

"And your parents?" Faron asked.

A sharp sucking of air gave her time to think and word her sentence carefully. "My father was gone most of the time. He was a sergeant in the army. My mother, God bless her, wasn't very loving, but she did the best she could."

"And yet you walk around carrying her insecurities – those which are not yours. It sits in your body as you make excuses."

"I don't want to have a disagreement with you, Faron. I have yet to witness your heart-warming smile and yet you draw me near you with your melancholy," she said. "I really can't wait for the others to meet you."

"I do that?" This was a surprise to him.

"Perhaps. But what of your decision?" She changed the subject.

"You are asking me to leave my home and travel to the unknown, to do business in a place where I believe there may be some hostility towards my kind."

Annie chuckled and waved her hand in dismissal. "Whatever gave you that idea? London is the centre of the world, darling. Jazz and dancing, trips to Paris. There are many Negroes in our fine city. Why, John Archer, a Negro, was elected Mayor of Battersea in London only a few years ago. A mayor, no less."

Faron looked out across the veranda to the palm trees breaking up the monotony of uneven rolling green. The wind picked up a little, making the palms dance. Voices of villagers echoed from beyond the bungalow's enclosure.

"Well," Annie paused. "I have some delights in store for my visitors. We are going to have a wild time tonight, Faron. Much to your taste, I would imagine."

"I must politely decline your invitation. I have a great number of things that need my attention and cannot wait," Faron responded. He hated all this familiarity. One invitation meant many more in the future.

Annie pouted.

He stood up and nodded. They both knew what they needed to know about each other. There was no more to be said or shared.

"If you must." She stayed sitting.

CHAPTER SEVENTEEN

With the Governor's invitation on his mind, Faron did not go home, but sought to rid himself of the recollections of the Bahia, his mother's wretched ways and Luíza's predictions. They had surfaced at the wedding and wouldn't let go. This invitation to England niggled him. Jojo had a new life and could manage the others if Faron took one lucky tailor with him. They could set up in London and travel back and forth. However, the isolation, and the track record of the hidden capabilities of the whites, filled him with dread.

All that had transpired served as a constant reminder that the prophecy was not done with him yet. He wanted to be normal. He wanted it to be finished. So, he needed a cure. The sameness of his existence wore him down. To accept who he was would leave him detached in bittersweet monotony. Faron snapped himself out of the memories that were spiralling into despair and moved faster across the plains. His gaze flew around the curve of the bushes as he headed home. Trees resembling black shadows reached towards the sky. He needed comfort. Relief. He lifted his nose and inhaled. Ahead, a lone man moved towards him. Faron waited in the shadows, eyes locked on his prey – a well-built man with heavy feet. Good. Faron wanted to fight the discord out of his head and body, so he needed to grapple with someone full of life. He put his promise to Jojo out of his mind, so he could rid himself of the irritation that compounded his spirit.

The man fought hard.

He shoved against his opponent with muscles that resembled mud huts.

There was a difference between his victims in Accra and those from the countryside. The Oburoni invasion had changed the Ashanti and Ga ways. The intervention of Catholic missionaries promising afterlife had made the locals lazy. They did not seem to appreciate life as they once had.

But this one did.

He clawed and bit at Faron's arm, then snapped it as though it were a piece of kindling. Faron lay under the large man, trying to avoid the heavy punches raining down on his face and chest. He could feel the ligaments in his elbow stretching around his humerus as it healed. Faron risked a smile – this one was furious indeed.

"I fear no demon. My Lord is with me. I will send you to him!" the man shouted, spit flying into Faron's eyes.

His fist slammed into Faron's jaw. Faron's tongue slid between three loose teeth. Blood oozed from his mouth as he spat them out. In response, Faron shot open his fingers and speared his right hand into the man's side, tearing through fat and muscle. He watched the brave man's expression change from anger to surprise as his eyes widened and his lips fell open. Faron forced his fingers further in, until the man gasped with pain. A familiar rotting smell moved through their entangled bodies. Confused, the man cast his eyes downward.

"I admire your strength," Faron noted.

The man's eyes returned to his opponent, with that familiar questioning look they all wore before they died. He shook at the smell of his own decomposing flesh. Faron lowered his eyelids. The taste of life in its very essence reverberated around his body. Muscle and skin inched around the exposed white spots of bone in his fingers and arms.

"I just need my fix. That's the way it is," Faron explained.

The man's eyes rolled to the back of his head. That big body shook. His mouth hung open, and a black tongue lolled out. His body trembled for a moment before bursting into grey ashes that slowly floated around Faron. Dust danced against the pull of gravity before succumbing to soil. Faron kept his eyes and mouth shut as the dust caked his face and body. Renewed flesh covered remnant bone tissue that had previously threatened to disclose the unfamiliar.

"What are you doing here?" The voice was soft and low.

Alarmed, Faron wiped the ashes from his face to see who was speaking. The grass underneath him no longer comforted his bones – instead, it allowed the hard soil and small stones to push against his restored flesh.

A young boy was peering at him.

Faron jumped to his feet to grab the child, but he backed off.

"What are you doing here?" the boy repeated. "This is my home."

Faron raised himself to stand tall.

The stick-thin boy had not yet gone through puberty. Black patches of hair sprouted around his body. Neither spoke. Faron's heart skipped a beat, unable to comprehend what was before him. He had never encountered "another." Invisible crickets in the grassland broke through the silence. The boy stepped sideways, exposing a protruding round lump on his upper back.

"You don't belong here," the boy said.

A slight resentment arose from hearing those words. Faron thought about grabbing the wretched creature and snapping his already malformed neck. This thing was not human. It sneered at him as though he were lesser. He had to keep it together – he sensed it was something of a child overwhelmed with fear and curiosity.

"I'm too fast for you. You can never be as fast as me." The boy grinned.

"Are you alone here?" Faron asked.

"No." The boy got on all fours to circle Faron. Sharp, curved claws aided stealthy footsteps as his paws dug into the soil. His head involuntarily tilted to the side. One arm dragged along the ground as he continued to circle Faron. The crescent moon shone down on the tips of the grass around them. Their dark figures blocked the entrance to the forest marked by groves of palm trees.

"There are others," the boy said coyly.

"Others like you?"

"Like me, and beyond."

Am I allowed to leave with no interference?" Faron asked.

"Is there only one of you?"

"As far as I know."

"You must be lonely."

"I am alone, but I am not lonely. Perhaps I can meet these others," Faron proposed, as slight relief washed over him. Other monstrosities like him existed. Perhaps they had answers. Had they been watching him? This creature was no match for him, but if it were as the creature suggested, then it was time for him to find out what the possibilities were and how these others existed. He had been in the country for over thirty years, and none had shown themselves to him.

"How do you survive?" Faron asked.

"We both feed, but I am full. Sometimes I am full up for a year." The boy stood up on two legs, revealing a flat hairless chest, like that of an ape. He patted his stomach and fell back onto all fours.

Faron did not respond. His eyes rested on the scattered trees that would shield him on the walk home. His bones ached.

"I will show you my strength soon," the boy promised Faron.

Faron wanted the boy to stop moving.

"I will show you how to eat and stop because your belly is full," the boy continued.

Faron scoffed. This thing avoided his questions and goaded him. It was unfathomable that he had been watching him this whole time. This deformed fool could not outsmart him. Faron wanted to wipe the smirk off the boy's face, but he knew that he couldn't.

"Can a belly ever stop receiving food?" Faron asked.

The boy stopped and raised himself up partially, as if to take a good look at Faron. He raised his claw-like hands in dismissal. "It's not about the food, it's about the feeling of satisfaction." With that, he crouched back

CORPO SECO

down on all fours and scurried away towards the grasslands without looking back.

Faron walked through the forest, deep in thought. It was late. Swaying trees whispered his secrets as he walked beneath them. The encounter with the boy had unnerved him. Clearly the boy was not a child, and neither was he alone. He had not revealed his true self. Faron never encountered "others." He had felt the presence of several during his lifetime in Bahia, but whatever they had been, they had decided to stay out of sight, as if they sensed his demeanour and feared him. The people of the Bahia whispered his name behind closed doors. Only Jojo had witnessed his power and lived. This boy had watched him fight and waited to see his abilities. This was not good.

It had been a long day. The invitation to London had left him deeply unsettled and the encounter with the boy added confusion to his somewhat peaceful and simple existence. Faron was not ready to go home to an empty house. He needed to be amongst the faces of the familiar. He decided to go to the compound of Mama Ekufuwa – a woman famous for her palm-butter stew which, according to Jojo, was second to none. It would be busy there. Although he couldn't eat the food of the people, he could have a lick during conversation. A good way to calm down and get back to the sentiment of the people. This day had been a cursed one, and in his rage he became unpredictable. If he hadn't attacked that unsuspecting man, none of this would have happened. He would still be in a non-complex existence. A twinge in the side of his stomach joined his sense of minor irritation. He would take his time to decide about England. After all, he was one of the richest men in the Jamestown area; even the

Governor understood the impact he had made on Jamestown. It had taken time to build up this foundation and establish himself since leaving Bahia. They knew this.

Faron looked down into Mama Ekufuwa's compound. It was too dark to see the pleasure in the patrons' faces, but the sounds of talk and laughter were enough. He joined the line of men waiting to order food and sit on stools in the cool air of the evening.

Red beans with plantains and smoked fish in large bowls floated high above the heads of patrons. Faron paid and joined three men walking towards an array of stools. It was custom to eat together; this encouraged conversation and goodwill.

A sudden waft of seaweed stung his nose. Faron stopped short. The men sat, comfortably unaware, and began to eat, while Faron stood transfixed as the shadow of a woman moved in his direction. It was as though no one else in the compound could see her. She swayed towards him until she was in full view of the kerosene lamps.

Her lips moved as she spoke, but he couldn't hear her. Small catlike eyes shone and blinked at him. Her hair fell in long plaits around her shoulders with a life of its own. Her full lips parted into a smile, as if she understood his stumped response.

"Will you drink with me?" he thought he heard her ask.

"I would do many things with you … with your permission, of course." Words escaped his mouth before he could control them, leaving him dismayed.

She gurgled softly as she touched his hand.

His stomach tightened.

"But first you must eat." She pointed to the waiting men in the distant dark who seemed not to witness her beauty. The plaits tangled and untangled themselves around her long neck. "You men want to eat, no?"

He blocked their view of her, not wanting anyone else to witness her beauty.

"We will drink together, sometime later." She paused. "I see you like shiny things that the Oburoni gives you." She tugged on the silver Albert chains secured from the buttonhole of his waistcoat and fingered his pocket watch with fascination.

"Where do you go?" he asked, concerned she would disappear and be lost forever.

"I go home. It is late," she replied.

"You're teasing me," he said.

She had chosen him, and now toyed with him.

"I will find you, don't worry." She smirked.

"When you do, you will not want to leave," he replied without altering his gaze. The urge was unbearable. He wanted to grab her, there and then, but what would he do? And who was she? The smell of seaweed and salt oozed from her pores. She stood oblivious to her surroundings – a woman out so late amongst the men in the compound.

"Perhaps. We shall see," she answered, and turned away without looking back.

He watched her drift into the darkness through a crowd of men who didn't seem to notice her. The sitting men called out to Faron, declaring that they had almost finished their food and he should join them. Faron sat with them, scooped up a ball of red beans, and placed the tip of his tongue into the gravy.

Chapter Eighteen

Sweat trickled between Faron's shoulder blades as he strolled through Jamestown's mid-morning heat. Dust gusted around the feet of pedestrians on the beaten-down pathways of the main road. The locals acknowledged Faron with respectful nods. A young boy had paid a visit to the house in the morning about a quarrel at Scissor House that needed his attention. Jojo had sent the boy asking Faron to join them – the new apprentice was becoming a nuisance and there might be an error in the accounts. Faron had no doubts that his tailors were faithful and dedicated. Scissor House was the best tailoring business in the region.

The tailors saluted Faron as he stepped into the Scissor House building. He made his way through the two sections into the back office. He pulled out the dark-blue hardback ledger book. Its leather spine and corners sported a few scuffs with blue curly patterns on the page edges. The first page revealed the supplier's name: Frederick W. Khan, Account Book Makers, Lithographers, St Johns Square, London, EC1. He paused at the address that he often ignored when working. Loud chatter erupted from the sewing room. Faron settled in his chair to go over the finances. It didn't take long to spot the discrepancy.

"Owura, I heard you were here." Jojo's face appeared at the door.

"Nana ba, I hear we have a problem," Faron said.

"None that cannot be solved today with your presence."

"If money is missing, somebody has either forgotten to provide details of the sales or thinks that I am thoughtless," Faron replied.

Jojo shook his head. He moved to the desk and opened the drawers to grab the tailor's notebook, his hands primed to open the pages as he leaned forwards over the desk, scouring for evidence. It bothered Faron to watch Jojo struggle with his eyesight. He wondered if his new wife would accommodate Jojo's physical differences with patience.

"We have to talk about this new apprentice," Jojo grunted.

He continued to peer into the notebook, mumbling to himself. Asi if by chance, Obo, the new apprentice pushed his head through the door.

"Owura, I heard you were here." Obo's voice rang loud and excitable.

Jojo did not look up from the notebook. Faron sensed that sometimes the man writhing in poverty was the first to disrespect the hand that fed him.

"Here it is!" Jojo lifted the notebook and pointed to his find. "Four suits and twenty kabas with slits. It's here. I forgot to write it in the ledger, but I wrote it in the notebook."

"I will make a kaba when I am left alone," Obo said with a grimace.

"What do you want, Obo?" Faron asked.

"He came here because he knows that his work is not good and that I am reporting him for coming in late every day this week," Jojo said.

Obo's smile disappeared. "Who is speaking to you? This is not your office. This is not your place."

"You are the one who is stealing materials, and you know I am about to discuss this with Mr Vivo," Jojo continued.

"Stealing materials?" Faron exclaimed.

"Look at you. You stress yourself out with all this accusation!" Obo said rolling his eyes to mimic Jojo's.

"Obo …," Faron said.

"Why do you have him here?" Obo demanded. "He can't measure properly. He wants me to do all his dirty work."

"The gods will curse you for your disrespect!" Jojo raged.

"Obo!" Faron slammed his fist into the table. "Obo, please take your unfinished stock home with you. You can find somewhere else to sew it. You are not welcome here."

Obo gasped. "But you have not heard what I need to tell you about this man. He cannot do his job properly–"

"And you can? You have been here for two months and already you want to drive the oldest-serving member out," Faron breathed.

"He does not respect me. He does not give me proper material to sew."

The air in the room suddenly thickened.

"Open the window in the front when you leave the building, Obo. Thank you." Faron answered.

Obo stood for a minute, dumbfounded.

The men watched him leave in a huff.

"He was trouble, I tell you. A lot of trouble. He never wanted to do anything, he kept arguing that he was a tailor and not a servant," Jojo ranted.

A draught picked up inside the room. A mess of fragrances filled Faron's lungs. He shifted to the doorway. The tailors were not in their seats. They stood around, thrilled and excited.

He could smell her.

She stood tall amongst the men. Her dress drew the shape of her breasts and hips. Danso's fingers held each end of the measuring tape. Crouched under her, his eyes darting across her midriff as he called out the measurements for his colleague to write down.

She turned her head slightly as though sensing him.

Their eyes locked, she smiled.

The tailors hastened to their seats when Faron entered the room. The humming of the foot pedals started up concurrently.

"I see you are being taken care of," he said.

"Hmm." The sound came from the back of her throat. She brushed back the long plaits falling over her face.

"We have the finest tailors in Accra." Boastful words flew from his tongue without his intending them.

"Really?"

"Well, you chose to visit us."

"That I did."

Danso stood up straight with the measuring tape hanging loose from his fingers.

"When will it be ready?" she asked.

Danso hesitated. "Tuesday."

"Tuesday?"

"Yes, Awura," Danso replied.

"Danso is our best tailor for the kaba and slit," Faron said.

She looked around the room at the tailors pretending to work. "This is such an inspiring place. I'd love to see the rest of the establishment."

Faron held out his hand. She placed her moist hand in his. He led her through the two rooms, trying not to linger on the remarkable glimmer in her eyes that accentuated her dark complexion. Faron's desk caught her attention. She pulled away from him and traced its outline with her fingers. She bent over to sniff the wood.

"It's mahogany tambour." The words lodged themselves in Faron's throat, and he found himself coughing to clear it.

"I love it," she exclaimed.

She turned around and walked back towards the entrance. Faron followed her.

"This is your first tailor house?" she asked.

His brows furrowed. "What do you mean?"

"Don't you want a second tailor house?"

He laughed. "What would I do with it?"

"No one will have what you have, if you have a second establishment."

He chuckled and asked. "Where have you been? No one has what I have now."

"A man who is content? How is that possible?" she retorted.

Faron moved in, but she stepped back. They held each other's gaze.

"What kind of man only wants one tailor shop and is satisfied with the foreigner Oburoni sharing all the monetary power?" she asked.

His eyes narrowed at her audaciousness.

"The Oburoni has no dominion over me. No one has."

"His king and his weapons give him power. What gives you power? Why should he respect you? Bow to you?"

This woman clearly knew how to rile a man.

She let out a throaty and contemptuous laugh and walked out of the building.

He followed her to face the unforgiving glare of the sun. "You found me easily?" he asked.

"You and any other," she retorted, kicking the dirt from her shoes. Her sharp tongue and casual manner did not sit well with him.

"Where do you go now?" he asked.

"Home."

"Where is that?"

She pointed in the direction of the only cemetery in town and winked. Fear, curiosity and lust – these were the feelings she toyed with. He gently took a few plaits in his hands, lifted them to his nose, and sniffed.

"What are you doing?" She slapped the plaits from his hands.

"Seaweed," he answered.

She stared at him … through him. Her honey-glazed eyes searched his, and then, without a word, she walked away.

"Tuesday!" he shouted after her. "See you Tuesday."

* * *

Jojo's wife prepared food and sent it to the house every other day. How was he supposed to eat? Whatever discussions took place between Jojo and his wife, she didn't listen to Jojo. She made sure Faron was never left hungry. Kwabla, the security watchman, received the food and usually ate it alone in the yard. He looked forward to it. To eat another woman's cooking always brought men many pleasures.

Today Kwabla joined Faron at the table.

Kwabla ate in silence while Faron pretended to sip on cognac. It burnt his throat. It was important that he didn't just sit and stare at Kwabla while he ate. He always had to make sure people were comfortable around him. The cognac did not cause him to gag. That would have been a sore sight for Kwabla. He knew Kwabla didn't trust him, but his dependability was absolute. Kwabla ignored the spoon lying neatly next to the plate. He tucked into the kenkey with proficiency and accuracy. His fingers became graceful machines cutting through the appropriate portion of kenkey cornmeal dumpling and scooping up just the right number of fried fish pieces to fit into the palm of his hand. He eyed Faron before dipping the kenkey into his mouth.

"Thank you, Owura. The ancestors will bless you for this."

Faron guffawed. "You don't think the ancestors have abandoned us in our quest for other gods?"

Kwabla's hand did not go back to the kenkey but fell on the table. "Owura, you cannot say such things. We do not disregard our ancestors – every day I speak to my grandfather and to my mother. I ask them for guidance. To open the path for me, to bless my children," Kwabla said.

"You may, but many of the people are now ignoring their ancestors," Faron retorted.

Kwabla slowly looked around the room. "The ancestors have worked for you. They are in your favour. Your people have been blessed."

"We are blessed with skills from being slaves, Kwabla. You are blessed with being born into freedom. We were blessed with Mantse Ankrah's generosity to our fathers when they arrived here."

"Owura, do you speak to your ancestors? Do they regard you?"

Faron thought for a minute. He had not thought about whether he was regarded – more abandoned and rejected. And yet Kwabla observed him as an outsider and determined that he was blessed. "Perhaps they do, Kwabla. But they do nothing for my people in Brazil."

Kwabla chortled, but the corners of his mouth did not turn up. "Owura, I would say that to live in a house as big as the Governor's and to own Scissor House are signs that the ancestors are watching you. The town respects you, Owura. You have done well and are blessed with eternal youth. It is time to thank your ancestors."

Faron did not remove his gaze from the shutters of his large dining room. He listened to Kwabla's words. Kwabla was a middle-aged man with a list of regrets to his name who believed that working for Faron brought him good luck and prosperity. Jojo stated Kwabla had the gift for protecting others. He had hired him as soon as the house was complete and now, it turned out, was Faron's only company.

Faron thought about why he had invited the night watchman to sit with him at the table. Kwabla did not express surprise – he merely sat down and ate. Perhaps he already knew how Faron was feeling. Throughout Kwabla's working evenings, his wife, sons and grand-children visited him with messages, arguments and negotiations distracting him from the monotony of his job while Faron sat encased in the grandeur of his colonial home. Sometimes Faron could hear Kwabla arguing with passers-by if they loitered in front of the house or owed him money.

Kwabla gently placed his empty cup on the table. "Owura, I must go down now, or people will think either you or I have met our death."

"Did you enjoy the food?" Faron asked.

Kwabla stood up and nodded. "Yes, Owura, I enjoyed the food, the plate, and the table."

"But not me?" Faron laughed.

"I enjoyed you too, Owura. Don't give up on your ancestors. If it wasn't for them, your father wouldn't have survived the journey on the boat."

Faron retired to his study as dusk promised moonlight to all those in need of solitude. The world outside slipped into silence. There was no need for light in the study, Faron knew the location and identity of every obstacle. It was a common occurrence to sit alone, contemplating the rest of his journey. He didn't feel that good about the events of the previous few days, but the encounter with the mystery woman Faron did want to recall. Her long neck, moving plaits, oiled skin and full lips. Her reticent manner had unnerved him. She spoke with a quiet arrogance, as if he was a mere pastime. He had smelt salt when he showed her around Scissor House. He touched the slime on her thick plaits. Had the deformed boy sent her to him? Was she one of the others that he had talked about? A curious tingling crawled to the surface of his skin. She hid her true self from him without understanding what he was. Perhaps she had no idea what she was dealing with. If that was the case, this would certainly add a layer of complexity to his life that he had not anticipated. He found himself trying to impress her. He couldn't help it. She would find out in time that he was not like most men. He was not as weak or short-sighted. He was a man of two continents. She would come to him. She would come to him because that is what she did.

Chapter Nineteen

Faron spent the day overseeing the spring cleaning of his home. Mid-morning, he realised he did not even know the mystery woman's name. It was only Wednesday.

On Thursday, Faron found himself a spectator of the fife and drum brass bands. The Governor had organised a military march to mark the first legislative elections in Accra. Faron sat amongst his contemporaries, beyond the British colonials in their white uniforms, his whole body wet from the high summer torridness in the stands. He thought only about her as the band played for the British, neglecting the traditional songs others were accustomed to.

Friday and Saturday were busy days at Scissor House. Clients came and went, picking up kabas and ballgowns for the weekend. Faron assisted the tailors in collecting orders, dispatching clothes, and receiving and counting cash, while clients negotiated, argued about sizes, and were re-pinned. This was the only time he interacted directly with the public. Most of the people of Jamestown had never met him. If you wanted to speak to the owners of Scissor House, you would have to be there over the weekend. Jojo remained the recognised face of the company.

Monday.

Faron stayed at home to make fufu. He remembered the first time he licked the cassava-and-plantain dish a few years after arriving in the Gold Coast. It left a bitter taste in his mouth; in hindsight it had been a joyous and memorable occasion of discovering taste. He could not swallow but he could lick. Fufu he was told should always be accompanied with soup and was a traditional Saturday dish. The men insisted he swallow and not chew the soft, clean, chewy texture. It amused them to see him lick instead of placing the ball-like solution into his mouth. He rolled the lumps under his tongue until out of sight of the others then spat them into the grass. Jojo joined him at the house, declaring cooking fufu easier than managing the other tailors. He needed respite. This pleased Faron as for once they could revisit the old days where they cooked and bickered before retiring for the night.

Jojo placed the root-based plant in boiling water while Faron brought out the mortar and pestle from the storage cupboard in the yard. Once the cassava finished boiling it was placed into the mortar. Jojo grabbed the long, wooden pestle and dunked. Faron reached into the mortar in-between the pounding to help mould the cassava. Jojo spoke about a fight that had happened near his compound between two families. Faron half-listened. The thick dough-like mixture needed to be completely smooth. An hour passed before he scooped out the mixture and shaped it into smaller balls. Jojo finished frying the chicken for the soup.

Faron sat down at his carved-oak draw-leaf table. Jojo entered, carrying a gold-trimmed, lidded soup tureen. He placed it on the table. Faron licked the fufu, searching for the twinge of bitterness. Jojo served himself okra soup with fufu and ate without lifting his head. A slight tartness hit the roof of Faron's mouth. He smiled and watched his only friend struggle to bite into the chicken bone for lack of teeth. Age lingered unnoticed until challenged.

Tuesday.

She didn't appear.

Faron stood outside Scissor House early in the morning, conversing with the owner of the hardware shop across the road. He waited for the first tailor to arrive as irritation set in. After demanding an unnecessary reorganisation of the kaba display on the wall, he decided to go home at midday to get away from the mockery of her desertion.

At home in his study, Faron pulled out a stained handkerchief he'd had in his possession on the day she had visited Scissor House. Her hair had left a residue on his fingers when he'd touched it, which was still on the handkerchief. He slowly rolled it open on the table to unravel a lock of black curly hair. His face darkened. He rubbed his damp brows. The house was warmer than usual, so he took off his shirt. He focused on his breathing, drawing in through his nose and exhaling through his mouth. The world receded until all sounds and smells were shut out and there was only his breathing. The seaweed had dried up in parts. He leaned in to sniff it.

Faron took a walk with the handkerchief in his possession. He stopped to smell it from time to time and found himself getting on a bus to Cape Coast. A hub for markets. An area full of sailors and labourers. No place for a woman unless she was a trader or prostitute. As he watched the changing terrain on the four-hour journey, he could feel himself boiling with anger at her audaciousness. How dare she toy with the emotions of the tailors and treat him like a fool. The way she had kicked her shoe in the dust and said "you and any other" … Who did she think she was? The fact that Danso eagerly dedicated himself to her kaba and that she had not shown up to collect or pay for his work. Nobody was allowed to enter their premises and humiliate them.

The bus driver argued with a passenger. A woman behind him hummed a popular local song. The man next to him had his head against the glass and was snoring. Faron couldn't believe what he was doing. Had he gone mad? He told no one what he was up to. He had better things to do but told himself that he had to see this woman. To look into her eyes one more time. Cape Coast was a long way from Jamestown. Perhaps she found it difficult to take the bus or maybe she had run out of funds. Either way he would see her and find out. Who was she, and what was she up to?

The port was full of low-class dockside palm-wine bars where foreign and local sailors drank and got merry. He sniffed the handkerchief and stopped at a small bar smelling of fermented wine and vomit. The bar was half-empty. He spotted her. She sat entertaining a gentleman. His eyes narrowed. A ball of heat ran across his chest. Two ladies behind the bar watched him approach the couple. One had shocking white plaits that fell to her thighs.

He pulled up a chair and sat down.

"You! How did you find me?" she gasped, pulling away from the man she was seated with. The man snapped his head back in surprise.

In the corner of his eye, Faron noticed the white-haired woman moving across the room towards them.

He pulled the handkerchief out of his pocket and threw it on the table.

"You need to go find your own woman," the man declared with a wave.

She picked up the handkerchief, unravelled it, and gaped at the mouldy mass of dried seaweed and hair.

Faron faced the man. The hazel in his eyes turned to black.

"Demon!" the man gasped, rising from his chair in panic. He backed away, bumping into the white-haired woman.

"I don't even know your name," Faron said.

The white-haired woman interjected. "You will know nothing about her unless she chooses to tell you."

"I must acquaint myself with your affairs ere I return to the routines of my own existence," Faron demanded.

"You are not welcome here," the white-haired woman declared.

"I am a paying customer like anyone else. Why would you count me as otherwise?"

The young woman's face was a picture of confusion. She glanced at the white-haired woman in silence. Her arms lay limp on the table. She had no power in this jurisdiction. The cascading plaits hid her expression.

He knew he had roused something in her beyond curiosity.

The white-haired woman spoke. "We don't like to be bothered –"

"I don't like games," Faron cut her off.

The white-haired woman glared at him. "Perhaps you should leave us to our own company."

"You're right," he replied. He turned back to the young woman that had plagued his thoughts for a week. "Although I didn't catch your name."

"That is not your choice," the white-haired woman snapped.

"No." He paused to look once more at the silent beauty who avoided eye contact. He didn't even feel like demanding the money owed to his tailors. "You're right. It's not my choice."

* * *

Faron remained in the confines of his own home recovering from the eight-hour round trip filled with pee stops, fare dodgers and bus drivers stopping to speak to other bus drivers. Passengers needing to eat or buy items. Faron settled back into his surroundings with the intention of blocking out his thoughts, and that included the faint sound of gossiping that wormed its way over the fences as dusk grew.

A loud banging downstairs interrupted his peace. He heard Kwabla unlock the iron gates. There was no movement for a while. Faron walked to the entrance. His face caught the light wind as the double-door entrance shutters swung half-open. Then he saw his visitor. She wore a one-piece kaba. Her hair wrapped in a green scarf.

Kwabla nodded at Faron and walked away.

"My name is Loiyan," she said.

He moved towards her but stopped short.

"How did you find me?" she asked.

"Have you paid my tailor for his hard work, or do you intend to waste his time too?"

She smoothed her hands along her dress. "I came to Swalaba this evening before they closed. I paid him. I have taken my clothes. My kaba is beautiful and fits me like a glove."

He could hear her heart beating.

"Are you going to let me in?" she asked.

"Why do you want to enter my home?" he retorted.

"To speak with you," she whispered.

He unbolted the second door. She stepped in. Her eyes glanced around with eager curiosity. He led her to the parlour. She stopped next to a parlour chair boasting an upholstered yellow-and-blue floral motif. "I like this chair," she said, running her fingers along the nail head detail on the edges of the upholstery. Then she sat down and requested two cups of water.

Faron sat opposite and watched her guzzle the contents of the cup. Water seeped down the sides of her mouth. She ignored it.

"You live alone in this big house?" she asked, placing the empty enamel cup on the side table next to her.

"Who is the white-haired woman?" Faron said.

"Akala. She is my mother," she answered.

"So, there are two of you?"

"How did you find me?" Loiyan asked.

"I showed you how. Don't you remember?" Faron replied.

"I have never seen you in that area before," she said.

"Not everyone needs to know me," Faron answered.

She stood up and walked towards him. Her hips swayed. "My mother did not want me to come here or speak to you. She says you are strange."

"Your mother has never met a man like me before. She is just scared of the unknown," Faron answered.

"Fear is not something we understand," she replied, kneeling next to his feet. She laid her head on his lap and said, "I felt something with you, I wasn't sure … but now I am."

"Why?"

He was a little taken aback at her immediate intimacy. She did not seek permission. Her childlike behaviour confused him. This stunning woman now rested her head in his lap as though he was safe to be around. A bold and deliberate move, yet naive.

"You found me. How did you do that?" she asked, interrupting his thoughts.

Faron gently took her soft hands. His eyelids grew heavy. He pulled her up to his chest. He caressed the warm flesh on her face. He placed his lips squarely on the extra plump of her lips and kissed her. He tasted salt.

She made an incredible noise deep in her throat – a breathless gasp.

"You'd better go back to your mother," he murmured.

"Now that you have kissed me, you can't keep your name from me," she whispered with a smile.

"Faron."

"All of it."

"Faron Oliveira Vivo. Once a Brazilian, now an African."

"Faron Oliveira," she repeated as if memorising it. "Where in Brazil?"

"Bahia. What do you know of Brazil?" he asked, surprised. No one ever asked where in Brazil simply because they knew nothing about the country.

"Did you come to this land alone?" she asked.

He caught himself for a minute. He almost let it slip that he was an original Tabom, which would be impossible because that was almost seventy years earlier.

"My parents came from Brazil," he responded.

"Ah. I see. Do you have plans to go back?"

"How would I do that? Of course not. This is my home."

"Can I have some more water?" she asked with a wink.

CHAPTER TWENTY

The tailors at Scissor House waited to give Faron the news. They did not take turns to explain what had happened – instead, they shouted over each other. Danso grinned uncontrollably, clapping then raising his hands to the sky. Eventually, Faron understood that Loiyan had visited Scissor House and gifted Danso an enormous tip as a sign of appreciation for his handicraft. She had claimed it was he who was the best tailor in Scissor House. The other tailors vigorously disputed this proclamation. The reason being, they said, she had not yet experienced the pleasure of using all their services. If all the tailors in Scissor House were tried and tested, only then could this declaration stand. Jojo brought out an extra chair from the back for Faron to sit on. The tailors continued sewing and arguing for the rest of the morning. Danso called in every trader that walked by to acquire snacks – Nkati Cake, a caramelised peanut snack bar, and Kofi Brokeman, sumptuous plantain with roasted peanuts. He thought nothing of sharing his newfound wealth with his colleagues. Faron pocketed some of the snacks for Kwabla and joined in the chatter. The men joked about their wives and their hunting skills with him. He watched as they flirted with female traders and bowed to elderly women picking up their outfits.

Later that afternoon, a soldier entered the shop, interrupting the twaddle that had gone on for most of the day. The soldier automatically greeted Jojo, assuming he was the owner. His actions caused all chattering to cease. Jojo stopped him and nodded in Faron's direction. The soldier apologised profusely before announcing that Governor Piggersill had requested Faron's presence at the headquarters the following day. There were grunts of approval around the room. British officials did not interact with locals on a day-to-day basis unless they were royalty. Faron, however, was familiar with many of the foreign officials, although the Governor's request in this manner came as a surprise. He wondered whether the Governor was aware of previous liaisons. They were probably pushing for a decision. Faron didn't want his tailors to get a whiff of the offer. It would spoil everything they had worked for together. But the soldier's visit brought the issue to the forefront again. The tailors were wondering what the Governor of all people wanted from them. Jojo escorted the soldier out of the building, and the excitable chatter drowned out the music of the pedals. Faron watched the starched uniform swallow the lucid flow of the soldier's steps as he walked away. The tailors deliberated. As far as they were concerned, Scissor House was in for some good news. Sewing pedals knocked furiously in recognition.

There was much to think about once he got home. The sound of locks against the steel gate coincided with Faron closing the shutters to the house. A nightly ritual ignited by Kwabla's clockwork devotion to rules. Faron locked the entrance door. The latch snapped and shut out the outside world, instantly urging Faron to bed. There was much to look forward to and discuss with both the Governor and the tailors. New territory to uncover in the quest for success. Faron didn't know when he fell asleep, but his dreams took him to the coastline. He found himself standing by the ocean observing a woman from the back as she combed her hair. The yellow comb dragged and snapped at her strands then bounced free as it separated itself. He watched the lull of repetition, not realising that with each move of her hand he was being drawn closer to her. As he got closer, he could see that she was naked. Her breasts shifted in rhythm with her hands dragging against her scalp. She turned around. He did not recognise her. The comb dropped to the sand. Faron picked it up to hand it to her, but she was gone. Almost immediately he found himself standing in his parlour. Next to his gramophone were two records. They lay hidden in the cupboard next to a collection of sheet music. Faron opened the cupboard door and found that his records were missing. A cold sweat came over him as he tried to remember the last time he had played them. Nobody would dare steal his collection. A sharp hissing sound filled the room. He turned to see a green bush viper darting across the floor towards him. He leaped back. The viper lifted itself up, slowly transforming into the woman from the beachfront.

"What do you have for me?" she asked.

He looked at the yellow comb in his hand and stretched it out for her.

The woman hissed at him in anger.

Faron woke up startled. His body and bed were soaked in sweat. The sun flickered through the shutters. It was a relief to hear the neighbour's rooster crowing. He did not dream much but this troubled him. Was his mother trying to reach him, or maybe Luíza? It would be interesting to hear Jojo's interpretation. His mind ran to Loiyan. They had not arranged to see each other but he knew where to find her. He wanted that feeling again. Her bright eyes, curved lips and flawless skin without so much of a crease in it. He stepped out of bed and stretched his hands to the sky.

It took less than three hours to get to Cape Coast this time with the help of his neighbour, Mr Lartey - a respected businessman and lawyer, Mr. Lartey was the proud owner of the steam-driven French Gardner-Serpollet, which had been originally acquired and brought to Ghana by the British Governor in 1902. Mr. Lartey, accompanied by his driver, regularly drove the car to church on Sundays. However, after much persuasion and the exchange of a generous sum, he reluctantly allowed Faron the privilege of using the car for a single evening, with his own driver at the wheel. To Faron's delight, the journey took considerably less time than before, making the experience all the more enjoyable and efficient. Another bus ride was out of the question. He was not feeling rested – the dreams had left him exhausted. They set off late afternoon with Faron dozing off on the journey, leaving the driver to navigate and entertain himself along the way.

Life swarmed around the port with labourers and officials. Trucks and cars moved in and out. Faron didn't have much time as he had to get back to Jamestown and return the car to its owner before midnight. He left the driver to find the bar.

Local labourers heaved in the bar, drinking and eating. Loiyan was nowhere in sight as he looked around and moved towards the back of the building to the outside kitchen. Akala was not amongst the women and children preparing food. Even though he did not care for the woman, if she had been here there would have been hopes of finding Loiyan. The more he searched the more he wanted to see her. Faron walked across the rocky shoreline, thinking about his dream. He passed traders calling out to him to buy their catch of the day. The fishermen sat by their canoes smoking and listening to gossip. The sun stood at the edge of the sea attempting to disappear in the distance. He carried on. Distant waves dared him to enter the ocean. He wondered what had possessed him to come all the way down to Cape Coast once again. Goosebumps picked up on his arms, reminding him of the increasing distance between him and the car as he kept up his search. He could see another small crowd of fishermen and traders packing up. His last stop. After this he had to go back.

Men packed items into a truck and women helped each other loading what was left of their wares onto their heads. He recognised her instantly. Her plaits fell around her shoulders as she lifted a large box to balance it on a rounded cloth perched on top of an older woman's head. The woman moved on, nodding her goodbyes. As if feeling his presence, Loiyan turned to face him. Their eyes locked. An instant giddiness entered his body. Her eyes flickered for just a moment. Faron looked around for Akala.

"She is not here today."

"Where is she then?" Faron asked.

"Busy," Loiyan answered.

They stared at each other for a moment as the traders moved around them preparing to leave the area. It was time to go home.

"It is late," she said.

"This place is far," Faron responded.

Her eyes revealed nothing. She merely waited. He looked out into the ocean. There were no rocks nearby like in his dream. Now that he was right in front of her, relief overcame him. All he had needed was to see her. Nothing more. He moved closer to her.

"Do you know why I am here?" he asked.

"You are a man. A simple creature. There is always only one answer to that," she replied.

Her arrogance matched his. Her words were intended to get a rise out of him, but he wasn't going to play into her games. A beautiful woman such as her was used to bringing confusion to men. He could feel it. He was stuck. He did not know what to say to her. Never had he been left without a response to any woman or man before.

She held out her hand with a smile.

"Come. I want you to tell me about the Bahia. You never told me."

Faron took her hand.

"I will tell you stories about Bahia. It is the most beautiful place in the world." Faron felt himself swell with pride. They walked along the beachfront together. He described the dense rainforests with their rare species of trees, rivers and mangroves, beaches, coral reefs and great natural pools with clear shallow waters. Her eyes followed his mouth and facial expressions as he talked. She questioned him many times about the mangroves and folklore of the indigenous. She asked him about the bôto – the shapeshifting dolphin of the Amazon that changed into a man who seduced women. Her body stiffened while listening to his confirmation of its existence.

"A man cannot create life. Your story is a lie," she interrupted.

Faron laughed. "There are many truths and untruths that everyone claims but no one has seen."

"No! The Oburoni has inserted a non-creator into the story. The bôto does exist, but she is a woman, not a man. The seed of the bôto can only change in the water and not the land, so there is no need to procreate as the child cannot survive on land."

"I have never met the bôto. I wouldn't know what happens when he copulates."

"Men come from women, women do not come from men," Loiyan insisted.

"That may be so but that is the story I know," Faron said.

"Did the Oburoni bring his God to the Bahia?" she asked abruptly.

"Yes," he answered.

"And what of the people left in Bahia? Now that they are no longer slaves – did the Oburoni leave with his gods and go back to his lands and people?"

"No, Loiyan. They did not leave."

"Then why don't you go back and help your people?"

"I cannot." He sighed. "It is not that simple."

She let go of his hand, folded her arms and pursed her lips, staring out into the twilight.

Time was running out. He wanted to see the fullness of her face again, but she had her back to him. The heaviness that had sat with him all this time had lifted. His mind buzzed. His feet sank into the sand. He imagined what it would feel like to put his lips against her skin and taste her again, but the driver would be wondering where he was.

She looked up at him. Her eyes shone bright as a paraffin oil lamp.

"I love to hear your stories of the Bahia. Thank you. I have learned so much."

Faron nodded.

He arrived in the early hours of the morning, waking Mr Lartey. Faron paid the driver and thanked him for his hospitality and insisted on walking home. The night sky spread out above him with only a few lamps on the streets to guide him, though he was not concerned. He needed to get his fix before going home. The few hours he spent with Loiyan had filled him with the feeling that taking risks didn't seem that precarious. She made him feel invincible. As he walked down the quiet streets his instincts picked up the guilty footsteps of a man who did not deserve what he had. Faron quickened his pace. He would be quick and discreet for tomorrow was another day and he needed to be full of vigour.

* * *

Loiyan waited for him in the front garden with Kwabla. The blue kaba outlined her curves courtesy of Danso. Her hair had changed. Neat cornrows snaked from her forehead down to the nape of her neck. The tip of the plaits coiled playfully above her breasts. She clapped her hands like a schoolgirl at the sight of Faron walking through the gates after work.

"I am so thirsty!" she exclaimed.

Heat rose from the pit of his stomach. Her neck was long and slender like her hands and legs. High cheekbones with a delicate facial structure. She commanded his attention as he watched her move in front of him to enter the house.

She drank five enamel cups of water one after the other.

"How long were you waiting for me?" he asked.

"An hour."

"I'm usually at Scissor House in the mornings."

She put the cup down then boldly placed her arms on his shoulders. His body's response to her scent was immediate. She leaned in to kiss him. He responded but didn't touch her – he knew he wouldn't be able to control himself. She licked the tip of his nose.

"You are my naughty secret," she chortled.

"Are there any men in your family?" Faron asked.

"No, we are six aunties and some cousins in our compound. No men," she replied.

"You're the youngest?"

"Oh no. Four others younger than me."

"Where is your father?" he asked.

"São Tomé." She blinked.

"Do you like my house?"

"It's the biggest I have ever seen." She laughed.

"Do you want to see the rest of it?"

"Oh yes!" She clapped her hands in excitement.

Faron led her upstairs. She peeped into all three

bedrooms, exclaiming, and commenting on the furniture. His bedroom was waiting for them at the end of the short corridor.

"What a beautiful bed!" she called out, freeing her feet from slippers, and immediately jumping onto it.

"This is a feather mattress." He heard himself boasting again.

She rolled around on the bed, laughing, and tugging at the sheets before untying the mosquito net so that it fell around the bed to encase her. She grabbed him, tilted his head, and brushed her lips against his. Faron's body shuddered. This woman's presence made him want to climb inside her body and live there. He gathered her close, pressing his lips tightly onto hers. He gently pushed her back onto the bed and kissed her while she pulled him tightly into her. She arched her back as his kisses travelled around her chest. He moved over her, lifting her kaba over her thighs. He touched the smooth skin on her stomach and his mouth covered her belly button. His fingers travelled to the inside of her thighs, brushing against rough, scale-like ripples.

She pushed him away.

"It's a reaction to the feather mattress. I better go … I need some water."

She climbed off the bed in a hurry.

He didn't understand what had just happened but didn't want her to leave. "I'll get you water, don't worry."

She stood up to flatten the kaba against her body.

"Stay with me tonight," he insisted.

"I can't. My skin will dry out … I have an illness," she breathed.

He felt a flurry of confusion as she walked past him to go back downstairs.

Faron called for Kwabla to bring water to the parlour. Kwabla entered with another cup of water for her. Faron saw the relief in her eyes as she grabbed the cup from him. A look of disdain covered Kwabla's face. She gulped. Faron recognised the slight shudder that correlated with cravings – her inability to focus. It was the same when he needed his fix.

"What is it that you need in order to stay?" he asked.

"For you to behave."

"You and I cannot survive on two-hour visits. You live far from Jamestown. Break from the usual constraints and be honest … with yourself," he said.

Her knuckles whitened as she tightened her grip on the chair. She looked around the room. "I need water."

"I have given you water."

"No, more … lots of it. In the bedroom. If I am to stay here."

"In cups?"

"Slow down," she answered.

"I was going to invite you to meet a good friend of mine tomorrow."

"Oh? I know you have acquaintances but are they your friends?" She smirked.

"What does that mean?" Faron asked, surprised.

"Someone such as yourself …" Loiyan began.

"What do you mean by that?"

"I'd like you to come to my home too." She smiled.

Faron paused. She confused him. She said things that sometimes felt like she disapproved of him, and yet now she invited him to her home.

"Your mother doesn't like me," Faron answered.

"She will like you once I bring you home. We do this properly. You can tell her who you are. Impress her. Come with me tomorrow evening."

"I have promised an old friend to visit him in the evening. Perhaps you could accompany me, and we can arrange another time for your mother?"

"Certainly." She turned to leave.

Faron watched her, not quite sure why he was rooted to the spot.

She reached for the door handle. "I don't eat in the houses of strangers, so I guess I'll just have to watch you."

CHAPTER TWENTY-ONE

The Governor needed two hundred army uniforms for the Gold Coast regiment, itself made up of five battalions. Edward, His Royal Highness the Prince of Wales, was paying a visit to the Gold Coast Colony and the army was to be prepared and presented. This was good news for the tailors. The reputation of Scissor House flourished, as did the tailors' sense of pride and worth. The cost of kabas and suits would be raised once the orders were completed. Everyone in Accra would want to buy garments from Scissor House no matter what the price. Faron thought about the possibility of importing silk for the English wives. Business was good, and he was confident it would remain that way.

Faron sat in the Governor's office listening to the requirements and uniform specifications. One large desk stood at the centre of the room, while another at the rear was home to a Royal 10 typewriter. A metal filing cabinet stood against a wall.

Harold Piggersill's blond hair framed a face weathered by the elements, lending him a rugged and outdoorsy appearance. He straightened up the framed European artworks dotted against the whitewashed walls as he talked. The large portrait of King George V sat high above the walls away from the Governor's fiddling fingers. Faron sat with legs crossed, observing his fidgety companion. A knock on the door interrupted their negotiations. Annie walked in. She wore a sheer voile print dress with lace trim. She removed her straw hat revealing effortless curls.

The Governor asked, "My dear, have you come to get your answer to the Liverpool enterprise? We haven't started discussing that yet."

She laughed in response and gave her husband a light kiss on the cheek.

"Is it too much to check up on my darling husband during afternoon tea? How delightful to find you here, Faron." She removed the glove from her left hand.

Faron nodded. This woman had a way of pushing for what she wanted. The Governor wanted the army uniforms made first. Perhaps it was a test to see whether his tailors were good enough to do business in England.

"If you would allow me some time till after this proposal. Once it is completed, I will have a clear head and a better answer," Faron responded.

"Darling, would you come back later?" the Governor asked Annie. "Mr Vivo and I are ironing out the details of our contract."

"Of course, I'll be with Mary at the bungalow this weekend," she said.

"Good, I'm hunting with Charlie and the boys," the Governor replied.

"Don't bring any dreadful carcasses into the house, please," Annie said.

The men watched her leave. Faron got the impression that neither party seemed to be concerned about the other's whereabouts.

Faron left the office with a smile. Scissor House was going to roar to the heavens with the news he had for them. He stepped into the road and saw Loiyan standing across the street waiting for him. She wore a sleeveless summer dress with a lowered waist, accentuating her long body. She smiled at his startled face and strode across the tarred road, weaving her way around horses pulling carts to join him.

"What are you doing here?" he asked, surprised.

"Today you need me to meet your friend," she replied.

"Did you follow me? How did you know I was here?"

"Scissor House knows all your secrets, does it not?"

Faron decided he would have to tell the tailors not to share information on his whereabouts.

"I saw an Oburoni woman entering the building. An important one. What did she say to you?" Loiyan interrupted his thoughts.

This stunned Faron. Why would she think, out of all the people entering the building, that Annie and he would know each other?

"Do you know her well?" she asked.

"I know many people well. Look, Loiyan, I must go speak to my tailors, it's better we meet later."

"Oh no. I want to be with you. I won't disturb you. I'm free to be with you all day."

She placed her arm in his and smiled at the road ahead.

Danso fell to his knees praising the heavens upon hearing the news of the orders for the army uniforms. Jojo's fist pumped the air. The tailors hugged each other. Loiyan hugged the tailors, engaging in their joy. The local palm-wine seller was sent for. Loiyan poured akpetishie for the men as they revelled in their newfound success. The tailors drank and cheered about their good fortune. They talked amongst themselves and with every client that came in with a request. Both Swalaba and Jamestown would know the might of Scissor House by sunrise the next day.

The army needed skilful tailors. The African warrant officers' uniforms were distinguished by yellow braiding on the fronts of their jackets with a tahe palm-tree badge on the fez. For field dress, a khaki shirt, shorts, jersey and puttees were worn with a Kilmarnock cap. The Governor's order confirmed that Scissor House had the best tailors in the greater Accra region. It could even be said that their tailors must be better than those in England if the Governor would rather have the soldiers' uniforms made in Accra.

As the tailors discussed this perspective with their newfound friend Loiyan, Jojo pulled Faron away from the celebrations to the back of the building.

"Kwabla came here after his shift at the house, Owura," Jojo said.

"Why? I pay him at the house," Faron asked.

"He spoke to me about this woman you have brought here. She has been visiting you."

"I'm bringing her to your compound tonight, Jojo," Faron said.

Jojo's eyes widened. "To my compound?"

"Yes. I need your approval." Faron chuckled.

"This one here? You want to make her your wife?"

"You asked me to find a woman. I have found one. I don't know if I will make her my wife yet, but I think it's time."

"Kwabla is convinced she is a witch," Jojo replied.

"Is he losing his mind?" Faron laughed. "And he came here after work to tell you what?"

"Owura, he is afraid. He is afraid of this woman," Jojo whispered.

"How so?"

"He has the sight. His mother never washed his eyes when he was young. He came to me because he is concerned for you. He sees the slime she leaves on the ground when she walks," Jojo answered.

"Slime?"

"He is afraid, Owura. He says he will not work for you if she keeps coming back."

"I, Faron, do not drive him away with his sight, but a mere woman does? Maybe his *sight* has got the better of him," Faron snapped.

"Owura, I brought Kwabla to you because he understands the ways of the ancestors. If he is concerned, then I too am concerned," Jojo insisted.

Faron thought about how good it would feel to put a fist through the wall right now. He locked eyes with Jojo "Do I interfere with you when your wife causes problems?"

"Owura, why does she need water?" Jojo asked.

"Is that what he said? What else did he tell you?"

"She may not be what you think she is."

"I already know this, Jojo. You doubt me?"

"What does she want from you Owura? Has she been seducing you? Kwabla says women like her seduce quickly, they do not wait for courtship. Once you have been seduced, she will take over your mind."

"Jojo, I will find out who she is and what she wants." Faron paused. "Believe me, I'm on the job. But for now, I intend to enjoy myself. Is this not what you wanted?"

"Yes, Papa." Jojo bent over to cough. His body jerked. He moved his face away from Faron.

"Hey, hey, what is all this coughing? Is Afua stressing you out?" Faron asked.

Jojo waved his hand. "Bring her to the compound, Owura. I will tell my wife."

"No funny business, Jojo. Don't bring any men with chickens, goats or cowrie beads. We won't be staying long."

"We have to go and see someone about this woman," Jojo responded. He wiped his napkin over his mouth, folded it and put it in his pocket.

Faron's eyes went black. His skin drew tight, and he crossed his arms over his chest. He had a lot to figure out and the distractions seemed to be mounting.

* * *

That evening, the children in Jojo's compound greeted Faron with excitement.

"Mr Vivo is here!" They shouted.

Loiyan moved in closer as they made their way through the compound.

"Owura, are you a seamstress at the Scissor House?" a young girl asked.

"Maybe," Loiyan replied, laughing and sweeping her plaits back.

They stopped at Jojo's in-laws' home. His father-in-law sat outside with men, drinking and pondering on life's tribulations. Faron handed him an envelope of money and stopped for a momentary discussion. Loiyan intertwined her fingers in his. The scent of her arousal flowered around him. A sensation rolled through his back and upper chest. He loved her scent. So fresh. So crisp. She made sure all witnessed her affections. Jojo's father-in-law accepted the envelope and rained blessings on Faron. The men's eyes filled with questions. Loiyan seemed somewhat awestruck at the attention Faron was receiving. He introduced her briefly. Lust and curiosity enveloped the men as they watched her. He wondered if she was unaware of her non-subtle ways. Nobody in this town knew him for any woman and she was making it clear that he belonged to her.

Jojo stood at the entrance of his hut waiting for his visitors. He reprimanded Faron for handing out money like water.

"Don't feed expectations, Owura, I can do without it."

"You live here, I don't. I get to go home. So, I don't have to do this every day, Jojo. Otherwise, what's it all for?" Faron responded.

"I didn't know it would be like this," Loiyan breathed into his ear. She squeezed his hand and beamed at him as they walked into Jojo's home.

They stayed for an hour. Afua told stories about Jojo's failings around the house for entertainment. Faron found it amusing hearing about his son from someone else. The glow on her face remained when she looked at Jojo – whether passing him water to drink or poking fun at him. He was still the only man in the compound in her eyes. He could see that his son clearly wanted for nothing and did not attempt to protest too much at his wife's decisions. Afua laid kelewele -fried plantain on the table for all.

Loiyan explained that she had already eaten her mother's food and was not hungry. She nudged Faron to eat. He shook his head.

"Afua has spent time frying kelewele for you. You need to eat," Loiyan insisted.

"Afua knows that I never eat kelewele. She made this for Jojo so that he could eat, not me," Faron replied.

Afua's perfect white teeth shone as she laughed at his comments.

"You will get used to it." Jojo spoke directly to Loiyan. He leaned forwards and helped himself to the kelewele, eating it all, and drank the cognac Faron had brought him.

Faron and Loiyan left when dusk threatened to hamper their way home.

They walked across Accra until they reached the beachfront. Loiyan slowed outside an abandoned shack along the grassy point just before the sand ventured into the sea. Waves crashed against the shore in the background. There were no buildings nearby and Faron wasn't sure why she didn't want him to go any further. Brisk wind rushed past the exposed parts of their bodies. He got sandblasted in the face by a gust of salty air.

"You don't live here – there is no one sleeping in that place." He nodded at the abandoned shack.

"No, that's not where I live, but soon you will see my home and meet my family. Just not today," she replied.

"And Akala will accept me in her arms," he said dryly.

Loiyan laughed. "Humour suits you."

Faron put his lips on hers. His tongue penetrated her mouth, caressing as heat roared through his body. A glow of euphoria entered her eyes. He nipped at her lower lip. She gasped. His hand tangled in her plaits and pulled her close. Her eyes closed. His fingers dipped under the folds of her bottom as he nibbled her earlobe. She trembled against him. He felt that she had planned to resist him but couldn't. Her body told him that she had already imagined this moment. The wind picked up around them. She moaned, wrapped her arms around him and dug her fingers into his scalp. Her breath was hot and desperate in his mouth. He squeezed her body into his as he devoured her neck. She gasped and pushed him away, a short, sharp and strong push that had him lose balance. This surprised him as he stopped himself from stumbling back. Their eyes locked. Her eyes flared then narrowed. She was unusually strong. She spoke in haste: "My family live by Lake Bosumtwi. That's where you will meet them."

"That's far from here," Faron exclaimed. "Another distant place to go to."

"It's my family home. We come down to Cape Coast to run our businesses," she answered.

"The beach bar?" Faron asked.

"Yes." She looked towards the restless ocean as it roared and foamed under the rising moon. "I must go now."

He surged towards her; his mouth covered hers briefly. "You like what I do to you. I can feel it. I can smell it. Tell me what it means for you, Loiyan."

She let him devour her neck again before placing her palms on his chest to resist once more. He grabbed her hands. Their eyes locked.

"I will go now." Loiyan yanked her hands away. She turned and ran towards the ocean without looking back. A figure emerged in the distance, hastening to meet her. The sand swirled around the woman's feet like a miniature storm as she drew closer. With an air of familiarity, she enveloped Loiyan in a tight embrace, as though they had been separated for an eternity. However, as her gaze shifted towards Faron, a frigid chill settled in the pit of his stomach. Her eyes, piercing and unyielding, seemed to delve deep into his very soul with an unnerving intensity, stripping away all his defences and leaving him raw and exposed. It was precisely as Jojo had alluded to—Loiyan was not entirely the person she portrayed herself to be.

CHAPTER TWENTY-TWO

The Governor's uniforms kept Scissor House busy. Jojo recruited three more tailors to assist. His Royal Highness the Prince of Wales's visit to the Gold Coast Colony was less than a month away, and the pressure was mounting. Only Danso continued taking civilian orders. Customers weren't happy about this. Some chose to visit Faron's rival on the other side of town, but Faron knew they would return because his business was at the border of both Swalaba and Jamestown, two vibrant areas filled with aspirational professionals. This was their time to shine. News spread swiftly around town about the Governor's order. Folks turned up just to get an update on how many uniforms had been completed.

Danso measured new clients planning on attending the parade. His reputation as the kaba king preceded him. The chief tailor for ceremonial robes, and expert in crafting the burnous cloaks worn for visits to Senegal and specifically for the Fulani passing through the country. Those attending and not sporting traditional clothes were measured for khaki tunics and trousers. Danso's new assistant, Fram, was a specialist in suits for all occasions. He knew how to make sure the lapels on suit jackets were not too wide, as they tended to be buttoned up high. Fram knew which clients preferred their trousers relatively narrow and straight, and he knew who liked shorter legs to flaunt their socks. He was also aware that the fashion was changing – for the parade, many were asking for wider-legged trousers called Oxford bags. Some of the younger men preferred double-breasted waistcoats and wore them with a single-breasted suit jacket. It didn't matter if the English had their suits shipped over – Scissor House tailors made sure nobody would know the difference.

Danso measured two men over the whirring of sewing machines. One of them, the shorter of the two, talked about the different access points to see the Prince of Wales. He asked if the tailors would be attending.

"We will be too busy sewing, my friend," Danso replied.

"How can you sew and not see the results of your work?" the short man gasped.

Danso shrugged. "Clients don't stop coming here because the Prince of England is coming to the Gold Coast."

"Well, you should be there to see the finished army uniform in action."

Faron greeted customers arriving to pick up their clothes. Jojo failed to arrive at the usual time. These days he was needed at Scissor House every day, all day.

"Well, Owura is here. You need to put it to him," Danso replied, nodding in Faron's direction.

The short man called out as Danso placed the measuring tape across his torso. "Owura," he called. "Mr. Oliveira Vivo!"

Faron looked up.

"Shouldn't these hardworking tailors be able to witness the procession and display of their hard work?"

Faron nodded. "Yes, I suppose, but who will run the shop?"

"Exactly!" Jojo appeared at the entrance. "We still have a shop to run. The whole of Scissor House cannot close on account of the Prince of Wales visiting. He will never go hungry. We need to eat and feed our families. We already have our own white Oburoni here. This one will just have extra clothes and feathers."

"Not everybody has to go. They can decide for themselves," Faron added.

There were exclamations as the tailors negotiated amongst themselves.

"I must go. I can tell you now, everybody must know about me," Danso declared.

"Everybody already knows about you," Jojo retorted.

Tailors and clients erupted in laughter.

"No, no, His Royal Highness the Prince of Wales needs to know about me. Pay attention to the Master of Africana." Danso grinned.

Jojo waited for Faron to finish packing the customers' garments before ushering him into the back office.

Jojo stood tall and wiry with dark circles forming half-moons under his eyes. He coughed through his revelation that Afua had suffered night sweats and terrible fatigue. The family rallied around with medicine and care, but he was going to have to go back home. Faron asked if he should accompany him to the house, but Jojo declined. Too many people with too many opinions and voices had him going out of his mind the night before. He needed to take over and make sure that the only help they received would be from his mother-in-law. No one else was to enter the house. Jojo had lost much weight all these years since getting married. His joints pushed against his skin and the coughing had increased. The burdens of responsibility weighed heavily upon him, visible in the furrowed lines that creased his brow and the weariness that clouded his eyes. Despite his efforts to conceal it, the strain of managing the affairs of his household and the demands of his work left an indelible mark upon his spirit. It dawned on Faron that amidst the hustle and bustle of their lives, he had unwittingly lost track of time. The once familiar contours of Jojo's face now bore the weight of years gone by, each line a testament to the passage of time and the burdens they had both shouldered. It was a sobering realization, a poignant reminder of the transient nature of life. Now was not the time for Faron to say anything, but he would once Afua recovered. A doctor would be sent for if she did not improve tonight. They walked to the front of Scissor House.

Akala stood with arms folded in the middle of the tailor's room. Jojo's body trembled instantly at the sight of her. Faron wasn't sure if it was the striking white plaits falling around her shoulders that made him uncomfortable, or if he knew a lot more than he was letting on.

"Mama, it's a pleasure to see you," Faron said, moving ahead of Jojo to greet her.

Akala's head swung around as she took in the room with a sudden sharpness and agility, as if her neck was elastic. Her eyes blazed with a feral fire. The atmosphere in the room was tinged with uncertainty. The men spoke in soft overtones as if not to disrespect her presence.

"Would you like to come into my office, Ms Akala? Faron asked.

She moved closer to the hanging gowns, shirts and kabas, querying the prices. "It's for my niece," Akala said to the tailors. A petite young girl with a caramel complexion stepped into the shop in excitement. Her bright hazel eyes had the men enthralled almost immediately.

"Auntie," she exclaimed, joining Akala to view the items. Akala pointed to a dress hanging on the wall behind Danso, and the young girl rubbed her hands with glee. Danso stood up to take the dress down while the young girl started a conversation with the tailors in the showroom.

"Jojo – are you Jojo?" Akala asked, looking straight through Faron.

Jojo put his hand to his chest as if he was unsure about his own name. As though her question was not meant for him.

She nodded. "Yes, you. It's Jojo, isn't it?"

"You don't belong here," Jojo replied.

Faron raised his eyes at Jojo's response.

Akala faced them. "Your friend needs to be cured, Jojo. He's an abomination."

A cold blast hit Faron as he watched Akala's lips form the word "abomination."

Jojo's hands rubbed his arms in response.

"You have to get him to confess what he is." Akala smiled.

"You are the deceitful sly one tricking men," Jojo snapped. His face reddened. His eyes flitted uncontrollably in anger.

"Are you afraid I will marry your daughter?" Faron scoffed.

Akala hissed at the men.

"She is life! You are not. You are a dry-bone corpse. The two cannot meet," she replied.

Faron's mind numbed. His palms grew damp. Blood rose into his cheeks. With a quick glance around the room, he noticed that the tailors had heard and seen nothing. The hazel-eyed girl enthralled them – it was as though they couldn't focus on anything but her.

"Without death there is no life and vice versa," Faron snapped.

"You sound like the Oburoni God, glorifying death for worshippers instead of life. You are a foreigner – they bring your kind on boats to influence our people so that we become like them through you. This is how they make our gods perish. I will make you evaporate before we go." Akala retorted.

"You are the one that is an abomination. Go back to where you belong and leave us alone. We don't need you here. We don't want your kind. We don't worship you. You hear me?" Jojo jabbed his finger into her face.

Akala smiled as she watched his finger.

Jojo coughed again.

Faron patted Jojo on the shoulder. He'd had enough. Loiyan would have a lot to answer for if she showed her face to him again. He wanted Jojo to leave the shop floor before he went into another coughing fit.

"Leave here!" Faron snapped. "Buy or make an order. When you finish, get out, otherwise I will throw you out by your neck."

With a low growl he turned away.

"You need to be rid of the curse. Only then can you see my daughter," Akala hissed after him. "I see you, Corpo Seco. You rot. That cure you are looking for – we have it."

Faron stopped in his tracks.

The cure. The one thing he needed.

"What do you want in return?" Jojo asked.

"Tribute. How can you abandon your gods for the Oburoni god? You do not let us go. We do for you. We are for you. We are yours!"

"Gods? What Gods? Where was God when my people were being enslaved?" Faron raged. "Where is the power of God for my people?" He faced Akala, waving his hands with each question. "You call yourself a God? What God? Where was your power when your people sold us? When we were on the ships? Where was your power against our masters in Brazil?"

Jojo looked at him in shock.

"These are not your people, corpse." Akala snapped back.

"This is my family and my house!" Faron shouted, pointing to the Scissor House floor.

"Give us our tribute, sick one" Akala addressed Jojo, "and you will get your cure … for your Papa." Her last words mocked him.

She turned to the young woman sitting with Danso and the other tailors in the corner and raised her hand to leave. They remained in conversation, oblivious. The young girl stood up in haste with apologies. Akala stopped at the entrance.

"You will get your cure," she said and disappeared.

"That is Mammy Wata," Jojo declared.

"Is that the name of some sort of witch? She just called herself a God." asked Faron.

"Mermaid. She is a mermaid."

209

The two men sat in the back room, lost in their own thoughts. Loud chatter from the showroom floated in and out of their environment. Jojo did not elaborate much on the mermaid revelation. Faron knew about mermaids – the story of Iara, the woman with green hair and copper skin who lured men to their death. He had not thought that there would be the same story here in the Gold Coast. He had never come across Iara and thought it to be a tale to scare men away from beautiful women.

Jojo coughed into his handkerchief intermittently. Faron stared out of the clouded window, thinking about the cure. He did not want Jojo burdened with his problems anymore. He wanted out of this endless torment. If he could get the cure, then he would leave Jojo to run Scissor House and go to England. He did not want Akala bothering the tailors. Now he understood that "others" mixing with humans didn't work. It brought a magnitude of problems. He wondered if Loiyan knew his truth. Akala, an angry woman living with bitterness, wanted to get rid of him. Loiyan was soft, loving and embracing. It was time for her to tell him the truth. How could Akala know so much about him? Did all the "others" lurking around in the Gold Coast know about him too? For the first time, Faron felt vulnerable. He looked at Jojo, who sat weary and silent.

"Jojo, go home to your wife. Afua needs you," Faron said.

Jojo coughed into his handkerchief.

"We need to get a doctor to see about your cough," Faron continued

"I have not been feeling well for a while now, Owura. For a few weeks. I must go home and lie down."

"Why haven't you spoken of this before, Jojo?" Faron asked.

"For the animal who does not have a tail, it is God who sweeps his body."

"What kind of answer is that? Do I look like an Oburoni philosopher?"

"You will need a night watchman, Owura. Kwabla is not coming back," Jojo answered.

"He left?" Faron asked surprised.

"If he didn't, he will not be working for you now, Owura," Jojo chuckled.

Faron laughed, even though he didn't mean to.

*　*　*

He waited for her.

It was as Jojo said. Kwabla disappeared without a word. He took his money from Jojo and did not return. It felt as though the hollows of the walls deliberately echoed the sound of Faron's footsteps throughout the house. Three galvanised metal washtubs full of water sat displayed in his bedroom courtesy of Kwabla before his abandonment.

Banku, a popular dish of fermented corn and cassava dough, with piping hot fish, sat on the table waiting to be eaten. She arrived with a red-and-white cloth wrapped around her. A separate cloth covered her breasts. Her moving form reminded him of a snake curling in the grass. He thought he saw her plaits swirl autonomously around her neck, but he couldn't be sure. She cruised across the compound to greet him. A flush of heat simmered through the knots in his stomach. He opened his mouth to breathe as she walked towards him. She kissed him on the mouth and spread her palms on his chest with a smile. He led her up to eat.

Her laughter filled Faron's home with buoyancy. As always, her presence soothed him. He watched her take the ball of banku from the serving bowl and place it on her plate. She cut through the banku and swiped it through the ground pepper and tomato soup before putting it into her mouth.

"I love fish," she said, "and greens. Anything with greens."

"I know," Faron replied.

"And why can't you eat with me, my love?" Loiyan asked.

"I'm quite full. I ate while I waited for you," he answered.

"Ah yes, of course you did," she replied nonchalantly.

Loiyan's plaits shifted. She grabbed two hanging in front of her and threw them over her shoulder. She moved her gaze back to the food on her plate and popped a single fisheye into her mouth. Faron brought a piece of cloth out of his pocket. He got up and pulled at the two ends, stretching the cloth around Loiyan's face, covering her eyes. She giggled as she adjusted the material for comfort. He took her hand and led her upstairs to the bedroom. She removed the blindfold and looked around the room. Three clawfoot tubs sat filled with water.

"Why aren't you afraid of me?" she asked.

"There are many things I saw in Bahia that were far more destructive. You are not something to be afraid of."

"My mother is right about you. You are not the same as other men."

"You are not the same as other women," Faron retorted.

"You show no surprise at any of my ways," she said.

"I have lived to see many of God's creatures – good and bad."

"You should fear me."

"I fear no one," Faron replied.

"You are not in Bahia now. You are in the home of the gods."

"Your gods deserted me and my people years ago," Faron said.

"Then hear my secret to silence your unbelieving tongue!" Loiyan's eyes flashed.

"Yes, about your thirst for water."

She blew into his face, her breath warm and moist. He ran his fingers over each of her plaits. A tingling sensation ran to his temples. The smell of seaweed would sit in his fingernails for days. His fingers traced from her lips down to her chest. He tapped the gap between her breasts and pressed his lips softly against her skin. He was sure there was only one emotion driving her.

"The man who knows me answers only to me," she commanded.

He stroked her face, hovering over her so that his rapid breathing was the only thing she could hear and feel on her face.

"Mammy Wata. I am Mammy Wata," she whispered.

"A mermaid?"

"A god."

He remained still in her embrace. He could feel her blood gushing through her veins. Her heart pummelling against her ribs. She smelt of the ocean breeze, palm trees and saltwater. He exhaled, trying not to be overcome by her scent. She was a creature of the universe that humans could not explain. They were similar in so many ways. She pressed her breasts against him and leaned into his body.

"Lie with me," she said, moving backwards onto the bed. A sudden sweet fragrance filled the room. Faron recognised the scent of the encyclical flowers that sometimes covered the branches of the macucu trees in the Amazon. Loiyan's whispers melted his interior, intoxicating him as he moved with her before taking her down to the bed. Their eyes locked, and for a moment there was silence.

"What are those scattered black dots on your face?" she asked, pressing her finger gently on each one.

"Freckles."

She laughed. "You look as though someone sprinkled black pepper onto your face."

His tongue shot into her mouth, and his hands grabbed her plaits. She arched her back. The need for her overtook him. His mouth was warm on her flesh, and she responded, matching his hungry moves. Her plaits loosened themselves from his fingers and moved around him.

"What is it that you want from me, Loiyan?" Faron growled.

"Obey me. Come when I call. Do as I say. Serve me," she purred.

Faron laughed. "I serve no one."

Loiyan shoved Faron, throwing him to the end of the bed.

"You have no choice. You are mine." She scowled. Her plaits curled and rose above her head in defiance.

His eyes narrowed. "You came to me, remember? I don't need you. You came because you wanted something from me. You and your mother – your people. I don't know what this game is, but it ends here. You underestimate me."

"No." She dusted herself down as she moved off the bed.

"What do you really know about me, and why are you here?" Faron demanded.

"Do you want to be cured?" She spoke low.

"I think you know the answer to that question."

"Then tomorrow come home with me and we will sort out your itch."

"My itch?" Faron scoffed.

Loiyan threw back her head and laughed at his reaction.

"Why does your mother want to cure me if she hates me so much?"

"She wants you cured if you are to serve me."

"Serve you?" It was Faron's turn to laugh.

"You do not have to fear what I am." She said, stripping off her clothes. He watched until she stood naked. He adored her so intensely that he felt a weird kind of fear creep up on him. She climbed into the tub filled with water and lay down. Her head back with her eyes closed as if he was not in the room. The water engulfed her. Assorted colours rippled continuously up and down her body. She lay still as though she was sleeping. He wanted to see every part of her, touch every inch of her, but he couldn't move. She shifted. Water cascaded onto the floor.

"How does your body change form?" he asked in a low voice.

"It is practiced from birth," she replied.

"But how do you do it?" Faron insisted.

"It's not something I can explain." She opened her eyes and pulled herself up and out of the clawfoot tub.

"Are there others? Apart from your family?" He looked around for a towel.

She sat on the bed, water dripping off her naked body.

"There are those that stay in the deeper ocean. That's what my mother once was. They do not step on land. They can shapeshift into other forms in the sea."

This fascinated Faron. What would happen if he needed his fix around them? Would they disintegrate into dust in the same way? A familiar twitch in his right side indicated his pleasure at the thought. He didn't know why but he could not bring himself to touch her. He watched her through lowered eyelids. Her breasts, thighs, skin all enthralled him. He spotted a towel hanging over a chair and grabbed it.

"We live in the lake now," she said.

Lake Bosumtwi was inland, perhaps a three-day walk. No wonder she stayed by the ocean. Faron had never been to Lake Bosumtwi. He pictured mermaids swimming naked in a lake. A slight spasm ran through his torso. The hunger was beginning again, and he did not know why.

"Are there any men?" he asked, wrapping the towel around her.

"They remain in the deep waters to guard our seed. The seed is the empire," she replied.

"So, there are many of you?"

"You ask too many questions. There are those who are out to destroy us. There are not as many of us as there used to be," she answered.

"Why is that?"

"I don't know, but the people of this land neglect us and give devotion to the Oburoni – the white man and his gods."

He gently blotted a drop of water that trickled down her cheek. "How does that affect you?"

"The Oburoni has brought the worship of death to our shores. He makes our people wear it around their necks. In worshipping death, women are no longer of virtue. He draws life away from us," she said.

"Loiyan, do you know what I am?" he asked her.

"You need to feed on our people to live. You must be cured. You cannot hurt people. We cannot allow it," she said.

"I don't do this on purpose, Loiyan," he breathed.

"I know this. I will come for you tomorrow and we will get your cure in Lake Bosumtwi. You are home now where you belong. I bring you life, Faron. Life to your death."

She stood up without drying herself and put her clothes back on.

"How do you know about me?" he demanded.

"I have to go home," she replied.

CHAPTER TWENTY-THREE

Afua sat against the wall of the front room with a short cloth covering her body. She talked with her mother, who wandered in and out of the house calling for nieces and nephews to bring or take away whatever her daughter needed. Jojo and Faron moved into the compound.

Jojo's sunken eyes had a dullness to them.

"Have you lost weight, Jojo?" Faron asked.

"Afua is better. She eats for me," Jojo replied, and pointed to a stool for Faron to sit on.

"I don't like the look of you. Dr Mensah will visit you tonight. Your wife is well, but you seem to have taken on her sickness. I don't like it," Faron said.

"How are the uniforms going? How many left?" Jojo asked.

"Seventy-five more and we are done. A few late nights are all we need."

Jojo nodded.

"Have you done any … have you been feeding lately?"

"No. This woman has brought too much confusion into my life."

"Is she curing you or killing you?" Jojo asked.

Faron stayed silent. Months had passed with just one feed. His preoccupation with Loiyan seemed to have curbed his appetite.

Jojo interrupted his thoughts "The neighbours cannot find out. Nobody can know what she is – they will kill her and you, Owura. The people fear her."

"They fear her and not the Oburoni?" Faron scoffed.

"It is no laughing matter, Papa. I don't trust them. I don't think you should go to Lake Bosumtwi."

"I will go and get my cure. I owe everyone in the Gold Coast that," Faron answered.

"You owe them nothing," Jojo retorted.

"Why have your people stopped worshipping these women? Were they your gods before?" Faron asked.

"Those that live in the bush. They are the ones still worshipping. There is only one God, Papa. Everything else is evil."

"Including me?"

"You were raised amongst bad people. It was not your choice."

"What would you have me do, Jojo?"

"Don't go."

* * *

She came for him wearing plum-red lipstick. A mane of hair fluffed around her shoulders like a ball of cotton. His insides twisted in her presence as if he was addicted to her. He remembered how his fix slowed down after meeting her. Tremors unsteadied his hands. Since Annie's proposition, the contract for soldiers' uniforms and Loiyan's appearance his needs had waned. The seizures, sweats or headaches that crept up on him as signals had slowed. He wondered if she was responsible for this. Perhaps that was why his body responded to hers the way it did. He thought about her all the time. She enveloped his senses even when she was not around. He did not go to bed that night as they agreed to meet early in the morning for the long journey on foot.

Faron understood Jojo's concerns, but it was time to face "others" in this country and find out what they were about. Perhaps Akala would answer all the questions. He wondered how they would cure him. What would they do to him? How would they do it? He thought about Mamãe hitting her head and falling slap bang onto the floor. It pained him now as much as it did the first time. His anger towards his mother had now been replaced with mixed emotions as he made his way through the forest with a beautiful woman at his side.

As they trekked deeper into the untamed backwoods, the city's constant buzz faded away. In its place, a symphony of nature began to play—the rhythmic chirping of crickets, the soft rustle of leaves, and the distant call of birdsong. Loiyan talked and laughed as they moved deeper and deeper into the woodlands. She never asked him any questions about his condition and displayed no curiosity. He wondered if she knew what he did. What he was capable of. She didn't fear him. He regarded the curve on the sides of her lips, the creases in her long neck, the sparkle in her eyes, and allowed himself to think of Ambrosina. The girl never stood a chance with him – not against his mother. What had he been thinking? He should have known his mother would intervene, but had refused to believe that she had certain capabilities. As the sun began to set, they found a clearing and found shelter under the thick canopy of trees. Faron chose to sit across from Loiyan, his muscles tense and his gaze constantly flickering between her face and her hands.

"You wish to study me?" She asked.

"No. I wish to maintain my dignity."

Loiyan erupted with laughter.

"I understand your apprehension, but you are a powerful man in this country. I am a mere woman with very little prospects."

"You tease me?" Faron growled. Her words pricked at his skin, igniting a fiery anger that threatened to consume him. A surge of indignation gnawed at him from within. She knew his desire for her and yet played with him, relishing in the power she held over him. He lay down on the soft grass and closed his eyes, shutting her out from his sight as he tried to make sense of his conflicting emotions. After a moment of silence, Loiyan carefully maneuvered herself to lie down next to him. Her body radiated warmth and comfort as it curled around his, her arm draping over his waist as she nestled herself against him. As the night wore on, not a single word passed between them, their embrace speaking volumes in the deafening silence of unspoken emotions.

As the soft glow of morning crept through the dense trees, they awoke from their sleep, their bodies attuned to the demands of their journey. Without needing to discuss their basic necessities, they continued on through the forest, navigating its winding trails with an unspoken understanding. As they traversed the vast expanse, it was essential to stop at the small villages along their route.

While Loiyan sought out water to quench her thirst, Faron took brief breaks to ease his aching muscles. However, amidst the hush of their journey he wondered if it would ignite his hunger.

As they journeyed on, Loiyan's shoulders slumped and a sense of hesitancy in her every movement increased. In the silence that engulfed them, she stole quick glances at him and offer tentative smiles, her eyes betraying a vulnerability that left him unsettled. Like a flower wilting under the weight of an unseen force, her demeanour seemed to wither away until all that remained were remnants of her former self.

"How many days?" He broke the silence as they walked through the dirt roads.

"Just tonight. Tomorrow we will be there."

Throughout the day, he had struggled with his anger, almost using it as a punishment, but deep down, he couldn't bear to see her transform into sadness. He needed to break the tension, so he took off running without warning, leaving her behind in surprise. He could hear her falling behind as he surged ahead. Finally coming to a stop, he turned around to find her already facing him, her unwavering gaze filled with fierce determination. The smile on her face was bittersweet, a mixture of love and inner turmoil. "I'll always be by your side," she whispered, her words laced with both warmth and apprehension. Faron's heart swirled with conflicting feelings as he watched her move ahead of him.

"You'll have to keep up with me," he joked, hoping to lighten the atmosphere. But as she turned to face him, her eyes held a depth of emotion that betrayed her brave words. "I promise to do my best," she replied.

As the sun dipped below the horizon on the second night, casting the world into a blanket of darkness, Faron held Loiyan tightly, feeling her pain weighing heavily on him. He knew Akala's disapproval of their relationship was straining Loiyan and it only added to their own struggles. Despite the tension between them, they found comfort in each other's arms. But as they lay in the grass together, a sense of unease lingered between them. Akala's visit to Scissor House remained unspoken, but its presence was palpable. Faron made a silent vow to be the epitome of politeness and restraint. He would do anything to ease her burden, to shield her from the pain of familial disapproval. In that moment, amidst all the hidden secrets and quiet acceptance of their love, they found a sanctuary in each other's embrace.

At the first light they greeted the new day with a quiet determination, ready to face whatever challenges lay ahead. A spiral-horned antelope stood still in the distance, watching them rise up between the bushes. Its shaggy, reddish brown coat accompanied short legs. Faron recognised the waterbuck. They were near the water now because waterbucks did not respond well to being dehydrated. They moved gracefully through the open roads and grasslands, their shared swiftness surpassing that of ordinary humans. Despite their awareness, they remained silent on the matter, the unspoken acknowledgment hanging between them.

"This is Ashanti land," Loiyan said, as a red-chested cuckoo chirped above them. "We do not disturb the people and they do not know we are here."

"I thought you wanted them to serve you?" Faron replied.

"My family are not indigenous to the lake. You will meet those that are. It is mainly the Akan people who live in this spot."

He suspected she enjoyed feeding him this information. She spoke with pride and authority as she pointed to the villages they avoided while moving through the thick brambles and bushes.

As the day neared its end, a sea of circular blue suddenly burst into their horizon, The lake stretched for miles, mountain views heaved around the other side of it. A stretch of green pastures filled the sides, rising steeply, covered with trees and bush. It was a beautiful sight to see at sunset.

Loiyan pulled him down a gentle rocky slope next to the shoreline. Absolute silence filled the space around them as mist settled on top of the waters. The humid air cooled as dusk approached.

"It's beautiful, isn't it?" she said, looking out into the endless blue.

"As beautiful as Bahia," Faron answered, catching his breath.

"Antelope God." She answered.

"What does that mean?"

"The water is God and saved the life of an antelope. The hunter chasing the antelope did not return. He stayed with the magnificent …. as we do."

"As beautiful as Bahia," Faron repeated.

He gathered her close, kissing her deep and long. The painful sorcery of her lips overcame his body. She ripped his shirt to caress his smooth chest. Faron ran his hands along the length of her body pulling her clothes away. His lips captured her hot flesh, his hand stopped over her heart. It was beating fast. She pulled him into the water. He cupped her bottom and raised his hips against hers as they lowered into the water. Loiyan straddled her legs around him, impatiently dragging him into the depths of the freshwater lake. Lust ripped through him.

"You're delicious," he groaned.

Heat roared through his body as she surged against him. He did not stop to worry about breathing. This was a different kind of fixation. They twisted against each other. Faron felt himself falling further into the abyss. The water did not bother him. A bubble emerged and encapsulated their bodies. Their lovemaking transcended time and space. Nothing could describe this power that overcame him. Colours blasted around them, matching the explosions in their nervous systems. Loiyan's hair moved in all directions. Her mouth was permanently open as she gasped and moaned in delirium. Colours blinded Faron's senses, sending shockwaves through his body. He no longer existed as anything other than a body of nerve endings. The further down they floated the more the light above them dimmed. Faron wanted all of her. To own her. Claim her. Never share her. His hands gripped her skin. She belonged to him. The hunger between them grew. Loiyan put her hands around his neck. Her nails dug in and drew blood.

Her lips moved.

"Mine."

His stomach tightened.

A sharp pull at Faron's legs hauled him away from Loiyan into deep blackness. A sudden blind panic engulfed him. Water filled his mouth. He thrashed against the pull. Hands grabbed at him. Bodies banged against him. A pair of hands fell on his shoulders, pushing him further into the abyss. His body tried to adjust to the water filling his lungs. His irises turned black. He kicked against the hands around his ankles and thrashed out, grabbing a neck and snapping it. A hazel-eyed face floated lifelessly away from him. A sudden kick hit him in the stomach. Faron buckled. Hands thrashed at him, and he mustered all his strength and swam towards the surface, hoping that Loiyan had not suffered the same fate as him. Did they attack her? The mermaids would pay for Loiyan if she had been harmed. He would make these manipulative creatures cower in fear and suffer. He hit the surface gasping for air just as the flurry of splashes around him increased. Several hands grabbed at his body to wrench him down again. Sharp nails raked across his chest, drawing beads of blood. He could see the shore. He summoned his strength and whirled towards the shoreline so the mermaids would follow him. He was stronger above the water. The first mermaid to follow him did not expect him to turn and face her, and he speared his fingers into her chest. Shrill screams soon filled the air as he roared in anger. His bones snapped and muscles ripped as his body responded to his feeding. Another mermaid rushed at him face on to rescue her compatriot. He jabbed her in the eye with his finger. Bubbles formed in the water from her howls of pain. No one was going to stop him from getting to shore.

He waded back onto land, his feet becoming skeletal. Agonising nausea swept through him. His body mass stretched and moved, changing back to the original attire of the legend in Bahia. He was Corpo Seco – one that

Africa had not yet beheld. Stronger than any of the creatures in this place – older, smarter and more powerful. He bolted further into the bush, camouflaging himself between the trunks of the trees as his eyes adjusted to the darkness of Lake Bosumtwi and its surroundings.

The form of a woman wrapped around a male soon came into focus on the shoreline. There was no sign of Loiyan. The old hunger kicked in and had him quivering with excitement. His tasteful experience of the numinous Mammy Wata that all men feared. It was he who was all powerful. He did not depend on men or women to survive. He depended on their flesh. The mermaid's webbed hands wrapped around the male's shoulders. Her green Afro rose above her head like a halo. Her murky brown skin shimmered in the moonlight, changing to camouflage her against the backdrop of the lake. Was the man an unfortunate victim or a servant to her bidding? Were they alone? The others who were trying to kill him had not yet surfaced from the lake to come after him. The two lovers didn't hear him until he was upon them. The Mammy Wata squealed when Faron grabbed the neck of the human male and tossed him away like rubbish. She screeched, lashing out, her nails scraping across his cheek. He put his hand to his face. She sprinted to the water, but Faron was right behind her. He grabbed her hair. A pungent smell hit his nose as his skeletal hands slipped on the slime of her hair. He wrapped the hair around his arm and yanked the mermaid backwards, sending her flying back onto land. The human grabbed Faron from behind. Faron twirled around and grabbed his fist. The Mammy Wata pulled at the human male to get away, but his dissipation happened quickly. Her hands grabbed at dust. She howled in pain. Her eyes flashed. Faron salivated. He blocked her blows as she thrashed at him. Murky green surged over her transforming body. She hissed, revealing sharp teeth. She lowered herself onto the land. Her webbed hands formed into claws. She twisted herself around with her fin, slashing across his abdomen, almost cutting it in half. Faron pulled back, stunned. Blood oozed from the middle of his rotting torso, exposing deposits of white fat. The Mammy Wata smiled and spun her fin again. Two more hissing mermaids appeared from the lake. They recoiled at the sweet decomposing smell of the Corpo Seco. His bones rattled. He let out a bloodcurdling laugh. He was ready to get rid of these creatures once and for all. They scampered towards him. His stretched fingers snapped together, perforating both faces into dust. Their fins fell noisily to the ground. The smell of their rotten fins would soon grace those who needed to be warned. He turned to the remaining Mammy Wata. She swiped her fin at him once more in desperation. Faron grabbed it and dragged her, writhing and screaming, into the bushes. He remembered the boy-man's words "There are others." He thought of Loiyan lying in pain somewhere. He thought of his mother slapping him for questioning her.

"Where is Loiyan? What have you done with her?" he shouted.

The mermaid laughed at him. His fist slammed into her skull, making a hole that fitted snugly around his clenched fingers.

A surge of mermaids attacked him from behind, hissing in unison. They slashed their fins across his abdomen, face and arms. He leaped onto their bodies, turning the night sky into dust amidst the screams. With each killing, Faron felt the power surge into his being. He never thought his fix would extend to "others", only to humans – and now their energy encased his being. The rotting that swathed his body in anger did not disappear. This was a different experience. He transformed because he was angry and threatened, not because he was hungry. He acted on impulse. They tried to bind him with their hair when he called for Loiyan but he was too fast. The plaits only brought his assailants right under his nose. He shoved his hand into their mouths, pulling out the very smouldering essence of lifeforce from within. Their bodies shrivelled up almost immediately as if they had no bones. He did not stop to ponder it. Flesh and euphoria spread through his body and encapsulated his bones with catapulting speed. They would pay for taking his woman. Several attacked him relentlessly, attempting to drag him back to the lake. They had become twisted into unrecognisable forms.

"Stop! Stop! Please, please stop! Please!" Loiyan appeared from the bushes. She ran towards him, her hands waving in the air, tears streaming down her cheeks.

Faron's heart stopped.

"Loiyan, what did they do to you?" he asked.

"Please, just stop, they don't deserve this," Loiyan exclaimed.

Her face was red and swollen, with bloodshot eyes and a runny nose. A shabby cloth was draped around her body. He moved forwards but she shifted away from him. Fear and dread seeped from her pores. He could hear murmurs, disapproval, tension in the air. His body started to adjust. His skin formulated and meshed immediately around his body. She had witnessed everything. She now knew him as Corpo Seco and not just as Faron. He took a deep breath as his skin closed the gaps on his muscles. A half-moon shone over the rippling lake waters, but no mermaids showed themselves.

"Loiyan?"

She sobbed. "You can't kill them. You can't hurt them anymore. You must go."

"What happened? Did they hurt you? Where is your mother?" he asked.

"She's not coming," she said.

"What's going on, Loiyan?" Faron demanded. He stepped towards her.

She recoiled and shrieked.

"No, don't touch me! There is no cure, okay? There is no cure. You have to die."

His heart broke into a thousand pieces and melted into the mud beneath him. The fins of dead mermaids spread out around them. The boy-man's words lingered "You don't belong here." She had seen everything from the shadows. He swallowed hard. Jojo had warned him not to come and he hadn't listened. He stood still for a moment watching the tears roll down Loiyan's cheeks and understood her deception.

He turned away to follow the path home.

She followed behind him for a short time, probably to make sure he left the area.

He could hear her sobs as he walked away from her in silence.

"I love you, I'm sorry," she said after him.

Faron did not turn back.

CHAPTER TWENTY-FOUR

A group of soldiers arrived to pick up the completed uniforms from Scissor House. Faron assisted in folding the uniforms and fitting them into the wooden trunks provided, while the tailors hurried to complete the last twenty uniforms. Scissor House closed at midday for the whole week to make sure the tailors were not disturbed. Danso was free to help with the packing. Jojo stayed at home citing poor health. He promised to visit Faron at home with a newly hired watchman. The Lake Bosumtwi incident had happened three days earlier, and they had not spoken to or seen each other. Faron knew Jojo would not be happy to hear what had transpired. He wondered how to break the news.

Soldiers dressed as civilians arrived throughout the day to pick up the trunks. The last of the packing felt symbolic for the men of Scissor House. Faron was now undeniably one of the wealthiest men in Accra. After today his tailors would be better off than they had ever been in their whole lives. Jojo and his family had much to celebrate. Faron wondered if the tailors would spend the money on taking care of their relatives and then go back to asking for advances on their wages in a few months. Jojo never had that problem. He didn't suffer fools gladly and always made sure those in the compound knew that his money did not stretch for everyone. Faron watched the last trunk being loaded onto the horse and carriage.

Jojo introduced Bobo as the new watchman. He was a stout figure with ears resembling outstretched hands waving from both sides of his head. After the grand tour of the house and numerous explanations of what things were and how they worked, the three men sat on the stools next to the three-stone fire. Jojo and Bobo ate Afua's etor, a dish of plantains with yams boiled and mashed with palm oil.

"You don't want to keep some etor for Danso?" Faron asked.

"It is sweet tasting. We will finish it here today," Jojo answered between mouthfuls.

"Has Jojo explained your pay?" Faron asked Bobo.

"Yes, Owura. Thank you, Owura."

"Bobo knows the ancestors sent you to us. We learn from the Owura, and the Owura learns from us. This brings us prosperity," Jojo said.

"Praise them for the abundant flow of food to my family," Bobo replied.

Faron rolled his eyes.

Bobo left with a full belly and promises to turn up on time the next day.

"Owura, I don't want to hear what happened at Lake Bosumtwi. I know it was very bad. What I want to know is, what are you going to do now?" Jojo said as they stepped into the parlour.

"I don't like the way you hold onto doors and walls to walk, Jojo. What did Dr Mensah say?" Faron asked.

"He told me to take a rest and that is what I'm doing. After this, I go home. My appetite is back – that's a good thing," Jojo replied.

"It's over, Jojo. I won't be seeing her again. She's not allowed in this house or at the shop."

"Settle down and have a real family. Simple things make men happy," Jojo replied.

"Why are we having this conversation? You know one day I will move away. Perhaps this time to Lagos." He clicked his fingers. "Or Freetown – the place that used to be the administration headquarters."

"How long can you keep moving, Owura?" Jojo asked. "You must stop and accept your fate."

Faron did not reply.

"Find your peace, Owura," Jojo continued. "You're a good man. I know you. I believe there will be peace for you. You will not have to suffer anymore."

"Stop, Jojo. I am not going through this with you again."

"But I am the one who witnesses your suffering. You must be careful with spirits, not all of them are good like you. The ancestors will reward you in time," Jojo said.

"Am I a spirit, Jojo?" Faron asked. "The ancestors have ignored my people for four hundred years and the Oburoni God condoned slavery. Let's face it, my reward was Loiyan – she made me happy."

Jojo nodded. "We will visit someone. I have found a pure spirit guide who can help you find your peace."

"You better not have told anyone about us, Jojo."

"Owura, he sent for me. One of the best on the Gold Coast. He is a descendant of the old spirit guides and only works with royalty. I did not seek him out. He sent word to my compound – nobody sees this man. He is known through oral history only. Ordinary people do not meet him. He sent word the day after Kwabla left. Now I know your peace is coming. We must meet him soon. Stop this water woman from coming here."

Faron changed the subject. "Are you ready for the Prince of Wales's visit, Jojo? Will you be able to go?"

"I will rest now and be ready. Don't worry"

* * *

Danso bought himself a Singer Class 66 sewing machine with a mahogany cabinet. He patted the heavy-duty domestic machine with pride. The Deluxe Library Table No. 40 cabinet exuded luxury. Sewing machines represented the meaning of life for Danso. This sewing machine had two table leaves that opened from the centre of the cabinet and folded out to create a spacious work surface. Danso demonstrated this by reaching into the cabinet and pulling the sewing machine up.

"This machine is an engineering masterpiece, Owura. It can sew everything from silk to canvas. And you see the sewing machine itself is spring mounted below. Now we can sew more than just uniforms and kabas, Owura."

"You are quite the businessman, Danso. What about your other machine?" Faron asked.

"I have it in the back. I can take it home or rent it to another tailor."

"Owura, who is going to see the Prince of Wales when he arrives?" another tailor piped up.

Faron sighed. Everyone at Scissor House had received an invitation. The visit was only a week away.

He didn't want to hear about the visit or uniforms anymore. He had no time to himself. No time to think. Knowing that the Governor would request to see him only brought about anxiety.

"Anyone who wants to go should go," Faron answered.

It was not that late, but his body, worn from the intensity of finishing, organising and packing garments, demanded respite. No sooner had he rested his head on the pillow his mind shut down. The panic and finality of orders drained him. He dreamed Jojo insisted on knocking his knuckles on Danso's new Singer 66 cabinet to declare it an unworthy item. In response, Danso punched Jojo square in the face.

Faron woke up with a start. A soft knocking was coming from downstairs.

The soft knocking grew louder.

"Bobo?" Faron stood on the stairs and called out.

"Yes, Owura," Bobo answered in a soft tone, fully aware that he had woken his boss at a bad time.

Faron moved downstairs to open the door.

A frail Loiyan stood awkwardly next to Bobo. Her hair laced in a bun. Her face gaunt and drawn.

"Madame said it was very important and refused to leave, Owura." Bobo spoke with caution.

Faron nodded and waved him away.

"What do you want?" The fire in his eyes snapped and spat.

"Faron, I know that you are angry, and you have every right to be. Forgive me," she blurted. "There is much I need to tell you. Please, I am sorry."

"Are you done?" he asked.

Her hands trembled as she pulled her shawl around her shoulders.

"I know you hate me." She caught her breath. "I know you do. But I need you to know that I did not want this. I did not want it. They forced me. They told me I had to do it. I know you are made of so much good."

"Loiyan, go in peace. Do not come here again. Do you understand?"

She gazed at him.

"There is nothing for you here. Do not bring yourself here again."

"I love you."

Faron slammed the door.

* * *

The next day, Danso appeared in the back room of Scissor House holding an envelope from the Governor. The ledger occupied Faron all morning in his attempt to ensure all was back to normal. Dr Mensah was expected to visit Jojo mid-morning and he needed to make it in time to hear what the doctor had to say. It was a habit of ordinary people not to exact diagnosis given by doctors but to just state that they were unwell or feeling bad. This frustrated Faron because he was a man about solutions, and without a clear diagnosis the problem could not be solved. He needed his best friend back beside him at Scissor House. Danso placed the envelope on the desk and hurried back to his Singer 66. He was an extremely busy man with a backlog of kaba orders and was also responsible for locking the building. These days, he was the last to leave and the first to open. Danso liked it this way because he could work on his new toy for as long as he wanted.

Faron opened the envelope in haste.

Gentlemen: –

I am pleased to say that the soldier's uniforms presented to me by Scissor House for the "Visit of His Royal Highness the Prince of Wales to the Gold Coast Colony 1925" have received much praise. The workmanship has been of the highest quality. Our dealings with you have been highly satisfactory and we have found you most accommodating.

With best wishes for your continued success,

Yours very truly,

Governor Charles Piggersill

Faron put the letter down. A rollercoaster of emotions filled his being. The business had been more successful than he or Jojo had ever anticipated, and yet life continued to get in the way. Faron's thoughts drifted to the encounter with the boy-man. He forgot about his intentions to confront that thing to see if it had sent Loiyan to seduce him. Perhaps they too had been watching him. He wondered if they were in it together. Since all parties were aware of his presence, it was time to show them who he was. Sudden muscle contractions attacked his legs under the desk. His pupils flashed black in response. He gripped the desk and saw that his fingers were blackened and chaffed. He forced himself to concentrate on the hum of the sewing machines. This mermaid fix didn't agree with him. It was unusual for him to need another so quickly. A distraction. That's what Loiyan had turned out to be, but surely a distraction was not the answer or cure to his problem.

Faron spotted Dr Mensah stepping out of Jojo's compound. He hurried across the road, relieved to have made it in time. Dr Mensah congratulated Faron. The completion of the military uniforms was common knowledge.

Faron waited to hear his diagnosis.

"Tuberculosis. It's a young person's disease, I hear. He must have caught it from his wife. This thing is contagious so don't allow him into Scissor House yet. The mining areas have better facilities than here for this condition, but I don't think he is well enough to be taken there at this time. My suggestion for the moment is some serious rest and perhaps for him to spend some time nearer to the sea. The air is pure there."

Faron was grateful and relieved to get to the bottom of the problem. He just hoped Afua listened to the doctor's instructions. He said his goodbyes and went to see his son.

Jojo was sat upright, weary and thin in a single chair. A tan plaid blanket covered his legs.

"How are you keeping? I just saw Dr Mensah," Faron said.

"Yes … nice man," Jojo replied.

Faron pulled out the Governor's letter and read it aloud.

Jojo clapped feebly and chuckled.

"It's a blessing Owura, look how far we have come."

"If it wasn't for you, we wouldn't have even started this business," Faron said.

Afua entered with a large bowl of goat light soup and placed it on the table next to Jojo, who looked exasperated.

"How am I supposed to eat this if I am not well?" he asked.

"You will eat," Afua snapped back, rolling her eyes.

Faron burst into laughter.

"Tell him," she ordered Faron.

"I'm only here to bring the news. I must go," Faron said, getting up from his chair.

Jojo bent over the table, attempting a sip to appease Afua.

Afua shook her head and left the room.

The trees swayed around Faron. A slow rustle of branches swept up around him as he walked through the forest. Faron decided to seek out the boy-man to find out more information. He had decided against informing Jojo of his decision. It would only serve to frustrate and aggravate his condition. The pathway in the forest was not kind to his feet. Small rocks, stones and twigs took their toll. The walk through the trees always gave him time to absorb the aftermath of his cravings. It reminded him of the Chapada Diamantina, the steep cliffs at the edge of a plateau in Brazil – the most beautiful sight to behold in Bahia.

The trees spoke to him as they swayed in the wind, full of captured souls whispering thoughts that entered the minds of humans as they passed through. When entering and leaving the forest, Faron always felt as though a spiritual conversation had taken place. That connection made him feel vulnerable and human. He hoped to feel the presence of his loved ones. The leaves rustled in anger. The forest behaved as though it knew that he would never die. He could feel his mother's indifference. He could feel her resignation.

Thinking back to the Bahia and when he went through his change, he had witnessed no other like him.

NADIA MADDY

He was a lone ghoul. Representation of power and mystery in the Bahia lay at his feet. Across the waters on African soil, however, he was not alone. The land of the Ga, Ewe, Fante, Ashanti and many more harboured others in different forms. He was sure the boy-man was the key to Loiyan. Akala must have sent him. He would find out the intricacies of these African beings – their lust, power and weaknesses. The heat surrounding him grew oppressive. It sucked out his bodily fluids for its own pleasure. He was glad to move deeper into the forest, where trees shielded the ground and all that passed through it, protecting all from the greedy monster in the sky. Faron's hunger grew stronger as he ambled through. It was dusk when he finally reached the grasslands. He walked over to the spot where his opponent, the male human, had fought so graciously. A man of honour. Faron stood in the spot and inhaled. He felt nothing. No spirit. No aura. No energy. The earth and the wind had consumed the remains. He sat down on the dry grass to wait in silence.

The grass rustled a moment before the boy-man showed himself. He stood hunched on two legs. "Why do you come back here?" he asked.

"I have some questions," Faron replied.

Broken teeth cracked the smile. "I knew you would come back. But remember, this is my home. You don't belong here."

"Did you send someone to follow me?" Faron asked.

"No." The smile remained.

"Your others, did you send them to me?"

"They cannot exist or move without my permission."

"Then where did the mermaid come from?"

The boy-man hissed hysterically, dropping to all fours. He chased his tail like a dog – except he didn't have a tail.

Faron remained still. The thing's reaction intrigued him.

"Mermaids! Cursed creatures. Arrogant, sly, manipulative."

"Did one of them break your heart?"

Saliva sprayed from the boy-man's mouth as he raged.

"I destroy them! Rid the plains of their vile, seductive –"

"Why?"

"I feed on them, drain every withering drop. My others sell their fins in the market," the boy-man said.

Faron felt a sting of protectiveness for Loiyan. She must never venture out here.

The boy-man moved in closer to get a good look at Faron's face. Not all his teeth were crooked, Faron saw – there were two long, sharp incisors, perfectly shaped and gleaming white.

"Have you met one?" the boy-man asked.

"I have."

"Ah, kill her when you are done. Turn her to dust and bring the tail to me."

"Why would I do that?" Faron asked.

"What brought you to me?" the boy-man retorted.

"You will tell me about the others that inhabit this land," Faron insisted.

"Do you tire of the mortals?" The boy-man looked around. "Want to see my others?"

"Yes."

They made their way through the forest to an abandoned village. The four-legged creature appeared to be concerned with being seen. He climbed trees, hopping from one branch to another, leading the way. Sudden involuntary body tremors sneaked upon Faron as he strolled through the forest. He slowed his pace to hide the spasms from the boy-man.

"How long have you been here?" Faron asked.

"Over a hundred years. I came from the Maghreb. My master let me go. He was hated by his kind. He let me go so they wouldn't find me."

"Who are 'they'?"

"I am Imazighen, a Beraberata. The Umayyad Caliphate invasion, they tried to destroy my kind and replace us if we did not bow down to their God."

The boy-man climbed down from the trees as they approached an intense array of afrormosia trees surrounded by bush. The shadow of two figures suddenly emerged as though they had known Faron was on his way. So, there were more? He shook himself off and drew himself up before moving towards the shadows. The hunger was really creeping up on him now. The boy-man chattered loudly in another tongue as they got closer to the thick bushes. Another shadow emerged and, although stooped, it managed to look up. A woman in the last part of her childbearing years, with skin hideously burnt along one side of her body and face. One visible eye held his gaze before turning to the boy-man. Two shadows behind her approached him with intent, boys no older than seven or eight.

The boy-man grinned again, displaying his sharp incisors. "I am full."

Faron was ready. It didn't matter how fast they were – the rush of his fix was upon him and would curtail them. There was nothing that could stop him in the throes of urgency. Loiyan had distracted him from the sins of his soul, but he hadn't asked to be born into a world where the god you were told to worship claimed your suffering and pain were your own fault, or part of a bigger plan of which you had no choice. Loiyan's presence brought light relief to help eliminate the pain, but here he was once again, being who he was foretold to be. No regrets from a life that he did not choose. No allegiance to a god that allowed four hundred years of deprivation to continue, with a book to justify it all. He remained alive, being what he was, and that was all he knew.

The boys exposed the same sharp incisors as the boy-man. One of them snarled and pounced. Faron's hand was already up.

The boy hung in mid-air, choking and clawing at his own neck.

The boy-man barked at Faron.

Faron fixed his gaze upon the wretched creature.

"If you think yourself a black mamba, strike me," he shouted.

The boy-man pulled back, wringing its hands. "How do you do this without touching him? What is this force you have? You are not of this terrain!"

Faron arranged his fingers as though he were holding the boy's neck. The boy continued to gasp and struggle in mid-air. The smell of rotten eggs erupted from his body. The creatures stood aghast and helpless. It seemed all "others" were on a mission to eliminate him. This was a trap. They did not ask questions or want to hear his side of the story. Faron's gaze remained fixed on the boy-man. The younger companion whined. The burnt-faced woman watched without emotion. Faron tightened his hand into a tight fist. The boy's legs flailed in mid-air. His motions weakened with every kick until they came to an abrupt stop. His legs turned ashy white, and the odour of rotting flesh filled the space around them. The boy-man hissed at Faron until the floating boy dried up and turned to dust. The other boy screamed and hurtled towards him. Faron bent down and twisted around, slicing the tendons behind the boy's knees with his fingernails. The boy fell clumsily to the earth. Faron dragged the boy across the ground to the boy-man.

"No more games."

"No! No!" The boy-man shrunk back, tripping over the uneven grimy surface.

"No what?" Faron shouted.

"No more games. We will tell you what you want … what you want … us and them," the boy-man cried.

Faron threw the bleeding boy across the floor as though he were a discarded chicken bone.

"Begin."

"I did not send any mermaids to you. They rule near the waters, not inland. We have no contact with them. This is truth," the boy-man said.

"Why do they come to me?"

"I do not know. They are creatures of the flesh seeking adoration. Seducers and wanderers of land and sea, loyal to none. They seek to own and conquer men. They will tip the balance of this land, of this world! Destroy them when you meet them. Fill them with your pleasure and cut them in half when you are done."

"One of them really did break your heart!" Faron snorted.

"I know pleasure alone – I have no heart to break." The boy-man dropped to all fours.

"Why did you attack me?" Faron asked.

"This is our land!" the boy-man snapped. "Ours, not yours."

"I have no interest in your land or you. Why would I want to take your land?"

"Because all come to take and destroy … our lands, our minds, find out our powers, our ways, and destroy us for no reason. This is the way."

"This is the way with men, not with us."

He heard another voice speak behind him. "A father's love and a mother's scorn meet to unearth a demon that walks the earth in denunciation. The ancestors prepare the land across the waters for the soul to be redeemed."

Faron snapped around like a man possessed. Those words had been uttered by Luíza and had hung over his head for two lifetimes. No one else had said them since her. The burnt-faced woman stood by the parting of the bushes leading to the afrormosia trees whose trunks were as wide as several mud huts and whose knots resembled the knees of fat men. She observed him with a barely visible sneer. The trees around her stood tall, forcing their way into the heavens, a perfect home for any tree-dwelling creature. She turned and walked into a carved-out opening in the base of a tree. Faron dashed towards the home of the tree dwellers. Today, he would get his answers and stop the games, even if he had to kill them all.

A small fire was the only source of light. The floor of the tree was strewn with soft leaves. The faces of creatures with claws and curling tongues and burial mounds protruded from the walls against the faces of warriors and kings with pursed lips and wide noses.

"Who are you?" Faron demanded, as he entered the dwelling. A cold chill wrapped itself around his bones. The burnt-faced woman stood at the edge of the fire. The flames danced as they towered above them. Her one eye blinked rapidly, the skin around the empty socket charred and uneven. Faron noticed the blackened parts of her body creeping through the rest of her flesh as the flames rose higher. He stared, not understanding what he was seeing but knowing that it was no accident. Although the flames crackled and flourished, all around them was silent. He moved forwards. The burnt-faced woman stepped into the flames in response. He shouted, and she turned to face him. Her burnt body rose above the flames. She screamed as if suddenly realising she had stepped into the fire. Faron stopped to cover his ears against the horrific noise. Drops of burnt debris and hardened flesh fell around him, revealing her naked flesh. Faron looked up at her raised figure in the fire. The woman was no more. Instead, staring back at him were honey-glazed pupils surrounded by the colour of urine. Decorated cuts to the face, enhanced by a large golden zumam nose ring and long plaits intertwined with cowrie beads and buttons, flowed in the rhythm of the crackling fire. Faron shielded his eyes from the glare. A faint hiss of static filled the room, or rather his head. A vibration that demanded his attention but didn't allow him to think. Her wails stung his soul.

"Who are you?" he yelled.

"An entity older than you," she hissed at him.

It felt like a thousand tongues spoke at once in different languages to answer his question. His head throbbed. "How do you know about me?"

She lowered herself into the balls of the fire as it whistled in response and then stepped out of the inferno. Faron moved back. This was another kind of beauty that he had not witnessed before. He never contemplated the different looks of women in his surroundings or even within the continent.

She looked nothing like the women of the Gold Coast. Her headdress was covered with ornaments and metals shook as she moved closer.

"I want nothing from you. It is you who wants from me. You who seek life. I seek death ... relief from this waste," she moaned.

"Who else is with you and that wretched creature?" Faron asked.

"We keep to ourselves."

"Where is the master?"

"Why have you come here, cursed one?" she asked.

She moved closer with the intent of seducing him. The smell of myrrh and berries engulfed the room. Her nipples dark and erect. Her smooth, deep, rich skin tone shone as though she had been oiled for the occasion. "We can share our pleasure and our secrets. There are many in this land who would go against us, but you and I are from other places. Give me the death – and I will give you the life."

Dry leaves rustled and crunched under her feet as she sauntered towards him. Her body was silhouetted against the light of the fire that lingered to keep the heat in the damp hollow trunk. Blood red toenails, wide hips and thick, shapely thighs caught his attention. She lowered herself onto the floor, pulling him down with her.

Her bare breasts rubbed against him.

"What are you?" Faron asked.

"Give me death, cursed one," she whispered.

She covered his mouth with hers and sucked on his lips as he pulled her in. He squeezed every part of her, digging his nails into her flesh, drawing blood. She laughed as she moved against him, pulling his clothes apart. Flashing images of subjects bathed in blood confused his mind. Her nibbles pricked into his skin, sending shuddering sensations through his spine. Every puncture gave him immeasurable pleasure. His mouth was suddenly overcome with her swollen tongue. He opened his eyes as he realised it was sliding down his throat, choking him. He grabbed the back of her neck to pull her away as her tongue unravelled in his mouth. His strong grasp allowed him to throw her across the room, away from him. She landed on the insides of the trunk and scrambled like a cat. The head of her tongue – a cobra hissing with displeasure.

"You! You are the master!" Faron shouted.

The burnt-faced woman laughed as her tongue subsided and disappeared back into her mouth. From the moment she had kissed him, he sensed she was timeworn. Deep rooted but not strong. A deity he was not familiar with. Nothing was familiar in these lands. He had gotten more than he had bargained for, and aggravation set upon him.

The burnt-faced woman slinked around him on all fours like a cat. "Give me your death, corpse. The ancestors will reward you with life."

"What do you know about me?" Faron demanded. "I came here for information, and you give me half-truths, and now you want my power?"

Her plaits dragged along the floor as she strolled toward him.

"You were some kind of special bloodline, and now you hang from trees in the Gold Coast, sucking blood from rodents," Faron said.

"Speak with humility, corpse! We owe you nothing. You have already killed one of my own," a thousand voices snapped.

Faron watched her as she stood upright. Perhaps this was why he never met any others. They were all greedy, seeking more power, not satisfied with their own. The boy-man was nowhere to be seen. He had not entered the bushes at all. He must have been commanded to stay away. She was alone with him, and there was only one boy left. He sensed she was incredibly old and tired.

"If you thought the boy was worth something you would never have let him attack me. And you fail to answer my question. How do you know about me?" Faron demanded.

"You are your mother's curse. You spilled her blood," she answered.

"Some women have no business reproducing," Faron shot back.

"And what of your future? Will you give me death for life?" she asked.

"You live, and I die? You take my powers, you mean. Is that the deal?" Faron snorted.

"We can drive the invaders out from the Numidia, far away from Mauri people."

"Ah, you want my power to fight your invaders. Let me guess, they come with their gods," Faron said.

"They come to destroy my people's ways and massacre us!" she howled.

"You are a god, are you not? You have the power to stop it."

"Your mother's scorn has turned you into a monster. Do you wish to reconcile in peace, cursed one?"

She called him a monster. This creature who lusted for power and didn't have the capacity to help her own people. This thing called him a monster and suggested that he reconcile with the woman who had caused his pain from the very beginning. Faron's face flushed as he clenched his fists. The hideous yellow pigment surrounding her dark eyes turned a shade brighter. She leered at him, sensing his anger.

"I can send you to drink from the breast of your first love, and you will no longer have to suffer. The pain will go away. You will be human and committed to the ground to rise with the ancestors. Don't you want to be cradled in the bosom of the woman who can forgive you?"

"Forgive me?" Faron laughed. "Forgive me! She should be begging for *my* forgiveness. She opened her legs for her master and punished me for it. She accused me of not siding with my own people, but all she wanted was power, not freedom, through me! Keep your own cursed life."

"In your anger you are blind to your cure," she replied.

"What is my cure?" he asked, utterly frustrated.

"Kill Mammy Wata or sacrifice. Sacrifice your life to me. I will give you death," she answered.

"I don't want it." He turned to leave, but she leaped upon him. Her open jaws widened like a chimpanzee. The cobra reappeared. Faron shifted to one side and slammed her to the floor. She rose in the flicker of an eye and lashed out. Faron grabbed her hand and twisted her arm, bringing her to her knees. Unable to free herself, the cobra wrapped itself around Faron's legs, toppling him, but he did not let go of her hand. The cobra jabbed at his torso, missing, and hitting the floor. Faron grabbed the cobra's neck. The cobra wriggled as he started to draw energy from her. She squealed, suddenly realising his intentions. She couldn't concentrate on the cobra when he was extracting her spirit. The flames from the fire leaped haphazardly around the room. A thousand tongues spoke all at once in different languages, shrieking his name, bringing repulsion to the core of his being. He let go instantly.

"Give me death, and you will be rewarded with life, corpse!"

"You'll get nothing from me," Faron snapped, trying to compose himself after hearing his name in the most ancient of tongues.

"Your mother is waiting for you to return to her. Will you keep disappointing her?" she mocked.

Faron grabbed her head with both hands. He squeezed her mouth open as she struggled against him. She was no match for him. Age had made her arrogant and lazy after years of commanding her slaves to do her dirty work. No one could use his mother to mock him. He started drawing her insides out. There was no turning back after deriding him. No deity or being would match or ridicule him again. The fire blazed beside them as she thrashed until a slight mist appeared at the tip of her tongue. Her eyes widened as the flames crackled and died. The mist drifted away from its former home of mucus membrane and entered Faron. He closed his mouth and threw her lifeless body onto the floor. He could feel the energy of her spirit intertwine with his body tissue, fuelling his strength. He quivered and gasped as the mist gushed into his organs. Visions of bloodied bodies surrounded by endless sand flew to the surface of his mind, hunger, exhaustion, and running … running from something.

This creature had fled just like the boy-man had said, but he did not sense fear. What he sensed was fatigue – she had grown weary of change. She had once ruled. She had been the master, it was true. He saw well-decorated gardens with flowers and olive trees. A people far away, facing a large river that instructed their way of living. Faron steadied himself as the visions flashed before him. It was a while before he was able to wipe himself off, wondering if the boy-man was even aware of what was happening in his domain. The burnt-faced woman lay still and beautiful on the leaves covering the damp earth. She was gone, and his mother would never be mentioned again. He was no longer interested in finding out about others. It was time to go home.

The warm night air enveloped him with a welcoming kiss. It was a huge relief going back to Jamestown. The trees blocked out the skyline as he walked away. Now he understood why he had never met others. They were not meant to be seen – not meant to be discovered. All lived an existence beyond the borders of human life, interacting only to meet their primal needs. It seemed most were undesirables, at least to each other, almost uncontrollable. This was a bad time for them all. Every part of the continent had suffered invasion - their land and ways destroyed or driven out. They seemed confused, lost and driven to madness. He had felt isolated all this time but now the feeling of seclusion would leave him once and for all.

The boy-man did not reappear until Faron came back to the forest. He was ugly, slow and stupid. His lumbering, awkward body did not allow him to sneak quietly around the jungle. Faron heard him swinging through the trees before he and the younger one thudded to the ground in front of him.

The boy-man pointed at Faron. "Did you disrespect my master? I told you not to come back here."

"Get out of my way."

The younger one made it all too easy. He ran straight at him, jumping high in the air to land on Faron. They both fell to the ground. The boy's mouth opened, stretching to the back of his jaw, showcasing enormous fangs. Faron impatiently jabbed his fingers into his sides. The younger one, desperate to tear him limb from limb, writhed, snapping ferociously against him. A familiar smell arose from the body of the younger one, but Faron did not wait for the body to become pulverised. He threw it in the direction of the boy-man and dusted himself off.

The boy-man shrieked as he tried to rescue his follower by gnawing on his own arm and forcing it into the mouth of the boy.

"Since you want to hear the truth, know this. That mermaid will end your life as you know it!" the boy-man shrieked.

Faron didn't look back.

"I will find you wherever you are and wherever you go!" the boy-man screamed after him.

"And when you do, you will be dead like your master," Faron muttered.

* * *

He did not expect to see the figure of Loiyan waiting for him in his front yard. She sat by the entrance door, wrapped in green. Her skin dry and scaly. Her hair hidden under a tightly wrapped headpiece. The skin around her mouth and forehead was red and sore. Thick, leathery, scaly patches dispersed around her legs. Flakes were scattered all over her person.

Shedding.

Faron's jaw tightened. His body instantly hardened at the scent in the air – jasmine. He walked past her and shouted for Bobo, who appeared from behind the building holding a fanner filled with rice, clearly in the middle of preparing his evening meal.

"Yes, Owura!"

"Get this woman out of my compound," he ordered as he opened his front door.

A stunned Bobo remained standing.

"I have to speak to you, Faron," Loiyan said, walking behind him.

"Madame …," Bobo called, unsure of what his actions should be.

Faron opened his door and moved inside but Loiyan was fast enough to grab his shoulder. Faron put his hand on hers and thrust her out of the way.

Bobo put down the fanner.

"Faron, I have to speak to you!" Loiyan protested as she fell back, almost knocking Bobo over.

"Madame, it's time to go. Come on now," Bobo said.

Faron closed the front door behind him. He moved towards the parlour. A short, sharp scream filled the building. Faron stopped in his tracks. Bobo screamed again. Faron rushed back to the door and opened it, running blindly into the yard to find Bobo standing with Loiyan.

"She made me, Owura. She made me scream for her," Bobo said.

"What do you want, Loiyan?" Faron demanded.

Loiyan ran past him straight into the house.

CHAPTER TWENTY-FIVE

"Were you with another woman?" Loiyan snarled.

"No."

Her skin was shedding all over the entrance rug.

It pained him. Why didn't she just ask for water? Perhaps Bobo had refused to indulge her. Why was she shedding so badly?

"Why did you wait here, Loiyan?" he snapped. "You should have come back another time."

She answered him with dull eyes. "I am forbidden to see you."

"There's a surprise," Faron answered.

Loiyan swung her nails across his face, missing it by an inch.

Faron stepped back, stupefied.

"You can see no one else! I smell female. Don't lie to me. I will destroy everything you have!" she screamed. A burst of colour surged around her body.

"You can't. You didn't give it to me," he retorted.

"You test me?" she hissed at him.

"I am a man. I don't need your assistance."

"All men need my assistance. If you make me angry, how can you ever be at peace? You cannot exist without

256

me. Why would I want to be with a human who cannot be loyal? I can have any male I want!" she snapped.

"You are Mammy Wata. You declare you know everything, like the Oburoni God. So, you should know what happens to your people. You know whether I share myself with others. I don't have to tell you," Faron replied.

Loiyan screeched in anger. She stormed into the parlour searching around the corners of the room. Frustrated, she seized the sofa, overturning it as if it were a footstool. Faron looked on in bemusement. It was as though Lake Bosumtwi had never happened. That she had never betrayed him or put his life in danger. Loiyan threw the voile-patterned chair across the room, screaming about his infidelity.

"Hey! Let's stop this now, Loiyan!" Faron shouted.

She snarled like an animal possessed.

He grabbed her shoulders, pulling her away from the destruction. Her scent filled his lungs and tickled his throat.

"I'll kill you, I'll kill you," she raged, raising her hand as if to punch him.

"No, you won't." He grabbed her wrists, pulling them down.

Her eyes and nose streamed.

"I can smell something," she stated.

"That may be, but it isn't me lying with another woman." He overpowered her, pushing her against the wall. Her musk saturated his nostrils. In her hysteria it seemed she did not realise that whatever she involuntarily emitted from her body intoxicated him.

"You want to attack and kill me? You're not supposed to kill me, it goes against creating," he said.

"That is not how we kill." Her voice was sullen.

They stood against the wall until her breathing slowed, and the rhythm of each breath coincided with his. He let go of her.

"I need water," she whispered, collapsing into his arms.

As she trembled against him, Faron knew this time he could not involve Bobo in his drama. He took her arm over his shoulder, guiding her up the stairs to the bathroom. Her feet dragged, knocking against the steps. He cajoled her to keep going, and she panted and nodded.

She huffed as he helped her into the solid porcelain tub. The bathroom was a status symbol in the Gold Coast. Only a few had one in their house. At the time of acquiring it, Faron had not thought that his vanity betrayed his aspirations. The bathroom was a pointless endeavour, for most of the time he bathed in the backyard, just like everyone else in Accra. It was far more pleasant and involved less waste, with easier access to the outside latrine. He demanded a single bathroom with a fixed tub in his home as it was a sign of progressive thinking and wealth in the Gold Coast. But he never used the bathtub and had never dreamed that a woman would be the first to find herself in it.

He filled it with water. Her body fell heavily into the bathtub, causing water to splash on his dusty, worn clothes. She submerged herself and closed her eyes. As the water rose, colours, from grey-green to purple, rippled through her body. Her skin's texture hardened to resemble snakeskin as it incorporated the colours flowing from her navel to her lower body. Faron gazed as the skin of her thighs stretched and fused. A sudden rush of blood to his head unsteadied him. Heat rose from his core. An unfamiliar reaction created confusion in his mind.

She opened her eyes. "I love you," she said.

"I love you too," he whispered without hesitation. His lips came down on hers. He loved the feeling of her mouth against his. He pulled her wet body out of the tub. She straightened up, stretched her arms over her head, and arched to crack her spine back into place. He marvelled at the glow of her dark skin.

"Mine," she whispered as she nibbled his ear.

He soaped up her entire body and rinsed her off.

They moved to the bedroom. The place he had tried to get her to succumb to him for so long. It didn't matter anymore. Nothing mattered. In the moment no thinking took place. Only the senses signified that they were alive. That they existed in space and time. A fragrant smell enveloped them, growing thicker in the darkness as they slipped against each other's sweating bodies, fighting, gasping and bucking until they were both limp with exhaustion.

In the stillness of the dark, Loiyan spoke softly. "Understand, Faron, that we are not bad, but the confusion that surrounds our existence in these times creates fear and destruction. Both for us and our people."

"Is that why you allowed your sisters, cousins and aunties to try to kill me?"

She paused.

"It was thought that if the ordinary person on the street found out who you were, it would confirm the need to leave traditional worship behind. Our customs are perishing. We exist to serve. What is the point of us if we do not? You serve. We serve. All serve on this terrain. And when we die, we continue to serve."

Faron sighed. "Don't your people understand that humans don't like difference? They seek to destroy anything that is not uniform."

She lifted her head up and looked into his eyes. "It is the Oburoni religion that tells them so."

"No. It is the human way. They want to exist as far apart from us as possible. They fear us. They do not seek to love us."

She trailed his chest with her long fingers. She looked so achingly beautiful. Her loose hair, a thick curly mane, floated around her shoulders. That seaweed smell. Delirium.

He sat up beside her, took her hand and kissed it.

"It is hard to be away from you, but I can be with no other, Faron." She spoke with resignation. "I … I am not allowed to be here. If they find out, it will go against everything I have been taught. I cannot stay here like this for long. It is not good for me."

"I will fill the bathtub for you every night."

"I told them to give you a chance," she continued. "That you were not here to harm or destroy what we have. I told them but they didn't listen. I had no choice."

"Answer me this … do you stop my hunger?" he asked.

"No, I don't have the power. I have no power over you because I love you." She paused. "None of this was supposed to happen."

"Welcome to my world," Faron replied.

She visited him for three days, going back and forth, staying for as long as she could. Faron filled the buckets from the water pump in the yard. It dawned on him as he carried the buckets upstairs that his strength had not waned since meeting with the burnt-faced woman, and perhaps it was his lust for Loiyan that replaced his old hunger. The longing that engulfed him every so often had now petered out. The cramps in his legs and arms were not surfacing as frequently as they had before. Not having to plan where to go or what to accomplish was a light relief. He was sure that the incident with the mermaids and the burnt-faced woman had calmed his hunger. He was convinced that his needs had diminished since meeting Loiyan. For this reason, he could not let her go. He would do whatever it took to keep her in his life. Considering what had happened, he would now seek his new fix on the other side of the greater Accra region, somewhere like Aplaku. It would also be better if he did not see the boy-man again.

Loiyan had a surprise. She insisted on keeping it a secret. She slept in the bathwater all night to prepare herself, and pre-dawn she wrapped her body in white and asked him to do the same. It would take nine hours to reach Tema, a small village on the cusp of the sea. They moved through the forest with effortless pace. Their footsteps barely touching the ground as they glided past blurred trees turning nine hours into three. The baking heat cast shimmering shadows around them. The sight of Tema coincided with distant drumming. Loiyan quickened her pace. The melodious harmony of women's voices enhanced by the beating drums rapidly gripped Faron's core. Loiyan walked ahead of him until her form faded. His sense of time abruptly altered. She turned and smiled before light hurt his eyes. He raised his hand to cover them. A warm glow encased him, penetrating his arms, legs and torso. As if he was encased in a womb, balmy and safe. Muffled voices lingered. Sweet adoration meandered around his bones. A childlike fear swathed him as a sense of the unknown enveloped his heart. He removed his arm from his face to reveal a sea of women draped in white. They danced harmoniously to the rhythm of the drums. Faron looked around as the singing grew louder. Their faces were plastered in white clay, and each carried offerings. Hair adorned with white ornaments. Heat moved around his body. The women ignored him. An older woman suddenly dropped to the ground. She groaned and writhed about. Women surrounded her, chanting in a language Faron did not recognise. The women threw things onto the fallen one, but he could not see what they were. Smoke and drumming penetrated everything. The older woman rose from the ground as if being pulled up by an invisible force. Her eyes shot open.

She spoke with Loiyan's voice. "I bring healing and fertility to you. Your fingers will intertwine with mine when you tend the crops. Your feet will mirror mine when you walk to sell your goods. Your lovemaking will bring you ecstasy. The pain in delivering your offspring will simmer away with every drop of rain that pounds the plains around you. Your fertility will bring joy and abundance to your village. As women, you are faithful and loved. You have accepted the divine, and the divine accepts you."

The women stomped their bare feet zealously against the ground in response. The older woman fell once again to the ground before regaining consciousness. The women helped her up. Loiyan appeared. She nodded and moved forwards with her hands outstretched to Faron. It was in this instant that he suddenly realised his own insignificance in the order of events. He was in the middle of the dancing, and yet no one could see him.

Loiyan appeared by his side.

"It is beautiful, is it not?" she asked.

"They administer devotion to you?"

"I am their deity. I give life. I throw abundance into their compounds."

Faron remained silent. He felt different, as though his hunger had become distant from him. Oxygenated blood flowed in his veins. The wind picked up, and the figures around them grew dimmer. Loiyan placed her hand in his and squeezed it. They were suddenly standing on the same dusty red pathway as before.

"What did I do to deserve this special invitation?" he asked.

"You must understand the magnitude of my existence," she answered.

"What did you do to me during the ceremony?"

"I demonstrated who I am and what I am made of."

"What exactly is that?" Faron asked.

Loiyan eyed him as they ambled away from Tema. "I am Love. I am the giver of life. Could you feel me through your aching bones?"

"What do you mean, aching?" he said.

"Your bones ache with age. Your heart is full of grief and misplaced love."

"I am but a mere mortal … with deific tendencies," Faron chuckled.

"We are one of a kind, somehow," she answered.

She had taken something away from him, but he could not sense what.

Loiyan clutched his hand and led him away from the experience through the thicket towards the sandy beach. Turquoise waves foamed, slapping against the ocean shoreline. Salt. She looked back when he hesitated. The glaring sun tended to drain him of his energy. Lack of shade was a thing on most beaches. Loiyan continued to pull him towards the smell of seaweed. The sun smothered him while it shimmered on her. Hot sand flipped around their feet as they walked. She let go of his hand abruptly. Her body appeared to narrow. With the ocean in her sight, she walked rapidly towards it. Her thick plaits moved against her swinging arms. Faron blinked. The glare of the sun distorted his vision. The salt smell disabled his senses. He lost his balance and stumbled. Something was wrong. Loiyan stepped into the water, wading in, not waiting for him. His insides twisted as he tried to increase his pace. He gulped a mouthful of air and stopped. Salt. Loiyan dipped under a giant wave and disappeared. He was not afraid for her but the aggravation that set upon him was rising from his stomach into his heart. She didn't look back to see where he was or if he had followed her. What if he had turned around and gone back to the village? What if he didn't care much for the ocean? Salt. The taste of salt was on her lips and fed into his saliva when they kissed. He liked it and always wanted more but this … this intensity suffocated him. Faron stood looking at the empty ocean. He couldn't see her. She remained hidden without a care in the world while he dripped with sweat. He walked briskly towards the ocean and stepped into the rush of the water. It gnawed at and stung his feet as if a thousand red ants were descending onto his skin. Faron yelped and buckled at the pain. He looked down to see the flesh of his toes melting. The saltwater rushed over his ankles. He jolted back in horror and pain. The stinging sensation racked his entire body as he bent down to hold his ankles. The pain had him panting. He moved back onto the sand and fell to his knees. He had never attempted to swim in the ocean before and had had no idea that it would destroy him. The very thing that gave Loiyan her life would be responsible for his demise. She could never know.

He looked for shade along the coast and spotted a group of palm trees over a rocky surface. It was difficult to walk along the sand. His skeletal big toe caused him to limp. His breathing constricted as the sun hampered his vision. Loiyan conveniently forgot that she had invited him here. This was not how he was used to being treated – it was certainly not how women treated their men. How could someone just disappear into the sea and neglect a guest without so much as asking whether they were okay? She didn't even look around to check up on him. Faron stopped. Why should he walk halfway across the beach for shade and wait for this woman? What was wrong with him? He turned in confusion and wobbled through the thickets to the other side of the village from where they had come.

A man wearing a white wrapper stood waiting at the opening of the bushes and smiled at the sight of Faron.

"She will not come back until after dark," he warned.

Faron stopped. He eyed this short, stout man that spoke to him as though he knew his business.

"Pardon me? I don't remember meeting you before."

"No, you have not," the man replied. He waved his hand in the direction away from the beach. "The women are preparing your night stop. If you are not comfortable with the beach, then follow me to rest and wait for her."

"My friend, I don't know you. Who are you?" Faron snapped.

"I am what you call a priest. The medium of your lover," he replied.

"A priest? Whose hopes and visions do you sell? The Oboruni or the mermaids?" Faron snorted.

"Service. I give service," the man answered.

"How do you know Loiyan?"

"She chose me."

Faron's throat constricted. He realised this situation required restraint and he was a long way from home.

"Chose you for what?" he asked tightly.

"To serve. We have finished cooking. Come."

The village was full of women wearing white. Beads were wrapped round their wrists and ankles. The women stared as he moved past them to the big huts surrounded by trees at the other end of the village. Faron walked in silence. The man led him to a house overlooking the others on a small knoll.

A woman sat next to a three-stone fire, fanning the smoke in-between the pot and the stones.

"Red, red … you eat?" she asked as they approached her. A wide gap between her two front teeth appeared as she spoke in broken English.

"Very little. My stomach is not good," Faron replied.

"You see the gap?" The man leaned into Faron pointing at his own front teeth that revealed no space. "That is beauty. There is no woman in this village that has the gap as wide as hers. That is what my Mammy Wata did for me." He smiled and winked.

"Your name?" the woman shouted before they could enter the house.

"Faron," he replied.

"Abena."

"Your wife?" Faron asked his companion.

"Yes, my second wife. Mammy Wata is my first."

"I am wife to the gods, and he is husband to the gods." Abena laughed.

"Mammy Wata won't turn on her own, but she will cut off the head of those who turn on her own people."

The man led him into the house and pointed to the straw bed.

Loiyan appeared in the early hours of the morning before the sun had the chance to climb the sky. He woke to a flickering tongue sliding across his neck. Her hands travelled around his body. Her eyes shone as she put her fingers to her lips and mouthed that they must leave immediately. They shifted into the bushes without waking the villagers. Loiyan told him she wanted to show him a plot of land in Sakumono. They strode through the plains, occasionally stopping to take shade from the burning sun. He checked the folds of her luminous skin for scaling. She did not seem as concerned as he was. She chattered on and brushed away visible flakes. He allowed himself to be led but she seemed slower than usual. On all the walks that they had taken together, they had never admitted to each other that they both moved so much faster than humans. It was possible that she had tired from the events of the past few days. If she wasn't dehydrated, all was well.

The plot was surrounded by vegetation. Loiyan explained that this was where he could build his next tailor shop.

She wanted more for him.

"I can give you this," she said.

"How do you think it can possibly happen?"

"It's what I do."

"Can you stay with me forever?" he asked.

Her eyes flickered. "I need water, Faron."

"Jamestown is right by the water. You offer me land and wealth, but you don't offer yourself."

"I will always be yours – so long as you are mine."

"And if I betray you?"

She glowered at him.

He chuckled. "It is you I want. The rest I shall consider."

"How can I be happy with you if I can't do what I was born to do?"

"You can do anything you want. You are not tied to what others think you should be."

"I cannot end up like Akala," she barked. "My mother will die long before she is supposed to because she fell in love with a mortal."

"Your mother has the capacity to fall in love?" Faron scoffed.

Loiyan grabbed Faron's chin as if she wanted to snap his neck. Her swiftness took him off guard. Their eyes locked. He lifted his hands in defeat.

"I spoke out of turn. I apologise."

"I am the child of Mammy Wata and a mortal, Faron." Her eyes darkened as she let go of his face. "My mother fell in love with my father. He died prematurely. My mother did not go back to the seed in the ocean. She stayed on land. Her hair grew white. Her body weak. In grief, she refused to be who she was. When she desired to serve again, she was banished. There are rules. Now my mother is an elder among the lake Mammy Wata, not the ocean. Only I am allowed. My mother is making up for the time and respect she lost in her grief."

"And so, what do you propose?" For the first time, Faron didn't know what to say.

"You live near the sea so I can come and go as I please. I've stayed with you for three days. I am well because I prepared, but who can tell how long I can survive?"

"Let us go." Faron needed to process her words. Her stories. Her type of love. He was not mortal, but neither was he a sea creature. She had a lot to lose if she stayed with him, and physically she could not. They did not speak on the journey home. He sensed her yearning to touch him but holding back. He walked with her until they reached the ocean nearer to Accra – the familiar abandoned hut.

"Why do you come to the ocean here overnight and not stay with your mother in Lake Bosumtwi?"

"I am my mother's link to the ocean mermaids, the messenger."

"When will I see you again?"

"I don't know, Faron. My followers needed me. They called me here to accept their sacrifices. When they call, I must come. Now I must go and rest. You too should rest from our trip, my love."

The moon lit up the night sky, aiding Faron's walk back home, as did the lanterns carried by pedestrians.

Bobo opened the gates.

"A message for you from Scissor House, Owura, from Danso. Jojo is ill. You must go to his house tomorrow."

Despair hit Faron like a punch in the stomach.

CHAPTER TWENTY-SIX

The mud-walled compound was full of people waiting for something to happen. They greeted Faron – nodding their heads and shaking his hand in respect as he walked through the forming crowd. They all knew Jojo, but many had never met him. Faron was Jojo's right-hand man, and Jojo his adviser. They were a team.

Faron was led to the bedroom to find Afua sitting by the bed. Jojo lay listless. Faron sighed. His only friend. His only child. He had been so occupied with Loiyan and the others, trying to fix the unfixable. Jojo's health had deteriorated quicker than he had expected. He was supposed to have taken him out to get some sea air. Wasn't that what Dr Mensah had said?

Afua's face was crusted with dried tears. She sat shell-shocked.

"I will take care of everything. Just send word to Scissor House." He handed Afua an envelope full of twenty-shilling notes.

"The gods will bless you, Owura," she said, shaking his hand.

Faron sat beside her and waited.

The wind howled. Shouts were followed by volleys of rain that smashed onto the rooftops. People ran into different huts in the compound to seek shelter from the downpour. Faron observed his long-time companion turn frailer with every hour that passed. How was it possible that someone you had known your whole life could physically change overnight and become unrecognisable? On the plantation, slaves had mostly dropped dead with exhaustion or were brutally murdered. There was rarely a chance for disease or illness to overpower their bodies and change them. Jojo's long, lean, muscular body was swallowed up by worn sheets that left him looking like a shrivelled stick. Life was cruel. Jojo was too young. Faron felt a sudden rage.

"Are you hungry?" Afua asked, standing up.

He did not know why she asked this, but it would have been rude to decline the offer. "I'll have a little bit of food," Faron answered.

She nodded and left him alone.

Jojo was only forty-four years old. Jamestown had welcomed them with open arms and had them relishing opportunity at every turn. Accra gave Jojo the chance to thrive and provided him with the tools to do so. Faron recalled the first year they arrived. A radio announcement reported that the eye doctors were providing free eye exams. The eye clinic was swarming with people. Young and old waited their turn with incessant chatter, excited at the prospect of finding out whether their eyes worked properly, or whether they would have to wear glasses.

Jojo sat in a lone chair staring at the letters on the wall in the eye clinic. The optician pointed to each letter and asked Jojo to repeat what he saw. Faron explained to the doctor that Jojo had not received a thorough education and therefore could not understand the letters. The eye doctor grinned and ignored Faron's protests as though he were an overbearing parent. Faron soon found out that the big city was full of people who didn't listen to you if they didn't feel like it. Jojo squinted and slapped his knee in frustration every time he missed a letter. He wanted so badly to do well at recognising the letters, as though this was his chance to shine in front of Faron.

Jojo had liked to reminisce whenever Faron overstayed his welcome in the compound. Faron could not quite comprehend the need to be surrounded by people 24/7 but understood that this was the African way. For himself, he was happy to leave and enter the serenity of his home after spending time with Jojo and his family.

"The best thing about coming to Accra was getting my spectacles," Jojo had said.

"I didn't like them," Faron replied. "They made you look like an old man."

Jojo laughed. "Those spectacles made me the best tailor on the Gold Coast. Do not disrespect my spectacles."

"No, *I* made you the best tailor in Accra, because I taught you everything I know."

"You taught me, but you never sewed anything, Owura. I did," Jojo said.

"Those spectacles added twenty years to your looks," Faron complained.

"My wife didn't feel that way when she saw me. She saw a handsome, responsible–"

Faron interrupted his friend. "She didn't see you sleeping on the floor in Scissor House. If she had seen that, she would have left you there."

Jojo snickered. He loved to reminisce on their first few years building the business. He was proud of all they had achieved, and that he had finally secured himself a family.

"You like to build, Owura. I like to sew."

"Sleeping on that floor was not something I relished," Faron replied.

"Yes, but us sleeping on the floor meant we made money quicker because those mosquitos taught us that if we don't make money, they will suck us dry!" Jojo said.

"You forget the ants and the lack of latrine?"

"Oh! Owura, you remember that? Is that what made you buy the cement and hire the workers quickly?" Jojo asked.

"No. You needed help," Faron said.

"So, you don't want to sew, you just want to build a big house and live in it?"

"Yes, just like you live in your big compound with your big wife who keeps calling you away from me?" Faron mimicked her: "Jojo! Jojo!"

"Owura – try find a wife to look after you. Now I'm going to my bed for comfort," Jojo replied.

"I don't need that kind of comfort!" Faron waved his words away. "This is perfect for me. We are good."

Faron stood over Jojo. He sensed interrupted slumber. Jojo opened his eyes, but it was momentary. Faron wanted more. He wanted to wake him and ask what he thought about Loiyan's proposal to build another Scissor House. What he thought of the Governor's proposition to go to England, to leave Scissor House with Danso to look after. He wondered if his friend would approve of the idea. Jojo's breathing faltered a little, and Faron considered calling Afua. An emptiness crept upon him. He walked to the door to peek outside. A young boy sat eating banku on the steps. Faron told him to fetch Afua. The boy stood up, understanding the gravity of his position in all this. Faron moved back to sit in his chair and wait.

Jojo remained inactive for an hour before he took his last breath. Afua wailed over the bed. Relatives managed to pull her off but not until the furniture had been knocked out of place. Faron stayed in his chair, glad that he was the last person Jojo had seen. He wondered whether Jojo's spirit was hovering around the room while his wife prostrated herself in distress. He thought about Jojo's mother. She had waited a long time for her son to join her and, if what the Africans believed was true, he would be greeted by her and together they would shower blessings on all those that had loved them. Perhaps Jojo would fight for his soul. When the men finally managed to pull a hysterical Afua out of the room, Faron walked over to the bed. He looked over the man who had helped him build Scissor House. Jojo had been his son, his friend and his keeper. This man was the first real bond he had created since leaving Bahia. He whimpered unexpectedly then straightened himself. Luckily, he was alone. He took a deep breath, knowing that this was the most fragile moment of his prolonged life. He never once thought that he would have to say goodbye to Jojo. High-pitched cries filled the compound. Faron leaned in and kissed Jojo's forehead. He pulled a wooden spoon from his bag and placed it in Jojo's hands.

"Child of the moon – one day we will be together again. Thank you for your friendship," Faron whispered.

His eyes burnt. He took deep breaths to steady himself. Jojo had kept his secret. They both triumphed over the challenges others placed before them. Jojo was the wiser man. There would never be one as loyal and worthy as Jojo.

Faron unlocked the door and entered Scissor House. It stood cold and empty. African fabrics and gowns hung on the walls. Sewing machines sat grey and silent. He walked to the next room. The Prince of Wales's visit was upon them like a bad dream. He climbed behind Jojo's sewing machine and sat down in Jojo's chair. He placed his head on the table and lay there until the next morning.

Faron locked the front door after the last tailor entered that morning. Scissor House was closed to the public. The tailors sewed for the funeral. Food and drink flowed throughout the day. The men set to work until the last stitch. They sewed and discussed Jojo's good and bad habits all morning.

News of Jojo's death spread through the city, and so mornings were consumed with having to unlock the front door to listen to the condolences of the many visitors who had all come across the great tailor at some point in their life. Jojo's sewing machine stood silently in the corner, his spectacles and a few peppermints decorated his table. A hollow feeling engulfed Faron. He decided to leave the building in search of street food for his men. Danso and Ato accompanied him. As they walked through the streets together, pedestrians nodded and waved, shouting, "The Prince of Wales is coming. We will see the soldier's uniforms. We will see for ourselves at the celebrations!"

Mama Ekufuwa's compound was half-full of labourers and traders eating, talking and waiting for food. The aromatic smell of palm nuts saturated the compound. Mama Ekufuwa's daughters stirred pots and filled bread torn open in the middle. Faron, Danso and Ato waited until one of Ekufuwa's daughters took their order for tsitsinga, a goat-meat kebab. Mama Ekufuwa noticed the men and pushed her way through the crowd to greet the now-famous tailors from Scissor House. She held Faron's hand as she extended her sorrow at the news of Jojo's death, then ordered her daughters to also serve palm-nut stew for the men before they were allowed to carry the tsitsinga back to work for their colleagues.

Conscious of the time, the men ate without much chatter. They could not refuse Mama Ekufuwa's generous offer of a free lunch. They were proud to be recognised for their work and sat like kings on their stools as they ate in a hurry. Then they said their goodbyes and climbed over the mound to get back onto the main pathway.

Faron saw a familiar figure with unmistakable long white plaits standing in the distance. She stood tall, hands on hips, staring straight at Faron.

Danso grunted in disapproval.

Akala's eyes remained fixed on Faron.

He encouraged the men to continue without him.

"Tomorrow," Akala declared.

"What will happen tomorrow, Akala? I know you're dying to tell me."

"Tomorrow you will lose everything."

"You did not give me what I have."

"Then let Loiyan alone. Let her be!"

"What?" He took a step toward her. "What are you going to do? All these idle threats. What can Mammy Wata do to me? I'm not one of your pathetic humans besotted by your beauty."

"Your path should not be crossing hers. Leave her be!" Akala yelled.

"Why won't she leave *me* alone?" Faron replied.

"We will take her away from here," Akala said.

"And I will find you and kill you," Faron retorted.

They both stood their ground. Townsfolk walking past them crossed over to the other side of the road. Two strangers of the land, locked in silent battle. Some of the passers-by knew Faron, but the sight of Akala was somewhat unnerving to them. Children shouted "witch" at her and ran away as fast as their legs could carry them. Akala conceded by pushing past Faron to venture down into the compound. The smell of seaweed lingered on his suit as he walked back to Scissor House.

CHAPTER TWENTY-SEVEN

A crowd from the greater Accra region joined Jojo's funeral. Faron did not attend funeral ceremonies – they were a reminder of the undignified burial that had given him a life of endless fixation. He arrived at the compound in the early hours and sat observing all those involved in the funeral arrangements. Women encircled burning firewood and large grand pots, chattering and barking orders at each other. Aromas rose above the rooftops, sauntering into the streets and neighbouring houses. Jojo had no children, and yet the compound was full of infants running around, occupying themselves with frivolities. The elders insisted Faron sit inside the house. It was not a sign of respect for him to be sitting in the compound. They offered him drink and food while he waited, which he politely declined. Individuals roamed in and out of the house shouting orders at each other. They had to get everything right for the most important man in their community. The whole of Swalaba and Jamestown was expected. Faron made sure Afua wanted for nothing. His son's funeral would be the most

   extravagant the city had ever seen. His only request was that Jojo be buried with his spoon. Afua knew better than to protest. The Governor sent his condolences. It didn't feel so bad sitting amongst the chaos. The lifeblood of all that Jojo represented brought him comfort.

The instructions stated that Faron would be present at the gravesite after the funeral proceedings. They came for him – Jojo's cousins-in-law, brothers-in-law and others that Faron could not recall meeting. They guided him through the streets to avoid people stopping to give their condolences. The men discussed the funeral provisions, what went wrong, who was responsible and what needed to be done. It unsettled Faron to hear them describe Jojo as "the body." How were people so quick to distance themselves from the man they had shared a life with in the compound?

It offended him.

A wrought-iron fence in the cemetery separated the living from the dead. The smell of newly turned earth and cut grass lingered around them. They followed the sound of wails and sobs. Faron's heart thumped against his chest. Over the years he did not have to hide what he thought or felt but lately it crept up on him and he struggled to contain his emotions. He breathed through his mouth. He was going to have to fight to keep his composure. The crowd blocked Jojo's grave. Danso spotted the approaching men and waved to Faron. It was a relief to see a familiar figure. Danso would protect him from the chaos of grief. He greeted Faron with bloodshot eyes. He sobbed, pulling Faron through the crowds to the open grave. The closed coffin lay neatly inside the rectangular hole. All eyes were on Faron as he bent down to gather earth from the fresh soil surrounding them. He stood at the edge. He knew what it felt like to be under the earth. The clawing, the choking, the screams. Danso abruptly threw his arms around Faron and sobbed into his chest. The cousins-in-law attempted to pull him off. Faron was expected to say something, and everyone was waiting.

"Oh, my brother, my brother! Jojo was my brother!" Danso's grip tightened around Faron.

They tried to cajole Danso to let go of Faron's suit jacket. The numbness in Faron's body left him without any resistance. He couldn't speak and he was not going to entertain anyone today. Afua stood beside the gravesite. Her blackened knees dirty from kneeling. Her eyes rested on Faron amidst the confusion. She needed him to end this tortuous moment. Faron prised a weeping Danso off his shirt. He nodded at Afua and moved beside her. He threw the earth onto the wooden coffin. Afua let out a wail, fell to her knees and tried to climb down into the hole. At that moment, the crowd pushed Faron out of the way to stop Afua from doing the unthinkable.

Mourners trailed back to Jojo's compound under the twilight sky. They straggled in, tired and worn, ready to eat and gossip before heading home. They each greeted Faron before sitting down, and those not entitled to sit inside the house entered briefly to pay their respects. The tailors sat outside in the backyard with the rest of the mourners. The room inside was reserved for important guests such as the immediate relatives and the local chief. Afua remained in the bedroom, grief-stricken. She had fallen into the grave and been pulled out. Faron had never seen a woman lose her mind like that before. That kind of dedication and love had him thinking about his own life. His mother's dedication was for what she could get. His father dedicated himself to no one. The slaves dedicated to themselves out of fear and scarcity. This single-minded commitment called love required sacrifice, responsibility and devotion. This was the humanity that Loiyan spoke of. This was the way of those who surrounded him. This was why sometimes he felt so alone, lost in his past. A past of disaffection, treachery and scarcity. He had allowed it to cloud his mind while attempting to find his place here. He had let himself down. Jojo had filled that void and given him all that he was lacking. In his bitterness he allowed his emotions and existence to be led by the past. He would do so no more.

* * *

The Prince of Wales arrived on the 12th of April 1925, en route to South Africa, and was met with great excitement from the people of the Gold Coast.

Scissor House remained closed.

Faron locked himself away with Bobo, refusing visitors all week. The tailors attended the festivities. This was bigger than Empire Day. They were determined to share the moment of pride for Jojo. Danso invited Faron to join them on the day. When he declined, the tailor insisted he would return to Faron's house after the festivities.

Jojo never got to see the ultimate reward for his hard work. An event that he had worked so hard for and never witnessed. This was a bitter pill to swallow. Faron reminded himself that Jojo was not the type to dwell on things and that he would have to do the same. The morning sun rose high into the sky undefeated; the distant hum of drums, loud cheers and car horns filled the area. There was nothing to block the celebrations out.

Faron retired to bed and forced himself into nothingness. No dreams, just still, dark matter. The peace that he had dreamed of felt as though it was drawing near.

The *HMS Recluse* arrived at Takoradi port, a destination that was under development and designated to become an important harbour for goods in and out of the Gold Coast. Takoradi was the perfect place to showcase successful development taking place in the country. The Prince arrived in his naval uniform and was met by the Governor. It was said that all were impressed with the soldiers' smart uniforms. The prince due to stay for a week travelled to Kumasi before making his way by train back to Accra. Locals played trombones and trumpets, music accompanying the dancing amidst the crowd. Linguists accompanied the Eastern and Central Province chiefs under state umbrellas with some carried on beds to meet the Prince on the polo ground. Danso said it was called "the great palava of Head Chiefs." The linguists of the Ga Mantse presented the Prince with a golden stool before the racing at the polo club. Faron was grateful for Danso's insistence on seeing him after the events. It gave him time to recuperate and think about his options, and to witness something he had not attended. He broke the news to his closest tailor about the Governor's offer. Danso listened in silence.

"You do not seem excited, Danso?" Faron queried.

"Are you going to take the offer, Owura?" he asked.

"It looks likely, there is nothing left for me here, my friend," Faron replied.

"There is everything left for you. Jojo has left much for you, and I am still here. You would leave me?" Danso choked on his words.

Faron did not understand how a grown man could get upset over him leaving. He was young, would marry and live his life. Did he not know this? Besides, time was always a factor in moving away, and Jojo was no longer around to hire people who "didn't ask questions."

"I will be back and forth, Danso. I will always come back, and I will stay with you when I am here." Faron appeased Danso as he wiped his eyes.

When Danso was gone, Faron proceeded to write to the Governor and his wife, thanking them for their patience. Upon further consideration it was truly a delight to take up their offer. Faron signed and sealed the envelope with a sigh of relief.

CHAPTER TWENTY-EIGHT

He remained at home.

His side hurt.

His bones ached.

His flesh crawled.

He lay in bed staring at the cobwebs in the corners of the ceiling. There was no sign of any spider.

He awoke in the dark to hollow silence. Moonbeams shone through the shutters. The town slept. Crickets chirped. A lunch invitation from the Governor lay neglected on the wooden floor. He had to get the previous two days out of his head. The weight of his body held him down. The world turned when he opened his eyes. Sleep engulfed his body and lulled him into a trance. The things he saw.

"Owura, I know you don't like to eat but fufu solves problems," Bobo protested as he handed Faron a small plate of food.

Faron took the food into the dining room and sat down to contemplate his state of mind. He licked the ball of fufu. Joy. The joy of preparing and sharing food with loved ones. The joy of conversation or silence while eating. The sour tang against his tongue caused a delightful sensation. A miniscule capacity to taste. Some humanity left. He was okay with that. He dared to take another lick.

A short knock at the entrance door stopped his indulgence.

"It's me."

Loiyan.

In his grief, he had blocked her from his mind, believing their love could not stand the test of time against any of the others, or even the humans. How could they pull through against all the enemies they had acquired in their forbidden quest for love? He was better off alone. Better off leaving the Gold Coast. It would be best for everyone.

Her breasts pushed against a white sleeveless vest. An unusually large multicoloured wrapper was draped around her waist. Cowrie beads snaked around her ankle. White beads adorned her pinned hairstyle, broadening the shape of her face. Why did his body heat up every time she was in his presence?

Her eyebrows rose in surprise at the food on the table.

"You are eating?" she asked incredulously.

He rose from his chair and pulled out another for her.

She moved unhurried.

"Are you going to feed me?" she asked.

"I don't know if there is any food left. My watchman brought it in."

"Where is the soup for the fufu?"

He smiled and wondered if there would ever be a time where he would not have to restrain himself when he was around her.

She leaned across the table and took his hand.

"The people love you, Faron. Your watchman even brings you food that his wife cooks and shares it," she gushed.

"It is not love, Loiyan. It's pity," he replied.

She leaned away from him and sighed. "I am sorry for your loss, Faron. I know you loved Jojo. He was your brother. He will watch over you now and protect you more than he could before."

"And you know this how? Did you speak to him?" Faron scoffed.

Loiyan stopped for a moment, contemplating her next words.

"There is something I need to tell you."

She knew something about the afterlife. She had proof and would show him right there and then. He sat tall, ready for the revelation. He remembered he too had something to tell her. He was leaving and most likely would not be back for a long time.

"I am with child," she said.

Faron froze. The blood drained from his face. A familiar coldness ran through his being.

"I am with child, Faron," she repeated.

What did she know that he didn't? Was she involved with other males? What kind of lie was this? What was she hoping to achieve?

"Is this your game?" he snapped.

"What game?" Loiyan asked, surprised.

"You cannot be pregnant," Faron growled. His vision blurred as he tried to regain his composure.

"Why not? Mammy Wata is a fertile being. We are life."

"And I am death!" Faron raged.

He grabbed her by the arm to haul her out of his house. Jolts of pain snapped around his eyes. His vision faltered with every movement.

She pulled his hand off her and threw an immediate backhand slap that stung his jaw.

He pushed her towards the door, trying to get her out before he did something terrible.

"You lie to me," he shouted.

She slapped at his hands to get away from his grip.

"You have been with another man!"

"What are you talking about, Faron? This is our baby," she exclaimed.

She threw another punch but missed this time. He was too quick for her.

"You deceive me," he yelled. He blinked several times to regain his vision. "No more lies!" he declared, making for the entrance door. He struggled to coordinate his body.

Loiyan cried angry tears.

"Tell me the truth, Loiyan," he roared as he opened the door. "You will tell me the truth."

"I dishonour my elders for you." Her voice was shrill. "I defy my pod for you. I defy Mammy Wata's rules for you!"

She grabbed the door handle and slammed them shut, refusing to leave.

She stood before him, bent and wheezing.

His rage dissipated.

"How is this possible?" Faron said. This was inconceivable. He placed his palms on his head and paced round the room. "I have never had any children, Loiyan. I have lived over two hundred years and have never had any children."

"I am Mammy Wata!" Loiyan slapped at her chest. "Know me, understand me, and respect me. Without me, there is no life. I create life. Life is wealth. I create pleasure. I am a woman. I am water. I am the giver of life. Don't question this, Faron!"

"If it is so then it is exactly as Akala said. An abomination." He raised his hands to the sky in despair.

"You regard what they believe?" Loiyan gasped, horrified. "That the child must be taken from me? The child must be banished from its people and home?"

"Who said this?" Faron's eyes turned black and narrowed.

Loiyan moved back to the parlour. She sat wringing her hands, rocking back and forth. "I am not strong like my mother. I have defied her and my people in the worst possible way."

She covered her head in her hands.

"Nobody is banishing anybody while I live and breathe here," Faron said, defiant.

"My mother, Akala, fell in love with a human. Do you not hear what I keep telling you? She disobeyed the code. She lived on land for too long. My father became a wealthy and important man in the community. He had a big house. Ashanti royalty invited him to visit their ceremonies. He was honoured with a stool. The more my mother stayed on land, away from her home, the more she aged. She loved him as if she was human. Gave only to him, my father. But he died unexpectedly."

She paused.

"Her hair turned white soon after they buried him. She fled to the freshwater mermaids in Lake Bosumtwi. But our people found me and took me away from her.

My mother searched for me and the only way I was promised to her was to make sure that I renounced my human side and joined the ocean."

"So, you don't live in Lake Bosumtwi?"

"I visit. I instruct. My mother has so much to prove to be accepted back into the pod." Loiyan's eyes brimmed with tears. "She knew, Faron. She guessed it as soon as it happened. This pregnancy is different. The baby, it grows so fast. I do not know what is happening inside my body."

Faron took a deep breath and swallowed hard. This was a side of humanity about which he knew nothing.

"I'm afraid, Faron."

He moved in and held her close. Her protruding stomach pushed against him as though it disagreed with their bodies connecting. He whispered into her hair, "Don't be afraid."

She buried her head in his chest. "They warned me. They warned me not to come here. They said I cannot be with you and have this baby. It is forbidden."

In bed, Loiyan slept on her front with her face pressed against the pillow. Her belly pushed at the mattress as though it was in the way. She should have been feeling discomfort, but she slept regardless. He watched her body rise and fall. Thick black cornrows. Smooth shoulders. He moved into her warm body. She stirred. He kissed the middle of her shoulders. He wondered what the human side to Loiyan was. Did she know what made her different to the other mermaids? Did she suppress her human side, or was it because of it that she had been chosen to lure him into their trap?

When she removed her clothes to lie with him her protruding belly shocked him. Joy expanded within his chest. Pain somersaulted in his abdomen. Loiyan took his hand and guided it over her stomach. It felt hard and round. Had he achieved in death what he could not in life?

"Us," she whispered.

Then she let his hand go and curled up into a ball with her back to him.

He wrapped his arms around her.

"I broke all the rules. Lying with you, falling in love with you, and now I am with child. What will they do with me once they take my baby away?" She spoke with a low voice as if talking to herself. Heat rose from her body like a furnace.

"Nobody is taking anybody away," Faron replied.

He raised himself to look over her shoulder.

Loiyan's gaze fixed upon the closed shutters.

He moved his hand to cup her stomach.

"It is ours," he confirmed.

"Maybe I should have the baby here?"

"You will be safer here."

There was no doubt in his mind that if they found her, they would kill her and the baby. She was harbouring an unknown inside her body. A catastrophe. Something that none of them could control. All trust was gone. As a mother she wouldn't be able to reason with their demands to get rid of the child. She wouldn't let them. He needed to come up with a plan.

CHAPTER TWENTY-NINE

The beach on the other side of town had a reputation for swallowing and spitting out dead bodies onto the sands. Its vast and desolate exterior proved safe enough for Loiyan's quick dips in the early hours of the morning. Waves crashed against the shore, drowning out the sound of birdcalls and squawks. Loiyan threw off her clothes and advanced towards the water as if she was the only one on the beachfront. Shallow seawater rushed around her ankles, she bowed down and crawled out further into the sea, on her hands and knees like a broad-snout crocodile. Faron watched with mixed feelings. His insides danced in tune with fear, sex and love, stretching against the skin on his abdomen and pushing against his ribs. Beads of sweat formed on his upper lip. Loiyan pushed herself around in a wave-like rhythm until a silver fin appeared and burst into luminous colours as her body bent into s-shaped curves. His heart thumped with a neediness that had him breathing through his mouth with force as he watched her.

The rapid expansion of her stomach worried him. Would the child need water as much as her? What would they be capable of? He looked around at the grassy knolls that surrounded the beachfront. There was nowhere to hide the baby around here. The Atlantic Ocean threw itself mercilessly against the rocks. There was nothing on this side of the beach to suggest any form of safety. If Jojo were alive, the child would have been in safe hands. Who could he go to that he could trust? They were truly alone in their turmoil with enemies they didn't need to have. This was about finding someone with no ulterior motive. But who would risk their life?

At home Faron urged the conversation forward. Loiyan's stomach formed the shape of an avocado jutting out against her clothes. He almost believed it was larger every time she came back from her morning swim.

"We have to find a place to keep our baby safe," he said.

Loiyan spread her legs as she leaned back on the chair to get comfortable.

"I will deliver the baby myself. We can trust no one."

"But you don't know how."

"I have witnessed childbirth amongst my followers," she replied.

"Witnessing it is not the same as doing it. We don't know what it is or how it will work," Faron said.

"I know someone …"

"Who?"

"A priestess … I will find her tomorrow."

"No, Loiyan! If she shares this information, it will be dangerous for us and the baby."

"Faron, I'm not asking you."

"You trust humans to keep your secret? When what we are doing goes against what your own kind believes?" he said.

"I choose only those who have devoted their entire life to me. I give them wealth and power. They will do my bidding. An elder who has been with me from birth, her bloodline devoted itself to Mammy Wata. She is the one I will call on. Mammy Wata instructs in dreams but it's not enough. She will know and respect my presence. It is an honour," Loiyan explained.

"As soon as our child is born, I must remove them from this place to keep them safe," Faron said.

Loiyan sat up and covered her swollen belly with her hands.

"Where?"

"I will find a place. Somewhere safe. Nobody can find our child, Loiyan. Nobody. It must be done. Don't worry."

Loiyan said nothing but her arms crisscrossed around her belly, and she turned away from him.

* * *

Faron gave Danso instructions to run Scissor House as his time was occupied by Loiyan preparing for the birth and finding somewhere to hide their child. Loiyan had stayed unusually silent after his suggestion. He knew she would resist him, but she had to choose safety even if she didn't want to give up on the hope of keeping it. If he had ever felt alone, it was then. No family. No future. Only enemies. Time was against them. It didn't take him long to realise the only folk to be trusted would come from her devotees. All Loiyan had to do was convince the mermaids that she had got rid of the baby and they would leave her alone. They would banish her but let her live. It was the price for their love. Faron felt a sense of dread. The responsibility was enormous. Having a woman give up everything she knew for him. What was he giving up for her? He feared that she would resent him for it. Loath him for her sacrifice. He couldn't pull out now, though, it was too late. Too late to save her. Too late to sacrifice his love for her and let her go back to her family.

On the day Loiyan departed to visit one of her oldest-serving members, he could not go with her. She would not allow it. It was unbearable watching her heave through the gates and walk through the streets of oblivion. She left in the early hours of the morning, before the traders arrived from the provinces with vegetables, fruits and grains for the market traders. Before the shopfronts opened their shutters and the factories lifted their corrugated iron doors up into the folds of the open doors, she ambled along, swinging her arms as if to mimic working women in a hurry. It was traumatic to watch a woman's body morph into something unfamiliar and witness it alter the very fabric of their habits and humanity. Faron did not know if this was what pregnancy did to every woman or just their union. Her belly grew with every initial blush of the sun against the cloudless sky and changed shape as it expanded. He always hid his alarm and instead chose to concentrate on creating comfort. He rubbed her stomach with shea butter and gave her his pillows to lie on. For the most part she did not feel any pain, just discomfort. Swimming allowed her to remain strong and happy. Afterwards she was content to stay inside the house and amuse herself with picture books and food. Bobo received a pay rise for remaining at the house for as long as he could. He became the day-and-night watchman, instructed to keep a log of those that loitered on the street and near the house on more than one occasion, and to keep track of unfamiliar faces. No one was going to take their child from them. Faron would reveal himself to anyone who tried to attack them, regardless of the consequences.

Faron sent a messenger to the Governor's office. With Loiyan gone and minimal time left to himself, he had to retract his approval of the offer. This was not a hard decision to make. Loiyan was not safe without him and would not survive in England. His money and wealth were here. He could not start again or guarantee their safety over there. There were those who had visited the King's country and came back with tales of splendour and entertainment, of colourful characters, cold weather and opulent living. Faron's curiosity was aroused, but the sacrifice was too great. They would have to leave for another destination along the coast – Sierra Leone, an affluent territory and home to Fourah Bay College, the first university of its kind in West Africa. An illustrious society awaited them with more business, attainment and enlightenment.

The visit to the Governor's office was short and sweet.

"We are disappointed with your decision," the Governor said.

"I apologise it took this long. It was not an easy decision to make. I had to consider all options." Faron remained standing with no intention of staying or encouraging further conversation.

"I hope you have made the right one," the Governor responded.

"I have."

The Governor presented him with a bottle of King George IV Scotch whiskey as a parting gift.

* * *

Loiyan did not come back the next day. This was bothersome but it gave Faron time to think about what needed to be done. In truth, their options were limited. Faron's mind cast back to when Jojo encouraged him to take a chance on strangers as if it was the lifeblood of their existence. Now he saw how many took a chance on him. His infuriation with Jojo's mother. His frustration with the whole village who encouraged him to take Jojo in as a young child. The welcoming celebrations held by the late Ga Manste Nii Ankrah of Otublohum. King Tackie Komeh I giving them land in Adabraka. Danso's willingness to leave his mother's house and join them in their quest to turn his vocation into a successful business. Everyone had taken a chance on him – even Kwabla. It was his turn to take a chance on them. His turn to trust, to have faith, to believe that somehow in this world, on this land, these people would not let him fall because it was not their custom.

Faron took the path he had been on with Loiyan to witness the festivities in her name. He plunged through the plains with speed. They did not have two or three days to spare. He hoped Loiyan would not come back while he was away. He had to arrive back home before dawn, to receive her when she arrived. The idea of Loiyan panicking in his absence did not sit well in his bones. He bounced against the ground, leaping and cascading, alerting wildlife to his chaotic frenzied rush. The village soon appeared within eyeshot as Faron circled round the back of the huts.

The man who had led him away from the beach before stood holding a staff at the edge of the bush between his huts. It was as if he was waiting for someone. He smiled and nodded at the sight of Faron.

"You knew I was coming?" Faron asked, almost disappointed at the lack of surprise.

"I knew someone was coming. Someone in trouble."

"My child …" Faron said earnestly.

"You will bring her, and we will do what is necessary," the man answered.

"Her?"

"Tell me your wishes."

"What do you mean 'her'?"

The man bowed his head in silence without looking up. "I await all your immediate requests, Owura."

Faron made clear his demands. That he would arrive with a child that would be taken in and looked after as if it were their own. Visitors might stop by from time to time to enquire about the children of the village, but it was none of their business. Those visitors must never have access to or be left alone with the child under any circumstances.

The man only interrupted him once.

"If the child is in danger in our village, we will have to give the baby up to the sea. To the ones who would protect her away from this land. To another coastline with another people. That is the only way. But we will only do that if they come, and we have no defence."

"Give the baby up to the sea? Don't you know if babies swallow saltwater they can die?" Faron asked, alarmed.

"No one gives a pig to a hyena to keep. It is me, is it not? Your faithful and loyal servant."

Faron did not answer. Was he doing the right thing? His instincts had brought him here and this man knew. He knew. So why now did he feel a sudden sense of dismay?

"If the cockroach wants to rule over the chicken, then it must hire the fox as a bodyguard, yes?" The man nodded, urging Faron to leave.

Faron had never been so unsure, and yet he knew this was where he would come with his only child. He snatched the man's hand and pulled him closer.

"If you know everything then you should know about me," he growled.

"Yes, I know. That you will kill me and my wife. My parents, my children and the whole village. But you will not have to. Please, go. You cannot stay here any longer."

Faron looked into the man's eyes so that he could see the reflection of Corpo Seco that Faron saw all those years ago in the Black River in the Amazonas. Then he turned and fell on all fours so the man could see him leap back through the forest.

* * *

She didn't appear for four days.

Faron couldn't breathe.

He didn't visit Scissor House.

It held the memory of Jojo.

It held the memory of her.

His chest tightened.

His hands shook.

He waited for her.

She had won this battle.

Changed him.

Human.

She was carrying his seed.

Fear.

Love.

Panic.

It rained on the fifth day. The deluge pummelled the rooftops. Wind battered flimsy front doors, whipped up branches from trees and howled over the sound of city life. He didn't hear Loiyan enter the house. He didn't even smell her. The rain masked the smell of seaweed. She appeared at the entrance, drenched.

"I needed the rain so I could come back," she spluttered.

He rushed to hold her. She felt thinner and frailer in his arms. Her belly jutted out like the aluguntugui.

"Where were you?"

"Our baby is ready to come, Faron."

"Already? How can this be?"

"Tomorrow."

"How do you know?" he asked, alarmed.

She took his hand and led him up the stairs to the bedroom.

He hadn't slept well since Loiyan had left the house. Vivid dreams of faceless mumbling voices dominated his sleep. This time he woke up around midday to an empty space beside him. Boisterous voices filtered through the house. He followed the sounds downstairs into the backyard. Loiyan stood with a short dark woman with beady eyes. She pushed her fingers through her head wrap to scratch her scalp. A large pot on a three-stone fire held bubbling water. The woman nodded in acknowledgment as Faron approached.

"I am having our baby here," Loiyan said. "Today."

"She is going to have the baby in the next few hours. I need water and cloth," the woman said.

Faron nodded. His throat tightened. Words were lost to him. His hands trembled as he moved back up the stairs to fulfil the old woman's request. He did not know how much cloth to bring or where to put it. Was she having the baby in the yard or here in the bedroom? He grabbed some clean cloth from the drawer and turned to leave the room.

Loiyan stood behind him. Her cheeks flushed as she held onto her stomach.

"She's pulling and scraping at my insides already, Faron."

"How do you know it's a 'she'?" Faron asked.

Loiyan raised her arms towards the bed and flopped onto it. She rolled over panting.

"Put the sheets down and bring the pot with the boiling water." The old woman appeared at the door.

Whimpering sounds escaped Loiyan's lips.

Faron dropped the sheets and rushed to get the pot from the yard. He came back to find Loiyan sprawled on the bed, her face contorted as she puffed through her mouth. The woman took the pot and blocked Faron from entering.

"You cannot be here. This is against all that we know. I must be alone with her."

"How long?" he asked.

"Four hours."

"What does she need?"

"Me."

Loiyan screamed.

Faron's stomach somersaulted. His heart pounded so fast he gasped for air.

"Four hours," the woman repeated.

Faron exited the house to find Bobo sweeping up the remains of the fire.

"Good morning, Owura."

"Morning, Bobo – please make sure you don't enter the house unless you are called. I have visitors and they must be alone. They are dealing with important matters. I will be back in a few hours."

"Is it your lady, Owura?"

"Yes, Bobo. She is visiting with her auntie."

"I will make sure they are fine. I will take care of it, Owura."

"Thank you, Bobo."

Scissor House opened its arms, waiting for him like an abandoned wife. The tailors clapped their hands in astonishment at his presence, clearly overjoyed to see him. It pleased them to fill him in with the latest gossip. Faron listened in silence, watching the hands on the wall clock move with solemn intention. He excused himself and sat in the office when the customers trundled in. The ledger book waited patiently in its favourite drawer. It had been a while since Faron had checked the books. He couldn't remember if Danso had been instructed on how to enter the sales, perhaps Jojo had briefed him on it. He had neglected his staff, and now that he was here, he sat at the desk feeling empty. A crack in the wall from the humidity changes was becoming apparent in the far corner of the room.

"Do you need a drink, Owura?" Danso peeped through the door.

"No, thank you, Danso. I will soon be gone."

Faron checked his English Karrusel pocket watch. He had spent two-and-a-half hours doing nothing. There was no point in staying there any longer. He would wait in his own house in his own parlour. He placed the ledger book back into the drawer. This was ridiculous.

The baby's cry echoed as Faron entered the courtyard. Bobo laughed and shouted, "Congratulations, Owura" at Faron running into the house. The bedroom door was wide open. Loiyan lay covered with tie-dye sheets while the old woman wiped the baby over with brisk strokes.

The woman smiled.

"It's a girl," she announced gently, placing the wrapped baby into his arms.

A wild lamentation in his native Portuguese left Faron's lips and spilled out into the room as he held his daughter close. Her bright eyes shone at him. Her short tongue poked through her lips. She gurgled unexpectedly, and Faron's eyes gleamed with gratitude. He caressed her perfect little face and found himself unable to contain the swell of emotion that filled his heart, until a sob tore through his body, and he whispered "she's beautiful" before burying his face into her neck.

"She's beautiful."

"She's ours, Faron."

Loiyan reached out for their daughter as tears spilled down her cheeks.

"How are we to be rid of her? How can you even do it?" she choked out, desperation clear in her voice.

"What do you mean 'rid of her'?" Faron said tentatively, checking the tiny fingers and toes for any sign of abnormality. No matter how hard he looked at them they remained simply human hands and feet.

"Must we do this, Faron? She looks so human. I had the baby here on purpose. If she were Mammy Wata, she would not have survived this birth. We can show them that she is more human and no threat."

"I don't know if that is a good thing. She cannot be like me."

Loiyan pulled herself up and tried to cajole their daughter out of Faron's hands.

Faron shook his head sadly and inhaled, knowing what must be done, despite every fibre of his being screaming against it. Loiyan attempted to take their daughter from him, but he held firm even as his tears ran unchecked down his face.

"We are doing this to keep her safe, Loiyan. I must take her now," he said with conviction, before gesturing for Loiyan to kiss their daughter one final time.

"Until this is all over. Give her a piece of your heart."

They hadn't stopped to think how hard this was going to be. The chaos and threat of what would happen meant they had been planning the practicalities and had neglected their true feelings.

"How can I kiss her, get close to her, hold her, and then let her go?"

"Because we are keeping her safe, not destroying her," Faron pleaded.

"I can't, Faron."

"Say goodbye, Loiyan. She'll be safe until we can get her back."

"She must feel the blessings of farewell to begin her journey," the old woman interjected, reminding them she was still in the room.

Faron put his daughter into Loiyan's arms. Tears rolled freely down her face as she placed multiple kisses on her daughter's forehead.

"We have not named her," she cried.

"We cannot," Faron replied.

"Then how will we ever find her?"

"How did you find me? How did I find you?"

It took all the strength he had inside him to remove their daughter from her mother and walk out of the room without looking back.

He raced through the forest, conscious that he might be followed. Who was to know if they were being watched? She was wrapped tightly onto his chest to withstand the speed. She made no sound as he bounded through the forest, wondering if the fate of his daughter would bring him answers. It was still hard to understand how this whole situation had transpired. How he became embroiled in a palaver like no other. He wondered if the forest would be his daughter's home and keep her safe from harm.

He sped into the welcoming arms of the man whose name was never volunteered. His gap-toothed wife stood by his side. She embraced his daughter in her arms and thanked him for the blessing of a child. Faron remembered his own past, and the way that taking on Jojo was an honour to the villagers as well as a responsibility and expectation. He wanted to tell the man that he would burn their village down if anything happened to his daughter, but the man's eyes told him all he needed to know. She would be protected. They said nothing to each other. Faron took one last look at the life he had managed to bring forth into the world. A miracle designated as an abomination. If she was his daughter, her resilience and stubbornness would help her survive. If she had her mother's temper and strength, nobody would mess with her.

The man ushered him away with a sombre face.

"You cannot protect anyone if you are far away mourning someone else. Please leave now."

* * *

The gate was open, the lock shattered on the ground, and blood splayed across the front yard like spilled palm oil. Faron's heart raced as he caught sight of Bobo's mangled body tangled in the bushes, his neck savaged with a massive chunk missing. Faron's heart beat wildly as he leaped over bloody prints on the stairs to get to his bedroom. His chest tightened with each step.

As he reached his bedroom, he saw the old woman slumped over in an unnatural position at his doorway, a lifeless husk. A moment later he heard it – the sickening slurping sound of someone sucking on sheets soaked in blood. He charged into the room and found the boy-man hunched over his bed, eyes wild with madness, half a bloody sheet hanging from his lips.

"Where is she?" Faron demanded, his voice hoarse.

The sheet dropped. The boy-man perched on two hind legs.

"My friend, I found you."

"Where is she?" Faron screamed.

"One tried to stop me downstairs, and that one there on the floor." He gestured towards the old woman's crumpled form by the door. "They are loyal to you, these humans, the way I was loyal to my master. Like my

305

children were loyal to me. But unlike you, I get full up." His voice rose into a wild shriek as he shook his bony finger at Faron. "You don't get full up!"

"Where is Loiyan?"

The boy-man wobbled as he tried to steady himself on the mattress. "Mammy Wata blood taste like bush meat, tough and stringy. Only good for occasional eating."

Faron raised his hand but not fast enough.

The boy-man leaped and dug his claws into Faron's chest.

Faron fell backward.

The boy-man opened his jaws, ready to tear open Faron's neck.

Faron pushed his fingers into the boy-man's back.

He felt the boy-man's jaws rip at his neck.

Faron's fingers tingled inside the bloodied components of the boy-man's flesh.

A mixture of fat and bloodied vessels stuck between the boy-man's teeth as he pulled his head away, blood dripping from his mouth.

The smell of rotting flesh filled the air.

The room swayed.

The boy-man wailed, struggling to free himself from Faron's grip as the rotting smell intensified. He opened his jaws again to the size of a gorilla, but Faron quickly pulled his fingers out of the boy-man, who fell to the ground writhing in pain, clawing at the floorboards.

Faron trembled. He put his hands to his neck. Blood oozed from the gaping wound. His muscles ripped around his body. His eyes felt like they were being pushed to the back of his head. Flashes of Jojo filled his mind and then, as quickly as they came, they disappeared.

The boy-man howled, scrambling to get up, his insides in clear distress. He struggled to get out of the room.

Faron's arms and legs trembled. His skin attempted to mesh scarring tissue.

Loiyan. What had he done with her? There was no sign of her, she must have got away. She was stronger than the humans.

The boy-man clambered onto the bedside table next to the window. His eyes fixed on escaping and healing.

Faron turned towards the stairs. He had to find Loiyan.

The neighbours' screams filled the air. The boy-man broke his own code as he jumped from fence to fence and house to house. He had to feed now to stay alive and rid himself of the decomposition that was taking place inside his body. Loud frightened male voices followed by thuds and howls of terror. Faron hadn't finished the job on the creature. There was no time for that. Now that the boy-man had exposed himself to the people, he would have to go into hiding.

Wind blew against Faron as he ran. People stood bemused and shouted greetings at him. Nobody ran in the street. Running was for hunters and children – not grown men. Some tried to stop him. Others asked what was wrong. He ignored them all. He had to get to Loiyan. There was only one place she could get to quickly enough if she was injured. The problem with that was that Mammy Wata would catch wind of her. Faron's feet barely touched the ground as he tore through the town. The journey to Cape Coast that took him four hours by car would take him less than an hour on foot. The human eye could not keep up with his speed. They could only feel the force of the wind against their bodies as he bolted into the bushes out of sight, plunging his way blindly through the woodland. Loiyan would have struggled to get to Cape Coast if she was wounded. She had just given birth and he did not know anything about the recovery, but he knew her determination meant she would be quick, though not as quick as him. He could not lose her. The boy-man's attack would send her straight into the arms of her pod, the only people who could protect her from him. She had no choice but to run to them, especially as they had just sent away their child. Her mind and heart must have been in a state of shock and breakdown. He needed to make sure she was alive. She was his life – his whole life.

Faron saw her from a distance at the edge of the pier.

Excited waves crashed against the steady wooden legs of the pier built with pride by the men of the country.

"Loiyan!" Faron bellowed.

The unmistakable hissing of Mammy Wata surrounded him. Faron turned to his left. One charged towards him with her claws out. Faron grabbed her. An agonising hunger swept over him. He sunk his teeth into her neck and gnawed. A sensual rush of satisfaction overcame him. He let her body drop to the floor. He looked at his bloodied hands as euphoria swept through his veins. The boy-man hadn't finished the job on him and now he was behaving untoward in his killings. Why was he gnawing at their necks with blood everywhere? He looked up in time to remember why he was there and moved forwards with excessive speed.

Akala stood ahead of him on the pier. She howled in anger at the sight of him.

"Loiyan!" Faron roared.

He hurried along the pier.

Akala's hissing filled his ears as she spun around so that her long plaits slashed against his abdomen like razorblades.

He drew back, but she pounced.

Faron threw Akala with all his might into the bodies of three approaching Mammy Wata. They fell back, toppling into the ocean behind them.

Loiyan lay at the side of the pier in a pool of blood. Colour vibrated around her body intermittently like a flickering candle. An unsightly gash in her left side left a gaping hole displaying bloody flesh. He could see that there had been a fierce struggle between her and the boy-man. The surface of her back was ripped and slashed. Faron whimpered as he moved in to hold her up.

She felt like a child in his arms.

"Whatever is left of me? Whatever I am, it is yours," he whispered.

Her head nuzzled in his chest and his into her hair.

A squawking long-tailed glossy starling flew past.

Loiyan gasped for air as she tried to speak.

"This is not how it is supposed to end, Faron. This is not what was supposed to happen."

"I know. I'm sorry," he blubbered.

"The tree-dwelling Asanbosam ... why did he invade your home?" she asked.

"I met him the night I met you. We had a disagreement."

Loiyan's eyes travelled towards the sea. Her plaits slapped against the floor as if they were caught fish starved of water.

"Our daughter may need to become human in order to survive now that we cannot walk boldly amongst our people and show them who we are," she whispered earnestly.

Amidst the hisses and screams, Faron noticed the boy-man tearing apart several Mammy Wata. The malicious creature had followed him to Cape Coast. After managing to grab hold of one of them, he sunk his teeth into her neck and watched as her legs mutated into a giant fin that revealed her true form. The other Mammy Wata lunged at the Asanbosam, who fought back viciously. Akala managed to scramble up onto the pier, knowing she was no match for the monster. She quickly glanced at Faron before surrendering herself and diving into the ocean. Some of the Mammy Wata swam past her towards land to do battle. A crowd of locals stood at the start of the pier pointing and screaming.

It was as the Mammy Wata predicted. This was an Oburoni God victory.

The demons were fighting themselves, displaying their true evil.

Loiyan's eyes flickered.

Faron tapped her body to stimulate her, but she was ebbing away. The screams and howls around them were no longer keeping her alert. He could hardly feel her heartbeat.

Faron caught his breath and let out a sob. His tears dropped onto her face. Anger had ruled and blinded his heart for so long. He believed in nothing. He had allowed the past to shape his future, but now his future was disappearing before his very eyes. His future was all he wanted. A home. A family. Love.

Faron wept as he struggled to lift her. Dead mermaids littered the pier around him. The Asanbosam shrieked with anger every time Faron moved. It was here for revenge and would not stop until it got to them. Mammy Wata blocked every effort with their fins, fingernails and hair, slashing at him from all angles to slow him down. The Asanbosam tried to block himself from the mermaids' relentless attack. He was fast but there were too many of them.

Faron smelt the fear and outrage of the humans as they threw bottles and sticks at the scene. Horror and panic filled the air around them. All on the pier were an affront to the Oburoni God. Some raised rosary beads to the sky. A few Mammy Wata worshippers gathered on the pier, creating boundaries with smoke and performing rituals. The people bellowed with terror and dread.

Faron repeated Loiyan's name as he attempted to descend the wooden legs of the pier with her limp body over his shoulder. He wanted to slip her softly into the ocean rather than throw her but there was no time. The Asanbosam's roars heightened at the sight of him leaving the scene, prompting Faron to jump into the endless rippling turquoise sea. His body hit the water. A flurry of bubbles hissed around him as the top layer of his skin peeled off. He bellowed in agony. His hands let go of Loiyan's body. She floated still and lifeless. He grabbed at Loiyan's motionless figure, but dizziness set in. He gnashed his teeth. An intense burning sensation crawled around his body. His face and feet swollen. Blisters formed on his skin. His fingers liquefied. His face felt like it was melting. Loiyan's still body floated away from him. This was his end, in salty ocean water with Loiyan.

He thought he saw Jojo.

The old man in the Amazonia with the spear in his neck.

Mamãe.

His mother called out his name with a soft comforting purr. She rocked him from side to side in their tiny bed before Sinhô arrived. The mother of the plantation stroked his hair and told him that he would rule the world and free his mother. Her lullabies soothed his soul. Safe. She wiped away bird feathers that drifted in from the outside that fell onto his face.

"Mamãe, please forgive me. I didn't mean to hurt you. I love you, Mamãe!"

Mamãe rocked faster and hummed louder.

Faron sobbed.

"I didn't mean to kill you, Mamãe. I'm sorry. I love you, Mamãe."

He returned to the Rio Negro, floating amongst the pirarucu fish and the caiman alligator – sailing into the abyss in harmony with life and death itself.

"Faron, Faron wake up. Wake up!"

Pinches on his arms and face snatched him away from the stillness of the river.

The sun prised his eyes open and glared at him.

Loiyan leaned over him, cradling him.

"He's okay now," Loiyan said, looking up.

Akala's face appeared, blocking out the glare of the sun's rays. Her eyes softer, resigned.

"The child is gone, and you gave your life for my daughter."

Loiyan's arms tightened around his body. Her scent intoxicated his being. Hadn't Mamãe been holding onto him a moment ago? Loiyan's plaits fell over his face as she leaned into him.

"Loiyan, you are here." His voice trembled.

She kissed him on the forehead.

"Because of you," Akala answered.

"Your curse is lifted, Faron," Loiyan said.

"My curse?" His voice was hoarse, almost entirely not his own. He tried to move, to sit up. Loiyan loosened her grip in response. He rubbed his eyes, unsure of what had transpired. His wet clothes were damp from the baking heat. Akala stood with two other mermaids. A crowd of noisy, white-clothed worshippers served as a barrier to the humans and the pier. Their chants could be heard far and near. Others danced and prayed amongst the dead carcasses while they were carried off and thrown into the ocean.

"We must go to Lake Bosumtwi, my love. We will build our home there," Loiyan said, brushing away seaweed from Faron's face.

"You are no longer the enemy, Faron. Loiyan has made her choice, and you yours. The demands of the ancestors have been met," Akala said.

The boy-man's body lay crumpled in a heap, wilted from dryness like a dead cat. Mammy Wata circled cautiously around it, shielding it against a lone figure. Another Asanbosam shrieked with rage and slammed his fists on either side of his head. Faron recognised him as the younger one he had let go in the forest. Fiery eyes locked onto Faron's in recognition. The Asanbosam growled, baring his teeth viciously. He rushed at the skinniest Mammy Wata. Her claws tore at his flesh as they tussled together. She ducked and dodged, managing to keep out of his grip until eventually she broke away. The other Mammy Wata stepped away from the boy-man's corpse, allowing him to take the dead Asanbosam's body without challenge. He threw himself onto it, howling and snapping at everyone around him. Gradually he lifted the corpse and took one last look at Faron and Loiyan before leaping off into the distance, his burden clutched tightly in his arms.

Akala moved to Loiyan and rubbed her forehead against her daughter's.

"It is over and now I must go back home to my pod and my people. There is much to explain."

Loiyan nodded and held her mother tight before Akala pulled away and moved towards the crowd of human women dancing fervently. One broke from the crowd and handed her something. She took it and moved towards the pier edge, taking one last long look at Faron and Loiyan before diving into the ocean.

Faron looked down at his body. His arms and legs were covered in a thick layer of watery, white skin that formed on the outside. He pulled at it with his hands. It peeled back like wet silk revealing smooth mocha-brown skin underneath. A sharp pain splattered across Faron's ribcage. He groaned. Loiyan held her hand out to help him sit up. Her cheeks flushed and her eyes glistened with tears. He had watched her fade away before his eyes, but she was alive.

"Am I dead?"

"No," she laughed softly. "You are very much alive. And very much human."

"How can I be human? It is not possible. I must be dead, and you must be dead too."

"The curse is lifted, Faron. My fate is that of my mother, but I am ready to live with it. Do you want to see how?"

She sat next to him and placed a broken mirror in his hand. He stared at his reflection. A man stared back at him, brown eyes wide with fear and surprise behind thick black lashes. His angular face was gaunt with scattered wrinkles that stretched across his weathered brow around his cheekbones. The menacing wild glint in his eyes was gone. Grey strands intertwined with black curls, a remnant of youth barely hinting at what once had been.

Faron slapped it away.

"What is this?"

"You are no longer Corpo Seco. You are only Faron. And I am only Loiyan, with a little of my mother in me. It is done."

"It is done?"

"It is done."

He was no longer Corpo Seco. No longer a living, breathing corpse. No longer hidden. No longer shameful. How could he live without being that? And his enemies?

"What about the Lake Bosumtwi Mammy Wata?"

"There were not many there. The few that remained have left. They go to Lake Togo first before Lake Debo."

"Where is that?"

"Mali"

He had survived it all, and with her. A sudden panic set in.

"We must get our daughter back if we are no longer who we were!"

"We cannot. She will have the remnants of who we once were, Faron. It is the sacrifice we made. Let her live her life without prejudice and slander." Loiyan's eyes dimmed. "Ours is tainted. She is safe amongst our people. They give us service. If we go to see her, someone will know. A villager will find out. It will be a rumour and the taint will begin. If we love her, we must let her grow up in a safe place where she is understood and cared for without history."

"The thing that you were fighting for … you've given up on it?" Faron asked, indignant.

"We must have a new way, Faron, otherwise we die. We must seek new life elsewhere and survive. It is our only option."

Loiyan stood up.

"She will know who she is. She cannot hide it," he said.

"And we must live in our own safety. Come."

Loiyan held out her hand with a smile.

Faron placed his hand in hers and let her lead the way.

ALSO AVAILABLE BY NADIA MADDY

THE PALM OIL STAIN

The Palm Oil Stain is a brutal tale of a woman's journey of love and survival. Set against the backdrop of the Rebel War in Sierra Leone, Shalimar escapes an attack on her village assisted by a South African mercenary the locals call Chameleon. Displaced in Freetown, Shalimar devises a plan to return home to locate her family while forging an unlikely relationship with Chameleon whose alcoholic abuse has left him bereft of any emotion. Shalimar soon learns her predicament was brought about by the betrayal of those close to her. Shalimar's decision to risk the wrath of the Rebels in the abandoned villages in order to find her family changes the course of her and Chameleon's life forever. The Palm Oil Stain is a deeply moving love story that relays the harsh reality of war, betrayal and redemption.

This novel is available in all major bookshops. Be sure to grab a copy and dive into another unforgettable journey.

Printed in the USA
CPSIA information can be obtained
at www.ICGtesting.com
LVHW090722260924
791981LV00010B/626

9 781399 993487